Hostie

All at Sea in the Ionian
With Rachel Lamb

To Diane with best wishes

Told by Frank Melling

 *Stafford 2022*

A Collie Press Book

For Bess

Copyright © Frank Melling, 2017

First published in Great Britain in 2017 by:
The Collie Press
Manley Lane Manley Cheshire WA6 0PB

Copyright © Frank Melling, 2017
The right of Frank Melling to be identified as the author of this Work has been
asserted by him in accordance with the Copyright, Designs and Patents Act 1988.

Cover Artwork by Mark Jarvis of Motografix,
The Boiler House, Alma Road, Rotherham S60 2HZ

Text and Design © Frank Melling

Layout by Geoff Fisher

All enquiries should be addressed to the publisher

A CIP catalogue record for this book is available in the British Library
ISBN 978-0-9527987-5-0

Printed and bound by
CPI Group (UK) Ltd, Croydon, CR0 4YY

Here's the story of my season's sailing in the Ionian –
and what a year it was!
I hope that you enjoy it.

Rachel

xxx

Introduction – and Thanks

FIRST, and most importantly, thank you for reading Hostie. An author is nothing without an audience and I am honoured that you should want to read this book.

Now to the story - because it is not as straightforward as it might seem at first glance. Please remember that Hostie is a completely fictional tale, set on an island which doesn't exist and with Rachel, the book's heroine, sailing a type of boat which I have invented. All this is fact.

What is also fact is that none of the characters in the book are based on real people, nor are the stories re-told versions of actual events.

So, sadly, there is no Tychos, no Serval yachts and you won't ever meet Rachel in a lovely harbour side Taverna either – although she would be good company if you did!

However, everything else is true. Hosties are wonderful. Lead Skippers are brave and competent beyond words and Engineers are sheer geniuses – they really all are!

The Ionian is even more beautiful than I describe and the sailing is better. Most of all, the Greek people are kinder and more generous than anyone could ever write.

There are dolphins and they do swim right next to your boat and look at you. The sky is as blue as Rachel says it is and the Ionian Sea as welcoming.

And to make the book fun, the fictional story is woven into real places, right down to the individual streets and tiny bays which actually do exist. So, you will be able to find Lefkas, Karya, Nydri, Kalamos, Sivota, the coastline of Meganisi and much, much more. Only Tychos is going to cause you a real problem because it doesn't exist!

You might even enjoy working out where the fictional stories finish and the fact begins.

So that's the background to the book. Now, why did I write it? The answer is simple. My wife and I sail in Lefkada, usually twice a year, and over time I have become really interested in the characters who make up the sailing community there. There are lots of Rachels, in various forms, as well as Lead Skippers like Mike and Engineers not very dissimilar to MG.

We have never sailed on a Flotilla but we have enjoyed watching them in action from the outside and they are fascinating. So, the first reason to write the book is that Lefkada is knee deep in really interesting characters – it's absolutely awash with them.

The second reason is that there are a lot of Rachels about, and probably all over the world too, trying to find themselves and discover who they really are and what they want to do with their lives.

Finally, I wanted to write about a place my wife and I love. Let me give you one example. One evening, we went for a meal on the seafront at Nydri and, when we sat down, I realised that I had forgotten my wallet and had only a single €20 note with me. I explained the problem to the waiter and told him that was all we could spend – and remember, this is a busy tourist area not a quiet little village in the mountains. He smiled and said just to order whatever we wanted and come back tomorrow to pay the balance. Think about doing that in any other part of the world!

Now to the thanks – and these are not just a form of words but are heartfelt. A huge number of people have been incredibly helpful in researching this book and without them the work would not exist. Some of them have assisted formally, in that they have been kind enough to allow me to interview them.

Others have just gossiped over a cup of coffee or by a boat. Because many of the conversations were candid and open I have mainly just used first names – and so I hope that you all recognise yourselves!

Everyone is equally important but I want to start with Ed because he took my wife and I from being dinghy sailors, who had done the requisite courses to sail in the Ionian, to a degree of practical sea sailing competency. Ed isn't Mike in the book – but his sailing skills most certainly are, as is his teaching style!

We have sailed with a number of companies in the Ionian over the years, and have had a good time with them all, but our favourite is Nisos so a big thanks to Rowan, Laurie and the lovely yacht "Maybe" from which I took a lot of the Serval's good nature and superb sailing characteristics. Cheers "Maybe" – and we'll see you soon!

Grace gave us a real insight into the hidden corners of a Hostie's life and Johnny was just as helpful from a Lead Skipper's point of view - as were Ollie, Brian and at least another ten of these super sailors. Jim, Ste, Pedro, Hubert and many more helped me to understand engineers – and how they work and think.

Zoe, Yorgos, Lynn, Theodor and Suzie all provided an invaluable insight into the role of a Base Manager and the commercial aspects of holiday sailing.

I wish I could name every single waiter, and waitress, who spent time talking to us between serving other customers - but thanks to you all.

A lot of the information in the book came from our experiences sailing and listening to other sailors but some didn't - for a very good reason! So, thanks to the Superyacht agents who were so helpful, but who were desperately keen not to be named for fear of being associated with something as down market as small yacht sailing!

A very, very, very famous London based department store was wonderful but would prefer their assistance to be discreet, rather than named. Particular thanks in this respect to Rukaya who explained how they look after special clients and especially how much posh pyjamas actually cost.

And yes, you really can ring up at midnight and have a package delivered to Luton Airport for your private jet to collect a few hours later.

Of course, the private jet you would need is the fabulous Gulfstream G650. I know this because Steve at Gulfstream, a true VIP in his own right, spent half an hour explaining what makes this aircraft worth every cent of the $75 million it costs.

Al, at Airbus Helicopters UK, was just as kind in explaining the needs of the rich and famous when it comes to choosing personal transport – and they are very different from us mere mortals queuing up to have our bags weighed at check in.

Baptiste, from Private Fly, patiently went through the very different way Gulfstream customers get on their planes compared to how we ordinary folk board an aircraft – and it seems to me that they really do have the better arrangements.

Baptiste was also incredibly helpful in calculating turn around times for London airports and flight times to and from Preveza which is the nearest airport to Lefkada. Surprisingly, I didn't have first-hand knowledge of sending my own private jet on a shopping mission!

However, the actual boarding procedure at Preveza Airport is 100% my creation with no input at all from him.

I keep using the word kind because it so apposite. During her tea break Jackie, from the Countess of Chester Hospital's A&E Department, explained what would hurt – and how - if you had just been kicked and cut your head open, and that's not information I had from personal experience either!

Jo and Jonny, of the staff at Boodles in Chester, were incredibly kind in letting me handle a range of extremely expensive necklaces. If you ever have a spare £20,000, and fancy a beautiful necklace, Boodles is the place to shop. Boodles' staff also shone some more light on the mind-set of very wealthy customers.

Which brings me to the most important acknowledgement of all – my wonderful wife, business partner, sailing companion and the editor of this book: Carol.

Since "Hostie" is written in the voice of a 22 year old woman, Carol and my daughter, Elizabeth, have acted as accuracy monitors so I hope that I achieved something like an authentic female voice to tell Rachel's story.

Lisa, Jennifer, Clare, Harry, Danny and Julia read early drafts of the book and were kind enough to make some helpful suggestions about how it could be improved.

However, it was Carol who has toiled over the text so that it is now in what we feel is a presentable form - and without me throwing my pram full of Teddy Bears too far!

We now self-publish all my books and since "A Penguin in a Sparrow's Nest" and "The Flying Penguin" have both been very successful, we wanted to keep the same team for "Hostie".

This means that the book was typeset by Geoff Fisher - a true, old fashioned craftsman and Chris Ganser at Photorestoration retouching.com did wonderful things with the images for the cover. Mark Jarvis designed the book's cover, his third for us now, and Danny Emmerson is our Account Executive at CPI, who print all our books. Together, they should all be beatified for their patience as Carol and I insist on re-doing things time and again until we are satisfied.

We hope that you will enjoy "Hostie" but please be reassured that the book is the best we can achieve. This is why we have used vastly better quality paper than you will normally find in a paperback book, and a larger format – despite Danny's advice that we could save money by following a conventional publishing route for paperbacks. My comment was that if we didn't love "Hostie" then how could we expect anyone else to like it?

So, thanks once again for reading the book and I hope that you have as much fun with Rachel and her team as we have had in creating her.

Make sure that you say hello if we see you in Lefkada.

For Carol with love –
and thanks for the Lefkas Canal

Contents

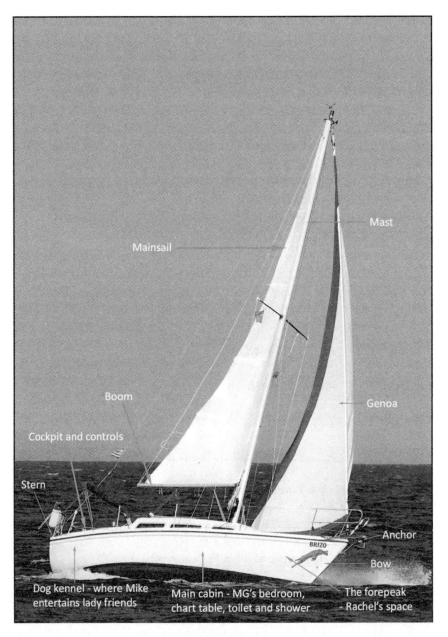

Mast

Mainsail

Boom

Genoa

Cockpit and controls

Stern

Anchor

BRIZO

Bow

Dog kennel - where Mike
entertains lady friends

Main cabin - MG's bedroom,
chart table, toilet and shower

The forepeak
- Rachel's space

Brizo – Serval 34
Under full sail heading back to Tychos

The Beaufort Scale

Beaufort Force	Description	Land Conditions	Sea Condition	Wave Height Feet/Metres	Windspeed MPH
0	Calm	Smoke goes straight up	Sea is like a mirror	0	0
1	Light Air	Wind direction is shown by smoke drift but not by wind vane	Ripples with appearance of scales; no foam crests	0.25 ft 0.1m	1-3
2	Light Breeze	Wind is felt on the face; leaves rustle; wind vanes move	Small wavelets; crests of glassy appearance, not breaking	0.5–1ft 0.15–0.3m	4-7
3	Gentle Breeze	Leaves and small twigs move steadily; wind extends small flags straight out	Large wavelets; crests begin to break; scattered whitecaps	2–3ft 0.6–1m	8-12
4	Moderate Breeze	Wind raises dust and loose paper; small branches move	Small waves, becoming longer; numerous whitecaps	3.5–5ft 1.1–1.5m	13-18
5	Fresh Breeze	Small trees sway; waves form on lakes	Moderate waves, taking longer form; many whitecaps; some spray	6-8 ft 1.9–2.5m	19-24
6	Strong Breeze	Large branches move; wires whistle; umbrellas are difficult to use	Larger waves forming; whitecaps everywhere; more spray	9.5–13 ft 3- 4m	25-31
7	Near Gale	Whole trees are in motion; walking against the wind is difficult	Sea heaps up; white foam from breaking waves begins to be blown in streaks	13.5–19ft 3-6m	32-38

What's a Hostie?

I never intended being a Hostess on a yacht. In fact, three weeks into the New Year I didn't even know what a Hostie was. I'd never set foot on a boat and I'd never heard of Flotilla sailing. The only reason I became a Hostie was that I sat on a phone and then fell off a couch. Well, that and an untidy guy with no manners and not a lot of common sense either.

I had gone to University because everyone else I knew went to Uni. My Mum worked in a bank and Dad was a teacher and we always did the right things together. I was a good girl at school, and worked hard, so I ended up going to a second rate University just because it would have been strange not to go – a bit like wearing wellies at a party, not exactly illegal but odd.

I was good at English, and got a B and an A in English Language and Literature at "A" level, but I was taught by teachers who loved their subject and so I loved it too.

My lecturers at Uni mainly loved themselves and I got more and more fed up with the politics and bitching which seemed to dominate my course.

I really tried to join in at Uni and be a proper student. I went to a few parties and got drunk like I was supposed to do. I had a puff of dope too but it made me dizzy, and a bit sick, so I didn't fancy a second go.

I also had sex at Uni - but not much. I knew I was supposed to get all foaming at the mouth and ecstatic and things but I always felt that I was having sex made at me, or maybe on me.

The worst thing was that I enjoyed sex more when I had been drinking. This made me feel terrible the following morning because I hate being drunk and what I hated even more was remembering that I had agreed to have sex with someone I really wasn't that bothered about.

Eventually I got a 2:2 - which is a second class degree. They gave me a scroll and a photo of a five second handshake with some guy whose name

I didn't even know. This was okay, but not exactly a bargain with a student debt of £43,000.

After Uni, I moved in with a man who had sort of become my boyfriend almost for the same reasons I had gone to University – because it seemed like the right thing to do. He wasn't bad looking and he'd got a 2:2 in Geography on a course which had been just as terrible as mine, so we had this in common.

He was training to become a manager at the local Tesco, which was a decent enough job, and so we shared a flat whilst I did a journalism course. Why journalism? Well, there aren't a lot of things you can do with a degree in English. I didn't want to teach and I liked writing so maybe journalism would be the career for me. The thing is, I wasn't sure - but I couldn't think of anything better.

Connor wanted sex regularly and, like everyone else, he wanted to do sex at me and I agreed because I thought that this was what I should do. Isn't that what all normal 22 year old girls do?

He used to watch porn all the time, and I really do mean all the time. There's nothing more guaranteed to put you off sex than watching a bloke staring at porn on his iPad first thing in the morning, while you're trying to eat your bowl of "Special K" and deciding what to write in your next assignment.

I didn't like Connor watching porn every second of the day. I wanted him to fancy me more than porn and I didn't know how to make this happen.

Eventually, Connor started suggesting that I was gay and he was good with the idea of me bringing girls back to the flat – if he could watch and maybe help things along a bit.

We had a big row and I said I was going back to Mum and Dad for a few days until things settled down. I intended to phone in sick to College, and stay at home for a week, but after three days I was missing Connor.

That's not quite right. I was more thinking of being back in wellies. A second rate degree. No job. So sexually incompetent that I couldn't keep a guy. How's that for success? The main thing on my mind was what else I could fail at. So I phoned Connor and told him that I was coming back. He made the right noises but, in all honesty, he didn't seem that bothered one way or the other.

It was dark when I got back and as rotten as the weather can get in late November – just above freezing and with that extra wet, wet rain which comes when there has been no sun for days. Connor shut his iPad off the moment I walked in so it was either a cultural programme on Renaissance art he was watching, and which he thought I might not like, or more porn.

He kissed me briefly on the cheek and I offered to make us both a cup of coffee. As you can see, I was a real multi tasker – sex toy, coffee maker and house keeper. I put the kettle on and then took my bag to the bedroom and dumped it on the bed.

I took the coffee through and sat on the couch. Connor didn't say anything so I asked him about work and how the training was going – really anything to try to reach out to him. All that I got in return were grunts.

To break the silence, I switched on the television and moved a bit further along the couch towards him – desperate if not for affection then at least a bit of companionship. We sat there, several miles apart, whilst the quiz show host beamed manically at the two families trying to win a holiday in Disneyworld or somewhere.

Connor was untidy, all day every day. Normally, I didn't mind finding things for him but this time, when his phone rang under the cushion next to me, I got quite irritated. I picked it up with the intention of telling him to take a bit more care because it was me that always had to find it for him.

His face balled up in anger as he snatched for the phone. He lunged at it but the couch fell over with me underneath it. In the semi-darkness, a text message came through. There was a picture of a slutty looking naked girl with her legs wide open and the message "See ya later xxx."

I crawled out from underneath the couch waving the phone at Connor like a gun.

I was absolutely hysterical and couldn't stop sobbing.

"You, you, you – bastard, bastard!"

I don't swear much at all so I couldn't think of anything ruder to say than bastard which I know wasn't very good but there I was, sobbing, with tears running down my face, and out of breath and shaking as if I had a fever.

As I sat there retching, Connor reached over and tore the phone from my hand.

He was surprisingly calm. "Fuck off then you frigid cow – fuck off now and find some lesbian to sleep with."

And with that he turned back to his iPad.

I scooped what I could reach into my bag in less than a minute and then walked past Connor. He didn't even look up when I threw my key to the flat at him. Yes, it was wellie time because for sure this was another one to add to the list of failures.

*****

I went straight home. Mum had put clean sheets on my bed and, during the next few days, when my pillow got too wet from crying, she changed it without saying anything.

Dad made me lots of milky coffee, put his arm round me and called me "Baby Bear" as we watched TV together. There were a lot of people worse off than me.

I e-mailed College and said I was having emotional problems and so I wasn't coming back - and I wasn't paying for the last two instalments of the course. They were really aggressive and told me that I had signed up for the complete thing and so I had to pay for the whole year - and that was that. There was no thought for how I was feeling - just where's the money?

So, I rang them and blubbed down the phone at the woman in accounts and then mentioned self-harm and this really put her into a corner. Two days later, I got an e-mail saying that they were going to make an exception – just this once.

*****

Anyone who says there's no work is just not trying. There might not be exactly what you want to do but there's always someone who will pay you for doing something.

My first job was as a Christmas Elf in the big garden centre near Knutsford. I had to wait by the door, smile at all the families and then make sure that they knew where Santa's Grotto was because, as my boss said, "Santa makes money for us..."

I liked smiling, and I liked the kids, but it was freezing. We had thin green pants, a jacket and a big floppy hat with a faded yellow flower on the front. The uniform had been used by a lot of other elves in previous Christmases!

We weren't supposed to wear any of our own clothes but my Mum went to an outdoor shop and got me a very thin top and tights, the sort that hikers use, and I slipped these on underneath the Elf outfit. The other girls were very impressed and so every Elf was wearing them by the end of the week and no-one froze to death. Mums are good news!

Christmas came and went. Mum and Dad were lovely but I was in that strange state where I had left home once, and been an independent woman, but now I was back as their little girl. No matter how hard they tried to avoid it, I was always going to be Baby Bear and as much as I loved being loved, it wasn't quite right.

After Christmas I got a job as a biscuit icer in a factory, on a zero hours contract. I was considered to be something of a high flyer because I had got my Brownie Hostess badge so I was put straight on to the cat biscuit icing production line instead of brushing up and emptying the bins.

The job was easy. The biscuits, in the shape of a rather tubby cat, came down an endless, moving rubber belt. One girl iced on two eyebrows.

Another girl stuck one eye on the face and the girl next to her stuck on the other eye. My job was to put a blob of pink icing, just down from the eyes, to make the nose.

On my left a big, fat, jolly girl, with a slightly lopsided face, iced the cats' mouths underneath my pink noses – all done beautifully, hour after hour after hour.

To be honest, I quite enjoyed myself – for about ten minutes. Then the relentless monotony of the never ending belt started to eat away at me. On the wall opposite the cat production line was a large clock. Its fingers ticked in whole minutes and I used to count them down like a slow motion space mission. Five, four, three, two, one – we have toilet break lift-off!

The other girls seemed to be able to separate their icing from the rest of their minds. It was incredible to see. They chatted and swapped gossip and laughed, and all without making a single mistake with an eyebrow or a smile: it was amazing.

They were very friendly, and tried to involve me in their conversation, but they knew as much as I did that they were on the production line for life – or until babies arrived – whilst I was waiting for the moment to escape.

Their kindness ate into me. They had little choice, except to ice biscuits, whereas I did - and this made me feel bad. It should have been another one of them putting the blob of pink icing on the cat's face – not me, with a University education.

After two weeks, I was asked to leave – not exactly sacked but told that it would be better for everyone if I left. The problem was the shape of the cats' noses because I had begun to experiment to add a bit of interest to the faces.

I had been taught how to apply the nose correctly. There had to be just the right amount of pressure on the enormous icing bag, to put a nice, round, flat nose underneath the eyes and in the centre of the biscuit cats' faces.

But I discovered something really, really interesting. If I pulled the icing nozzle off quickly I could make the nose stick out a bit, in a really cute way. Another good one was putting a bend in the nose so that the cat looked a bit startled or I could turn it up to give it a cuddly look.

Jade sat at the end of the production line and it was her job to pull any sub-standard cats off. As my experiments became bolder, the pile of reject cats was growing. During our 30 minute lunch break Jade came across to see me.

She really tried to be kind but was still firm. She was the Line Supervisor and there were too many sub-standard cats coming down to her.

For a few days, my noses hit the specification and then things drifted again and so I was summoned into the Line Manager's office for a talk. He was manically busy and this pressure helped us both because he didn't have time for any long discussions. It was simple. I was wasting my time and I was costing the company money by wrecking his cats.

I wasn't going to be offered any more work in the following week but I was a nice girl so he would pay me for the remaining six hours of the shift. But there was a bonus - a big bag of the sub-standard cat biscuits I had created.

I munched through the biscuits on the bus going home but kept a particularly lopsided one because it looked just like I felt!

*****

My Dad was determined to retire when he was sixty and he wanted to do something special to celebrate – climb Mount Everest, canoe down the Amazon or sail across the Atlantic in a little boat. Mum just smiled as the adventure magazines piled up. She loved him more than she loved herself but she knew, and he probably did too, that the actual adventure was going to be a cruise in the Mediterranean or maybe a bus tour of Iceland. After a sensible life, sixty was too late to suddenly start becoming an explorer.

With nothing better to do, I picked up one of Dad's sailing magazines and there, at the back, was a small advert tucked away next to the offers to mend sails and service engines. It was short and direct:

> ***Delfini Sailing Holidays. Very small, friendly sailing company wants well organised person to look after clients sailing on yachts in Greece. Terrible pay but lots of sunshine. No experience necessary.***

Then there was a mobile number.

There was no mention of me actually sailing anywhere and the thought of helping people on holiday sounded really attractive. I couldn't possibly be earning any less than I was at the minute and Greece would be a fresh start. I also wanted to work somewhere which was friendly and where I was welcome. Being shown the door for putting funny noses on biscuit cats wasn't appealing!

I phoned the number and got a recorded message saying that no-one from Delfini Sailing Holidays was available but that they would all be at the West of England Boat Show in two weeks' time.

So I sent a text – and didn't get a reply. Just as I was beginning to think of what dead end job I was going to end up in next, the happy face on my phone lit up. It was a text from someone called Dave asking me to see him at the Boat Show about the Hostess job.

The exhibition was at the Mercia Showground, where they hold all the big agricultural shows, between Shrewsbury and Market Drayton.

I left home early and parked in the field. Although it was midday, I'm sure that some God or other had forgotten to turn on the lights because it was a dark, bitterly cold winter's day. You know it's bad when you look up and see a patch of dark grey and think that the weather's getting better!

The admission was £12 and I felt really guilty as I opened my purse and counted out the two five pound notes and two one pound coins. My Mum had loaned me £20, and we both knew what "loan" really meant!

My Dad had given me a big hug and told me that I was certain to get the job. Now, I had £8 left in the world – and I needed £5 for petrol to get home. Wow, the life of international celebrity, Christmas Elf Superstar, Rachel Lamb – who can't even afford a cup of coffee and a muffin!

I asked the lady at the reception desk if she knew where I could find Delfini Holidays. She was all smiles, ran her finger up and down the list of exhibitors and then directed me to the far right hand side of the main hall, where she said there were some of the smaller stands.

I walked a few metres into the main hall and then stopped still. All around me, reaching for the roof, was a forest of gleaming boats.

Some looked liked James Bond speedboats, with massive outboard engines on the back and windscreens like sports cars. Others had masts stretching almost to the roof with great shining eggs underneath, hanging down like blobs of honey attached to long strands.

But the ones which were most impressive were the giant motorboats, almost the size of small houses. These sat on immense, artificial islands, and were guarded by tanned young men and incredibly beautiful girls, just about my age.

In the very centre of the hall was a boat wider than my Mum and Dad's house – it just stretched away out of sight. I walked slowly up to it, like one of the kids I used to take to see Santa. The most beautiful girl I had ever seen glided down to the velvet ropes and opened her lips into what you could mistake for a smile. The smell of very expensive perfume drifted across as she spoke. The words were, "May I help you?" but the message was, "Don't litter our extremely valuable carpet because real people want to see what we have to offer."

She wore an immaculate, intensely blindingly white silk scarf which carried a most delicate, sweeping silver "Starstriker Yachts" badge.

She repeated her question, this time slightly more slowly, almost pausing between each word. "May I help you?"

I didn't stutter but the words came out irregularly as if they were fighting for space in my mouth and didn't know which was first in the queue to come out. "No, I'm just looking because I hope to get a job on, I mean with, yachts, in Greece, with a sailing firm and…"

My mouth went dry and the words stuck to the back of my tongue.

Her smile didn't shift by even one millimetre.

"Yes…" and then she flicked the merest hint of a glance at my jeans and trainers – and they were my best ones too!

"Well, it's been lovely chatting to you," she purred through two perfect lips, each one of which carried the precise amount of lipstick necessary to enhance them to the next level of superiority over every other woman in the world, "but if you will excuse me now, I have to get back to work."

She half turned to glide up the carpeted stairs but I had to ask.

"I don't know much about boats yet, but…but how much is one like this?"

Her smile would have extinguished the sun and made it snow in the Sahara Desert. She hesitated again. "We like to think of the "75" as our mid-range yacht so when you have £4 million available, I'd love to talk to you about becoming an owner."

And with that she collected a single, microscopically tiny canape from a silver tray and floated up the stairs.

Wow! If this was yachting you could count me in. Of course, I'd have to go on a diet, and get a bit better at sloshing the make up on, but this yacht thing was certainly a lot better than icing cats' noses or being a Christmas Elf.

I wandered through the main hall, past more massive yachts with masts like trees, and came across a whole area of companies selling sailing holidays. The names sounded very exotic – Nisos, Sunsail, Neilson, Ionian Dreams, Knossos Sailing and a load more.

I stopped at the counter of the Nisos stand and asked a happy looking girl if she knew where Delfini were. She didn't but she spoke to a fit looking lad next to her – I really was starting to get excited about the whole boat business – and he pointed towards the hall about 75 metres behind him.

At first I thought that I had mis-understood him because the sign at the entrance said: "Boat Jumble" and inside it looked like a giant car boot sale – but for boats. There were lengths of chain and ropes and what looked like second hand car sat navs, but much bigger, and little rubber boats balanced against the wall but there, on the far wall, in a corner, was a big pin board with the sign "Delfini Sailing Holidays – We do Unique" and a picture of large, happy looking dolphin.

I threaded my way through the crowd and there were two men sitting on green plastic chairs, next to a cheap garden table. Neither of them looked particularly welcoming.

I walked up and said: "Excuse me. I'm looking for Mr. Rodgers. I'm Rachel Lamb and I've come about the job as a Hostess."

The older one of the two jumped up. "Oh Rachel, great to see you. I'm Dave." He was late middle-aged, with a wrinkled, worn face and stained teeth - but a big smile.

The other man was more difficult to describe. He was tall, over six feet, and lean, with shoulder length hair parted untidily down the middle. His eyes were almost black and I got the feeling that he was looking at me from somewhere a long way inside them.

His age was equally difficult to guess – not past 30 for sure but with a lined face that had seen a lot of use.

He spoke quietly, in an uncommitted voice. "I'm Mike Purser and I'm Lead Skipper. Pleased to meet you, Rachel."

He held out a large hand which, although he didn't do any of the macho man crushing, felt like a machine it was so powerful. The hand's skin was hard and rough in a way which I had never felt on any of the men I had ever met before. It was a hand that was confident about itself, strong, in control and the master of everything it came into contact with, a special hand attached to a physical body which didn't need a gym subscription to help it be fit.

Dave waved me closer towards them. "Come on in to our palace of fun. Good isn't it?"

He thrust a third, battered chair towards me. It was covered in blobs of black paint which had dried on in hard lumps. He wiped some of the dust from it with his sleeve and smiled. "Sit down, sit down Rachel and tell us all about yourself."

"Would you like to see my CV first? I'm afraid that it's not very impressive after University because I haven't quite worked out what I want to do."

My voice trailed off as I thought of my time as a cat nose icer and a frozen Elf.

"No, no, we're not interested in any of that, are we Mike? Tell us about yourself. We're a people company. People first and paper second, that's our motto – or at least one of them – isn't it Mike?"

Mike half smiled and nodded.

So I told them everything just about as honestly as I could. I told them that I regretted going to Uni. I told them what a bastard Connor had been and I told them I had been sacked for changing the specification on cats' noses. When I got to the cat bit of the story, Mike came out from behind his eyes and smiled – and I felt as if an elephant had been taken off my shoulders.

I sat on the edge of the plastic chair and got ready for the questions. It was Dave who spoke.

"Well, that all sounds great to me, what do you think Mike?"

Mike sort of half smiled: "Yes, that's great, absolutely great."

Dave was a lot keener. "You can read, and do joined up writing, you've got a brain and, to be honest, we've been looking for someone who was really good at putting cats' noses on biscuits - but we've been struggling to find anyone.

"You've got the job. You start the first week in April and we'll be working out of our offices in Ligia to begin with before we relocate to our main base in Tychos.

"Any questions?"

I sat there like a Cabbage Patch doll dressed in jeans, all floppy and with a silly smile on my face.

"That's fantastic and I'm so grateful but I'm not sure what I'll be doing. I can't find your website at the moment. I know that it's my fault for being dim but there doesn't seem to be a Delfini Sailing Holidays' site so I'm not sure." My voice trailed off weakly.

"I mean, I really do want the job and thank you, really thank you, but could I please just know a little bit more?"

Dave rocked back on his plastic chair until I was certain that the legs were going to break.

"Rachel, I want to be completely honest and open with you because that's how we are at Delfini, isn't it Mike?"

Mike had reversed back behind his eyes but nodded in agreement.

Dave continued, but this time in a bit more serious voice: "Being honest is the key thing in life and, honestly, we've had a few problems in the last year and so we're, er, sort of regrouping this season.

"That's why we've got a more focussed pitch than the other sailing holiday companies, you know, in here with the real sailors rather than all tarted up with the free drinks and pens and key fobs. Who needs all that when you're going sailing?"

Mike nodded again.

"Because we're in the process of restructuring, our rates of pay are a bit more modest than some of the other companies but there are special benefits. If you do well, I could see you being promoted to Senior Hostess with the chance to progress up our management structure."

I nearly burst into tears. Here was a job I wanted and I could do. Maybe I could be something more than just a cat biscuit icer.

I didn't know what to say.

In fact, before I could say anything at all, a guy arrived with a big box of plum coloured polo shirts. He grinned at Dave. "Pay me when things pick up. Gotta go. I need to meet customers with some money…"

He dumped the shirts on the floor and left.

Dave picked one up and passed it to Mike. "Nice stuff, he does really nice stuff. These'll be great."

Then he turned to me. "Here's your staff uniform. Have a dig around and find one to fit you."

Everything was going too fast. The last time I felt like this had been on a Year 11 skiing holiday and then I'd hit a tree and cut my lip.

I was starting to think that things couldn't get much worse but I still found myself with my head in the shirts searching for something which looked as if it would fit.

Mike got up. "Take your anorak off."

It wasn't a request but an order. I did as I was told. Mike dug around in the box and pulled out a shirt. He held it up to me as if I wasn't there. "Yup, that's the one. Just go behind the screen and put it on and we can see how it looks."

I didn't know what to say. There wasn't a hint of leering or smutty comment but just straightforward fact. Put your shirt on and let's see what it looks like. It was more like my Dad talking to me than a guy not much older than me.

I went behind the pin board, and checked that no-one could see me, but Mike and Dave were deep in conversation and I don't think that they would have been bothered if I had stood stark naked in front of them. I pulled off my top and looked down at my jeans. Oh God! There was a roll of fat hanging over them, only a little one but it was there. I was a lot nearer a size 14 than I was a 12 and now two men were going to look at me! Please, please, please don't let them notice how fat I am.

I almost crept out from behind the screen but no-one took any notice of me. After what seemed like hours, Dave said: "Yeah, that looks great. Leave it on.

"Ready to start?"

Everything was running out of control. I was in a Delfini Holidays' top, about to start work, and I hadn't even accepted the job yet.

"Dave, I mean, I mean Mr. Hodges"

I was interrupted. "Dave, always Dave, we're all part of the same team now."

"But…"

My voice trailed off. "But what about wages and things?"

Dave sat straight up and made a serious face. "Look Rachel, as I explained, we're facing a few challenges and, and let's be honest, you don't have a lot of experience in the sailing business, do you?"

My face dropped into a sad Emoji.

"Well, you should look at this first year as more like being an intern – you know, work experience but paid: the first step on the ladder of a new career."

I nodded like a Cabbage Patch doll which had suddenly sprung into life.

"So," Dave continued, "I'm not so much offering you wages but more expenses. We will try to be generous, won't we Mike…"

There was an affirmative nod from the second chair, "but you will have to be a team player. You can be a team player, can't you Rachel?"

I nodded silently.

"So, let's say that we give you €5 a day for expenses – personal stuff and all that – and I'll also put £50 a week into your bank account back in England when things pick up. That's fair, isn't it Mike?"

"Yes, I'd say that was very fair Dave – in fact, more than very fair – because you've not mentioned the free staff accommodation and free food."

"You're right as always Mike. Yes, there'll be free staff accommodation, free food and maybe a bottle or two."

My mouth was dry. It was time to jump out of the plane. No more questions. No more thinking about what I should or shouldn't do or what was right or wrong.

"Yes, I'll do it, please, but I've just got one more question. Will there be any opportunity to go on a boat?"

For the first time, Mike's face split into a genuine grin. "Oh yes Rachel, I promise you will go on a boat – you really will."

Then Dave gave me a big hug and Mike shook my hand again and there was another smile.

Where is the Ionian Sea, Actually?

DAVE cast a professional eye over me. "You look really smart, Rache, you really do. Nice top. Jeans. Yup, you look good to me and what does that mean Mike?" His face creased into laughter.

"That means it's Beer o'Clock."

"Look Rache, you're miles better looking than us two put together so we're going for a beer. All that you've got to do while we're away is give out these flyers, smile and sell a load of holidays. Think you can do that?"

"But I don't know anything about sailing or the Ionian or even where our offices are. I don't know anything about anything."

"Look Chief Hostess Designate, you've got an iPhone and Google. Get stuck in and we'll see you in a bit."

And with that they ambled off chatting.

I hit Google hard. The Ionian is the sea at the end of the Adriatic, opposite Italy and a bit down from Corfu. There are Inner Ionian and Outer Ionian Seas. The Inner Ionian is like an enormous lake 44 miles long and 23 miles wide with lots of islands in it.

Every picture had green, tree covered mountains shooting up from dark, blue black seas. It was only right next to the shore that there were the brilliant, aquamarine colours that I thought were everywhere in Greece.

On one side of the lake is the island of Lefkada – one of the biggest in the Inner Ionian. There was Lefkas Town which looked like a proper little town. Our offices, and I had already started thinking of being part of Delfini Sailing Holidays, were based in a small village a few miles from Lefkas called Ligia.

If you followed Google maps a bit further down the road, there was another small town called Nydri and about 29 zillion, million yachts in a long harbour.

In fact, every image on Google was a yacht picture. Sailing, parked up in some beautiful bay and very often with some stunning girl in a micro bikini either wrapped round the side of the boat or jumping into the sea. I reached down to the waist band on my jeans, had a quick feel at the roll of fat, and thought that was the end of cat biscuits!

The sailing looked so fantastic – brilliant sun, white sails and there was me, sitting on the front of the yacht, with the wind blowing my hair, sipping a drink through a long straw. It was a dream and what a dream! I was prepared to spend all day in the office, because that was what they were paying me for, but I did hope that they would let me go out with them occasionally.

Maybe I was about to become me.

★★★★★

The flyers were okay – but not brilliant. In fact, that's not really fair. They were terrible with spelling and grammatical mistakes all over the place. I thought of getting out my pen, marking all the errors and then giving the flyer back to Dave - but then I remembered the cat noses and thought that it was probably better to keep my mouth very tightly shut.

I soon learned that a happy smile was the key thing to flyering. Smile a lot and most people will take a flyer from you. The problems came when I was asked a question – or worse still, two!

"Where are you sailing from this year?"

Lefkas, Ligia, the seafront next to Blackpool Pier? I really didn't have a clue. I was beginning to get stressed and started scanning the horizon – how's that for sailor girl talk – for Dave and Mike. Then something clicked.

I beamed the smile of the truly confident. "We're working on the exact details just at the minute but we'll be in the Lefkas area, towards Nydri."

The first time I said this I winced, expecting to get verbally punched but the two lads nodded, took the flyer and off they went. Wow, I could do this!

I smiled on for an hour and then a middle aged couple came striding down to the stand, looking very focussed and full of serious intentions.

The man, casually but well dressed, held out his hand. "Hi, it's Anthony and Sally Walters – we sail with you every year."

I smiled and nodded as if I knew all about them.

"Well, we just want you to know that we feel really bad about what happened to Dave. What they did to him was terrible and so whatever he does this year, we're going to go with him."

"Yes, we are," agreed his wife, "it was shocking. How could they get away with it? They want locking up. It might have been legal but as far as I'm concerned, they're just damned crooks."

"Look," Anthony said, "I don't know what the cost will be this year but we normally pay around £3,000 so I thought that if we gave you 50% now this might help things along a bit. How's that sound?"

£1500! I had hardly even seen £50 and now they wanted to give me £1500. All this was getting far too much for me.

Anthony spoke again. "Dave probably needs cash at the moment so I went to the bank and sorted some out for him."

And with that, he turned to his wife who produced a large, brown envelope from her handbag.

"Here we go," she beamed.

I stood there holding it like the last person in Pass the Parcel, frightened to unwrap it and find out that it was a boy's toy.

The strange thing was that, suddenly, things were changing inside my head and it was a very weird experience. Instead of being given a timetable to follow, or lectures to attend, or a toilet break at 10.20 – and remember it's five minutes, so don't be late back – I was on my own. It was like falling out of the nest, flapping my arms and finding I could fly. I could fly, I really could.

Someone had given me £1500 and I wasn't frightened or stressed because it was down to me what to do next.

"That's very kind, incredibly kind, and yes, Dave will be very grateful.

"I'm new to Delfini so please forgive me for not knowing you personally but could you please be so kind as to leave your names and contact details so that Dave can get back to you?"

Sally had another rummage in her bag, found a pen and wrote neatly on the back of one of the flyers. And that was that.

"Don't forget to tell Dave we're right with him and we'll see him in June."

I looked at the envelope and then tucked it away at the bottom of my bag. £1500 was a lot of money to look after but I had just grown up.

I saw Mike coming for ten minutes before he reached me. Every few paces, someone stopped him for a chat and it seemed as if there was no-one in the show who didn't want to say hello.

Eventually he arrived at the stand. I was still handing out flyers and smiling until my face was aching.

"Done any good, Rache?"

"Well, I have given a load of flyers out…"

"Great – you never know when you're going to get lucky at a show."

"And someone left something for Dave."

I was trying to keep a straight face but couldn't.

"Oh yeah, and what would that be?"

"Nothing really – just a brown envelope."

Now Mike was joining in what was clearly a joke.

"And what would be in that brown envelope? Free tickets to Twicken-ham for the Six Nations? Six tabs of Viagra to help the poor bugger have some fun? No, I know - the brochure for the retirement home in Lefkas.

"Actually, it's probably a Court Summons for the money we owe."

"No, it's something else."

"Oh come on Rache, you're killing me. What've you got?"

"Could we use £1500 – in cash?" Had I really just said "We"?

"You are joking, you really are joking. Fifteen hundred sterling and at this time of year? If you're winding me up you're sacked – and I'll take your shirt off you, right here in front of everyone."

I felt so happy with the teasing and that Mike wanted to join in with the joke. For the first time in my adult life, I was on the inside with someone instead of having my nose pressed to the window looking in.

I reached into my bag and breathed a sigh of relief when I found the envelope was still there. I held it out to Mike and explained about the couple who had left it.

"Bloody good people are Anthony and Sally. Bloody decent, good people. They're the reason we're still here you know."

I waited a moment and then looked Mike directly in eyes. I had to raise my head, he was so much taller than me, but what I was going to say needed saying directly without anything getting in the way. I was standing at the most important cross-roads of my life and I needed to know which way to go.

"Mike, the Walters went on about Dave needing money and then they were talking about criminals. Has he done something wrong?"

I paused because I was frightened to ask the next question, afraid of pressing too hard and losing what I had just found and which was already becoming precious to me.

"Mike, I need to know because I am not going to get involved in anything dishonest. I'd rather ice biscuits for the rest of my life than do something illegal. Tell me the truth."

"That's fair enough Rache. Sit down and I'll tell you the whole story.

"Dave has been sailing in the Ionian since the idea of sailing for a holiday was invented. He knows everyone and he loves taking people sailing and so, over the years, customers kept coming back and eventually he set up on his own and the firm grew.

"The problem is that Dave never liked the business side of sailing very much. He could do it, and actually he was good at it, but his heart was always on the water, you know - being with customers and giving them a good time.

"Eighteen months ago, a bloke called Itkul Sadykov came down to our offices in Lefkas – in those days we had a proper office with a couch and a desk and all the other crap – and he said that he was looking to invest in a sailing company.

"He told us all about the other tourism businesses he had in his portfolio and opened his laptop to show us all the great things he was doing.

"The deal was that he would invest in the company and Dave would retire from the day to day running of the business and become more of a consultant – that meant that he could spend more time on the water. You can see how it went...

"Sadykov took us out for meals every night, and wouldn't take a penny, and he was driving a brand new Range Rover so he clearly wasn't short of a quid or ten.

"Then he brought in his assistant, a lovely looking girl, very smart – white shirt and black skirt, clean on every day – the real thing. Lovely American accent too.

"She was an accountant and would have charmed the birds out of the trees. She sympathised with Dave about all the boring paper work and just offered to do it all for him. No stress, no fuss, no questions – just give it to me and you go sailing. So he did.

"I know that this sounds as if Dave was stupid but it wasn't like that at all. They looked rich and successful and the bigger the business grew, the more hassle there was and the further away we got from what we wanted to do, and what we were good at - giving clients a good time sailing.

"If they made some money as well as us, so what? We'd got rid of all the things that were driving us crazy and that we hated - and we were out sailing with our customers.

"That's the thing. If you want something enough, then you'll believe anything to get it."

I thought about my relationship with Connor and nodded.

"At first, everything went really well. We got new computers and a posh coffee maker in the office, and a new van too. The boats all had a re-fit and were brought up to the latest spec. It all looked great.

"April, that was Sadykov's assistant's name, answered all the e-mails. We were crap at this in any case - but I happened to notice one particular e-mail because it had a red message across the top.

"It was a final demand for payment for sails from a company Dave and

I had dealt with for years. I asked April what was this all about and she just said that it had been a computer mistake by the bank, you know, the sort that causes delays in transferring money from Greece to the UK or something, I don't know what exactly.

"But it was the same thing again. I didn't want to believe that everything wasn't absolutely wonderful - and Dave didn't either. We were having a great time, the clients were the happiest they'd ever been and it was all too good to imagine that anything could be wrong.

"You've got to believe that, Rachel, it was just all too good.

"We packed up for the end of the season but left the boats in the water on our two pontoons until we could lift them a couple of weeks later.

"Sadykov asked us if we would drive to Athens to meet a Greek investor who wanted to put more money in the business. It's a six hour drive but we were dead keen and so we got cleaned up and headed south in the van.

"When we got there, Sadykov didn't turn up for the meeting but he sent Dave a text saying that he had been delayed and that he would see us the following day.

"It was no big deal so we had a meal and a few beers, and went to bed feeling good about life. The following day, we turned up at the restaurant where we were supposed to meet Sadykov.

"He didn't appear. Dave was getting a bit agitated by now and tried ringing and texting him but there was no reply so we thought stuff you, we'll have another night in the hotel and a few more beers.

"Things started to smell really funny the following morning. Dave tried to pay with the company credit card but it was rejected. The hotel receptionist was all smiles but you could see that she wasn't happy. Dave had some money in his jacket pocket from the tips he'd been given and I had a couple of hundred Euros on me so we paid up and left.

"We were both getting a bad feeling for what had happened and so we drove as fast we could and took a chance on the speed cameras which are all over the 951.

"When we got to our yard, the gates were closed and there was a big guy in a black windcheater outside. Dave went apeshit and told the bloke to clear off out of the way or there'd be trouble.

"The security guy started getting all tense and so I calmed everyone down before it all kicked off.

"After ten minutes, another guy came out with some more security blokes.

"He was just what he looked like – a lawyer.

"He asked us to park the van and come into the office – our own bloody office, would you believe?

18

"There were two other lawyer types there and a couple more of these big guys, all looking really keen to give Dave a smack if he gobbed off.

"I'll come to the end of the story because there isn't any point in going through the detail. It still gets to me, even now.

"Sadykov was a con-man and he had used Delfini as security for huge loans of over €2 million.

"The suits all claim that he is a legitimate businessman but the truth is that he's nothing more than a stinking, thieving conman - stealing from people who believe his lies.

"The loan was made to a company registered in the Cayman Islands and there was more chance of us flying than ever getting a penny of it back.

"The Swiss guy was actually quite pleasant. He said that St. Cergue International Finance now owned everything – as in absolutely everything. They owned the boats, the offices, the pontoons, even the bloody posh coffee maker.

"We could either pay the debt in full, there and then and immediately, and we'd all stay best mates, or he would accept the offer he had received from a sailing company based on the Costa Blanca.

"The thing that got to me is that everyone except us knew what was happening. It had probably all been done before with the same people involved. Park your car on double yellow lines and you'll get a fine. Nick a couple of million Euros from some idiots and you get taken out to dinner. It was just shit.

"Dave was in tears, honestly Rachel, he just sat there sobbing like a baby.

"I think even the Swiss guys felt a bit sorry for him - and maybe even embarrassed.

"The smoothie Swiss boss said how sorry he was about all this but business is business and would Dave like to buy the name back off them and start again?

"Well, Dave starts raging and shouting but I calmed him down because rolling round the floor getting a kicking from three big security guys wasn't going to fix anything.

"I asked the Swiss bloke what we would get if we bought the name back. He laughed and said everything that wasn't inside the compound which gave me an idea. It was the worst hand of cards ever but there was just a one in a million chance.

"I got my wallet out and said, 'Well, you'll have to do us a really good price because after paying for the hotel in Athens we're broke.'

"I unzipped the inner bit and shook out €11 and 70 cents in coins.

"They thought that this was great. Thick sailor with not enough money to buy a meal. Oh yeah, that was hilarious.

"Everyone joined in the joke – even the security guys - so we all had a really big laugh at how dumb me and Dave had been. How funny was that?

"Then the Swiss guy said. 'How about €1 and seventy cents and then you can both go and have a beer to celebrate your purchase?'

"My mind was running flat out because I'd had a thought. Not absolutely everything we owned was in Lefkas, you see. There were five old boats on our original base in Tychos. Sadykov had never seen them and he'd never been to Tychos so I tried to keep calm and think clearly.

"I smiled like an idiot and said that neither of us had a car and so could we please keep the van and anything else, like our shirts and wet weather gear which really belonged to the company?

"They were all enjoying the joke but it had clicked with Dave what was on my mind and so he just continued to sit there looking miserable.

"I told them that we didn't want any trouble in the future like someone taking the van off us or anything, so could they please write me a receipt, or whatever we needed, saying that we owned everything outside the yard, and did we need a witness because remember I'm really stupid and don't know anything.

"So they did, and we walked out of the gates with the worst kicking either of us had ever had – but still in business.

"And that's exactly what happened Rache. No word of a lie. We did nothing wrong except for being thick - and I guess that we're not the first people to let their hearts rule their brains."

I sat in silence because I didn't know what to say. Nothing in my life had prepared me for anything like this. Dishonesty for me was someone taking one of your yoghurts from the fridge in the kitchen at Uni or drinking more wine than they'd brought to the party. Now there was this. I didn't understand it and I was frightened.

Mike spoke again. "Rache, everyone is being really kind but we're living from hand to mouth until we get some money in. That £1500 you've taken is going to keep us from starving, it's that important.

"Come with us and give us a hand because we really need you."

I felt the tears welling in my eyes and I wiped them on the back of my hand.

"You really want me?"

"Yes, we both really do. The other thing is that you're the only one who's applied…"

And then he hugged me hard, with his long, strong arms, and kissed me on the top of my head.

*****

Dave came back and immediately sensed that things were not as they had been when he left. His eyes darted to Mike and he said: "You told her?"

Mike nodded. "Yes, everything."

Both of them looked at me and Dave spoke. "Well? What do you think? If you want out now, all I can say is thanks for coming – and you can keep the shirt as a souvenir."

There were no smiles on either of their faces.

"Look, it's not the money because all that I've got in the way of money is a giant student debt. I believe that it wasn't your fault and you seem two really nice people but…"

"But what, Rachel, let's hear the but now and get it over with." Mike's face was cold and uncompromising.

I suppose I should have felt bullied or intimidated – they were older than me and had done so much more. But I wasn't. I knew that I was at a cross-roads in my life and the choices facing me were all very different.

I could get a job as a classroom assistant straight away and start Teacher Training in September and be sure of a salary and holidays and enough money to rent a flat.

Journalism was still on the table too. If I went to see the Pastoral Tutor at College and told her about Connor, they would have had me back.

I knew that I didn't have to be a Christmas Elf for a second year. I could do better than that.

And now two men I had barely met were putting me on the spot to make a decision which was going to change my life for the better - or maybe for worse.

"The only thing I want you to tell me is that you can do it. Will I have a job a month after I come out to you or will it just go wrong? Tell me the truth."

Dave spoke: "Rachel, that sounds almost like a threat. It's me who's lost everything - not you. It's me that's got no future if this fails – not a 22 year old with a degree and a Mum and Dad with a house where she can live.

"We need you. We need your brains and we need your enthusiasm but I'm not going down on my knees to you or anyone else.

"We think that we can pull things round but we don't know for sure. If you want to come and try with us - great. If not, then thanks for coming and we'll see you around. But either way it's 100% your choice. I am not promising anything – I can't promise because I don't know."

There was a few seconds pause - but it felt like a day. Then the sign post lit up with great big flashing letters.

"I'll come, please and work for you and do my best but you'll have to help me because I don't know one end of a boat from the other. Are they called boats or yachts or are they ships?"

Dave wrapped his two hands around mine.

"Good girl, Rache, good girl. We knew you were quality right from the first moment we saw you, didn't we Mike? I said straight away, 'That's a quality Hostie walking down the row to us. I can tell quality a mile off…"

I smiled and thought about the €2 million scam and how good they both were at judging character!

"But you'll have to help me Dave, I don't know anything. What clothes do I need and what shall I bring?"

Dave beamed. "Knickers, Rache, Hosties always bring knickers but never enough. Loads of knickers. I've never met a Hostie yet who had enough knickers for the season so load up with knickers."

I really didn't know what to say after that so I just stood there, looking embarrassed.

Mike chipped in. "There aren't as many shops on Tychos as you're used to so you need to bring a couple of skirts, and a few tops and maybe a casual dress. You got a casual dress, Rache?"

I nodded lamely.

"And a couple of bikinis. Jeans are good too and a fleece because it sometimes gets a bit cold in the Ionian, and then all the girl stuff that you might need. Yeah, loads of girl stuff – and plenty of knickers like Dave said because you might not find exactly what you want on Tychos.

"And don't forget the flips flops. You really need some flip flops Rache – and knickers of course." Dave concluded.

They were rolling about like two eleven year olds at the knickers' joke and I couldn't help smiling.

"And write your address down before you go so that we know where to send your air ticket to Preveza and then we'll meet you there in April.

"You're going to have a great time."

And that's how I became a Hostie.

*****

I went home and told Mum and Dad that I'd got the job and they asked all the right, sensible questions about wages and contracts and holidays and where I was going to live but I said that Dave and Mike were still sorting everything out - that they were really nice people and that it was all going to be good. Dad knew better than Mum that I was going to Greece because it was more than a job. I needed to go to Greece to find myself – to find out who I really was.

Dave asked me to be ready to join them in the first week in April, before the sailing season started at the end of the month. Before then, I had to earn some money so I phoned the garden centre where I had been a Christmas Elf and asked if they had any vacancies.

As I have said, there is never any shortage of work so I got a job straight away cleaning the tables in the café. I needed the money but if I was going to be a Hostie, I also needed to learn so I watched how the staff interacted with customers. Interacted sounds all very formal but I really did concentrate on how the customers were served – what was said to them and how they were treated.

It was a very different atmosphere from being a Christmas Elf where I was expected to be silly and amuse the kids. These customers were all adults and they wanted adults serving them.

The café manager was very kind and when I asked if I could learn how to work on the till, she was only too pleased to train me. I was learning again – this time about cash and credit charges and how to work out what food customers were bringing to the till before they actually arrived. I became really good at spotting the difference between pie and chips and fish and chips as the trays slid towards me!

To be honest, they did everything they could to make me happy because I took a lot of work off the manager. After a couple of weeks, I was checking the suppliers as they delivered to us. With hundreds of burgers and fish fingers arriving every week it was a serious job and so I took it seriously. It felt completely different from messing about with cats' noses. This was a real job and, bit by bit, it was as if the fog which had been surrounding me for the last four years was clearing.

I liked the responsibility and I liked the work and it was only the occasional text from Dave or Mike which reminded me that I already had a job.

To keep me happy, I was allowed to help out in the kitchen and I learned how to make massive helpings of Spaghetti Bolognaise and cook burgers on the giant griddle. I had never cooked before but I liked making food and found I had a knack for it. Okay, I was never going to be a Michelin starred chef but in a couple of weeks I could make most of the things we sold and I felt good about this too.

This was the biggest difference between my old life and the new life. Instead of always having to do what someone else had worked out, I was being treated like, well - like an adult! At Uni, I was a 21 year old child and now eight months later I was expected to do things right and get on with jobs independently. I liked it a lot.

*****

One thing which was the same as Uni was the homework. I read so much that it was like my finals. Where to start? Well, the difference between boats and ships is that boats go inside ships. Yessss! Got one right!

And a boat with a sail is a yacht. And usually, there are two sails – the one at the front which is called a Genoa and the big one at the back which is the mainsail. Then there were rudders and keels and sheets which don't go on your bed but are ropes for moving the sails about, and stays, which are metal ropes to hold the mast up, and ten thousand other things - a lot of which made no sense at all. Who ever heard of a vang or ram's horn – except when it was attached to a boy sheep's head?

As I said before, I was a good girl at school and not frightened of work, so I really got stuck in and, although I didn't understand a lot about what I was reading that didn't stop me from trying. If I was going to work for a sailing holiday firm, I was going to learn about sailing.

I also watched some really scary YouTube films, where yachts were bouncing up and down with great big waves crashing over them. There was one with a girl at the steering wheel of a little yacht going round Cape Horn with enormous waves washing over her. And there she was with a bright red face, smiling and waving at the camera. Wow!

I really hoped that Mike would let me have a little go in a yacht at least a couple of times but I didn't fancy anything scary because, for sure, I was no action girl heroine!

*****

My Mum and Dad were very kind but they were worried – really worried. My Dad understood that I needed to go to Greece and so he was supportive and hid his unease.

My Mum didn't hide hers but she did her best to help in a practical way. My Dad bought me a big, Gore-tex kit bag, with extra compartments where I could separate wet and dry clothes and my Mum sorted out a really good medical kit and put this in a grey bag which had a lovely red flower on it. She loaded it up with paracetamol, Imodium and a load of girl stuff.

My Dad laughed when I told him that the only thing Dave had told me to bring was lots of knickers - but he had other ideas. He bought a really top quality anorak for me, which must have cost a fortune, and a very thin sleeping bag made from some stuff the SAS use so it was really warm but rolled up into a ball you could almost fit in your handbag.

Then, when Mum was out, he sat me down. He was serious – and I never liked that look at all.

"Look Rachel, going to Greece and working for a little holiday company with no money is not what I wanted for you – we both know that. But I also know that it's what you want so I've stroked your Mum's feathers and we're both going to support you.

"Go to Greece, do your best and let them know how lucky they are to have you.

"But if things do go wrong, or you're not happy or they don't treat you properly, then remember that we're here to help. Your bed will always be made. Our arms will always be open and you will always be our Baby Bear.

"And I know that the next thing I am going to say could cause a row but I don't want it to. Please listen to me and then do what I say without an argument."

Dad passed me a thin, fabric wallet.

"In there is €1,000. It's not for you to use. It's not to make life easy for you or to stop you making a success of the job in your own way or anything else like that. It's your emergency parachute – that's all.

"If things go terribly wrong, and you have tried your best but you know that you are in trouble you can't sort out, get a taxi to the airport and get on the first plane home and I'll be there when you land.

"I know that everything will go well but if the plane does burst into flames at least you will have a parachute."

I started crying and gave my Dad a big, long hug.

*****

I decided to do one more thing. My friends from school and Uni hadn't been much help when I had been really fed up and lost so I decided to just empty the cupboards of all the emotional junk which had done me no good so far. I sent a text to everyone to say that I was off travelling and couldn't be reached and then I posted a Facebook message saying more or less the same thing.

There would be no texts to pick me up and none to drag me down. No pictures of me on Instagram having a great time in Greece and no whinging ones either. Good or bad, failure or success, I was going to do this thing on my own. Win or lose, it would be my battle and I was prepared to take whatever Greece, Delfini Holidays and sailing threw at me.

Mum and Dad were a different problem - and in two different ways too! I was always talking to Mum on Facebook even when things were at their worst. It could have been big things or little ones but we were always messaging each other. She was really upset when I told her that for a bit, things would go very quiet.

My Dad hates Facebook and texting so there was no problem there – but he loves sending long, detailed e-mails written in perfect English.

He is also always wanting to help me and if he ever found out what had actually happened with Connor, I mean the actual detail and the words Connor had shouted at me, Dad would probably be in jail now for what he would have done to Connor.

I had to tell Dad, in a way that showed him how much I still loved him, that I wouldn't be sending e-mails and I wouldn't be replying to his either.

I didn't know what the internet and phone reception was like in Greece but I said that it was rubbish and that sending messages by Facebook or e-mail was going to be almost impossible. To say this to my Mum in particular, was really hard.

I was grateful that I had my Dad's €1000 parachute but once I used this I would have failed and I would have to start all over again. This time, there would be no turning back, no excuses, no-one to rely on except me. I looked at myself in the mirror in my bedroom and I was scared – but proud too.

*****

My Mum and Dad came to Manchester Airport and waited whilst I checked in. Dave had sent the tickets just as he said he would and even if I had never heard of the super budget airline I was flying with, the check in girl accepted them.

I went back to Mum and Dad for a last hug. Dad gave me a kiss on the cheek and said: "I love you Baby Bear. Remember, we're here for you day and night, the moment you need us."

Then I turned and walked towards security.

I love my Mum and Dad very much but now it was time to find out about me and what sort of person I was deep inside. I had to be able to look in the mirror every morning and like the person I saw looking back at me so, for fear of becoming too frightened to go on and ending up running back into their arms, I didn't glance back even once but headed straight for the security guy handing out the plastic bags for liquids.

I needed to flap my arms and see if I could fly – and I wasn't sure if I could…

3

You Expect Me to Sleep Where?

THE plane roared down the runway at Manchester Airport and plumes of spray spiralled out from the wing tips as we climbed through the dense, grey, clinging cloud.

We turned south but I couldn't see our house, or even anywhere near where I had lived for most of my life, because of the thick fog. I was glad because I didn't need reminding of my bedroom or my lovely duvet and the big bookcase with my teddy sat on the window ledge looking at me.

We climbed into a brilliant blue sky and I thought of spending the next seven months in the sun. I could do this!

The "Fasten Your Seat Belt" sign came on at almost exactly the same time as an Eastern European voice explained that there would be "a little turbulence" over Austria and that passengers should return to their seats immediately.

This was a good warning as the plane dropped what felt like 20 miles and then boinged up again, passing the bit of sky we had just been flying through! Then we skidded to the left, then the right and we dropped and climbed and skidded some more - all the way down the Adriatic Coast to Greece.

The elderly lady next to me was going out to her villa on Corfu and went paler and paler as we slid from one side to the other. I prayed that she wouldn't throw up all over my new jeans.

Come on weather. Where's the blue sky and sun?

*****

The next message was the one I always liked to hear. "Cabin crew, prepare for landing."

We broke through a dense, almost black, blanket of rain and mist and there below us was an equally dark sea, covered with angry looking waves each one of which had a white scarf on its head, waving furiously in the wind.

We bounced round towards a range of mountains, covered in fog. I couldn't imagine where the runway would be up there. Then there was another turn and through the window I saw that we were going back out to sea. Whoops! Has the pilot got his SatNav switched on?

The engine noise slowed down and we began descending fast over what looked like a huge lake. I stretched to see through the window. There, just on my left, was a long strip of dirty white, concrete runway covered in tyre marks.

I'm not frightened of flying but I always hold myself just that bit tense in the last few seconds before the landing. The roar died away to nothing and there was a huge clonk on one side of the plane followed by a second one as the wheels hit the runway.

Welcome to Preveza. I was here.

*****

I already knew that Preveza was a military airport which someone with a bit of sense thought would be great for tourists visiting the area. That has to be a better thing to do than bombing people. It also explained why there were none of the posh corridors which slide up to the plane, like you get at Manchester. Instead, some stairs were wheeled up to the side and we staggered out into a gale and driving rain. I pulled my anorak hood over my head - and said silent thanks to my Dad.

It was only 100m walk from the plane to the small terminal building but by the time I got there my jeans were wet. Wow! No wonder those mountains looked green.

Our passports were checked, actually they weren't checked much at all, by a nice policeman in a little booth. He had a glance at my scary passport face and then smiled – and I smiled back. It was what I needed.

I walked along with a girl about my age and she said that the baggage took just a few minutes to collect because there was usually only one plane arriving at a time. There was only a short wait and then the luggage came chugging along as it does in every airport in the world. There was my black kit bag carrying my life for the next seven months. It didn't look much.

I heaved it off the baggage belt and dumped it onto a trolley with my rucksack on top.

Mike had promised to meet me but I couldn't just rush out. The truth is that I was too scared. When he saw me, would it be to tell me that they had a better Hostie, or maybe he thought that I had turned all ugly since the Boat Show or perhaps he would have forgotten that I was coming or…

I just didn't know what to think or believe and, if my Dad had been with me and asked if I wanted to go home then and there, I would probably have gone. It really was that bad.

It took me a few minutes to get myself together. I had asked for this. I wanted it and I had insisted on having it so I pushed the trolley out of the baggage area at motorway speed and on to the tiny concourse.

And there was Mike, tall, confident – and with a big smile.

"Rache, great to see you. Did you have a good flight?"

He scooped up my kit bag, yes the one I had struggled getting on to the trolley, in one hand, slung it over his shoulder and then said: "Give us your rucksack. You must be tired out." and took it from my hand.

"The limousine awaits you, Madam…"

There was none of the security you see at big airports and so we threaded our way through the buses and taxis and there was a big white van with a large dolphin on the side and Delfini Sailing Holidays written in blue, cursive script. Other than a few bits of rust, and some dings in the back, the van looked quite presentable.

Mike opened the side door and threw my rucksack and kit bag into what was very clearly a working van. It smelled of oil and petrol and there was a big red toolbox, a few coils of rope and some loops of shiny wire. Against one wall stood a black and yellow plastic cabinet with dozens of little compartments and, next to that, a giant roll of what looked like blue kitchen paper.

The front of the van was divided from the back by a wooden wall. Mike cleared a huge bag of crisps and a bottle of water off the seat and flung open the passenger door for me to get in. There was more debris from bits of meal on the floor but I threaded my feet round these and off we went.

The rain was hammering down and the clouds were so low, I could have leaned out of the window and touched them.

Mike read my mind. "It's a bit blowy Rache but April's a funny month in the Ionian. It can be really nice, like an English summer's day – or it can be a properly chilly. Do you want the heater up a bit?"

We were struggling to talk because neither of us knew what to say. It wasn't really surprising because we had only spent one afternoon together and exchanged a few texts – that hardly made us best mates.

We drove away from the airport and past the warning signs every few hundred metres forbidding anyone from taking photographs and there was an old jet fighter, perched on a pole, reminding everyone that this was still a military base.

The van bounced along on the road past huge greenhouses and cultivated fields and then we climbed uphill. There were big pot holes everywhere. Mike saw me gripping the handle above the door and wincing.

"Rache, Greece isn't England. They're good people here – kind, almost too kind in some ways, and hard working but they've got big problems.

"Those stories you read about the country running out of money aren't bullshit – they're true. They've got a lot on their plate so as long as you can actually drive on the road then that's enough. A few holes can wait."

We arrived at a T-junction with a sign saying Agios Nikolaos. It wasn't really a town, more of a big village, and cars and vans were parked everywhere with not a double yellow line in sight.

Now Mike grinned: "The Greeks are more relaxed about a lot of things than the English, and top of the list is parking! Don't worry, you'll soon get into the lifestyle."

We drove out of the town and there was another deafening silence. I thought that I would try something non-controversial to talk about – and made a big mistake!

I turned to Mike and in my best party conversation voice said: "How did you become a Lead Skipper?"

"You really want to know?"

"Yes, of course…"

"Because I love sailing and I can't do anything better with my life. How's that sound?"

I didn't say anything.

"I sailed dinghies as a kid and I was very good. Everyone said I was Olympic material. But to compete in the Olympics you need a lot of money. My Dad was a gardener at the local college and my Mum was a dinner lady. They did their best to take me to the right competitions but we always had the worst boat with the oldest sails. I might have had the ability but I didn't have the equipment and so I was never going to win.

"I didn't hate school or anything but I just wanted to sail so when I was sixteen I left and got a job in a small marina and started to get a reputation for being able to sail anything in any weather.

"Then there was the financial crash in 2008 and a lot of boats were re-possessed. I met these lads who were getting good money doing boat re-possessions.

"You know, some bloke whose business was doing well and who'd borrowed a shed load of money for a flash new boat and then suddenly found out that he was deep in the smelly stuff and the bank had got all stroppy.

"So the banks sold the boats to debt collection companies, who really couldn't give a toss for anyone, and we had the job of getting the boats back. Any weather, day or night - good money if we delivered the boats to another marina.

"I tell you Rache, there were some seriously upset bunnies when they went down to the pier at the weekend and found their pride and joy gone and all they had left was a Court Order stapled to the dock.

"From there, I got into the boat delivery business – all over Britain, the Med, the Atlantic – even one to Callao in Peru so I've sailed round Cape Horn and that was bloody scary.

"Then I was delivering a boat to Corfu and met Dave and he said he was looking for a new Lead Skipper because his previous one had gone working on some millionaire's yacht in the Baltic and did I fancy a go at the holiday market?

"To be honest, I was in two minds but Dave was just so bloody keen and enthusiastic that I said I would give him a hand for a couple of months, because there was no delivery work, and then I ended up staying.

"I got to spend a lot of time on the water and I got real satisfaction from giving customers a good time. The more I enjoyed it the more I wanted to carry on doing it so that's how I became Lead Skipper. I guess that I am here for life now too, because I can't think of anything I want to do more than this.

"And that's really all there is to it."

I didn't know what to say. Everything was so new. The words, the ideas, even the idea of taking someone's boat and just leaving a bit of paper saying that they no longer owned it was incredible. I really was beginning to wonder what I had got myself into.

The road ran alongside the sea now and the waves were breaking fiercely on the shore, throwing a thin, salty mist onto the van's windscreen.

"It's beautiful out there Rache, sailing across the bay to Preveza. Today would be sparky but in summer you would have to go a long way to find anywhere more beautiful."

There was another difficult silence, probably only a few seconds but you know how it feels like hours and hours when you don't know what to say but you know you should say something.

Mike was just as uncomfortable as I was but he helped out.

"And on your right Madam, is the old Venetian fort and ahead of us - the world famous Lefkas floating bridge."

"You're kidding me. A bridge that floats?"

"Yes indeed Madam, believe your tour guide. This bridge actually does float and every hour it swings open so all the happy sailors, and a few not so happy ones 'cos they're not sailing with us, go through the Lefkas Canal and out into the Ionian.

"You'll love it."

I wondered when I was going to get the chance to love the bridge or the boats. I knew what I had signed up for – to be a hostess and keep all the customers happy when they came back from sailing, but I did hope that I would get some chance to go out on a boat.

I thought that we were going to die when we crossed the bridge! There were big, steel ridges all across the roadway and my teeth nearly fell out with the vibration as the van shook itself across.

To my left was what looked like a big canal and ahead there was Lefkas Town. I felt my tummy tighten with excitement. We were getting nearer to my new home by the second.

★★★★★

We drove along the harbour wall but there were only a few yachts in the water. On the other side of the harbour there was a forest of masts sticking up from yachts still in boatyards. They were balanced on their keels and propped up with massive pieces of wood. Some had men clambering over them whilst others were having paint rolled on to their hulls. Everywhere I looked it was busy.

We turned left at a little traffic island at the beginning of the town and now the road went alongside the biggest marina I had ever seen. There was space for thousands and thousands of boats – well, a lot anyway – and a big hotel with a guard. If this was sailing, you could count me in.

Then I remembered. I'd only brought two dresses and a couple of skirts. What would the clients think when they saw me in the same clothes every day?

Every tiny bit of space had a yacht in it. There were small ones, big ones and some enormous things with huge keels. The interesting thing was that they all looked almost the same. White hulls and decks and sharp bows sticking straight down at ninety degrees. They were obviously fantastic boats but they looked as if some of the boys in my Primary School had drawn them in art.

At the end of the marina, we turned right and headed out along a dual carriageway. There were still boats in yards but clearly this wasn't the posh end of Lefkas. Mike had gone quiet again so I just looked out of the window as people scurried across the road, heads down and with no thought of the traffic. I thought how few seconds they would have lasted crossing a dual carriageway in Manchester!

We drove on for a few miles. The road climbed and dropped and then opened out again and, next to the sea, there was what looked like a dump for boats. There were boats everywhere, some being painted, some with holes in their sides. There were engines under plastic covers, nylon ropes and coils of wire. This wasn't like Lefkas Marina – not even a tiny little bit.

Mike swung the van into the yard and parked in a small lake of light brown water.

He smiled: "He we are Rache. Risto's Boatyard - home to some of the finest tradesmen on Lefkada. It's where we're getting the boats prepped before we go to Tychos."

He saw the look on my face. "Don't let the looks fool you, Rache. I know everything looks a bit rough and ready but Risto keeps half the fishing boats in the Ionian on the water, and he's a pal of ours, so we couldn't be in a better place.

"Come and meet MG, our Chief Engineer, and say hello."

I opened the door of the van and then jumped as far as I could over the puddle - but still got splashed. The wind had picked up even more and the rain stung my face as I ran after Mike towards a rough concrete building at the back of the yard.

Mike motioned me under the tin roof. "Those are our boats, Rache. There's only the last two to do now – the other three are already on the water."

He waved his hand towards two boats balanced on their keels and supported on each side by three paint stained pieces of wood, each one with a wedge underneath it where it touched the boat's hull.

One had been freshly painted underneath, with a thick blue gloss, but the second one looked a lot less ready.

I didn't know much about boats so I was even more shocked than if I had been a hard core yachtie. Instead of the blunt shape of the other yachts, the bows on these boats swooped down in a beautiful curve and then swept backwards to a lovely taper at the rear. Each one had a big sticker of a huge spotted cat, like a leopard, on the bows, springing into action as if it couldn't wait to get going.

"Oh Mike, they're beautiful – absolutely beautiful. I've never seen anything like them on the web. They're so graceful and…

"And they sail even better than they look. And they're a bloody nightmare to maintain and they were £50,000 too expensive and Dave was a soft sod for buying them and they should have been sold when we were doing good.

"But yes, the Servals are the most beautiful small yachts in the world and customers love them. If MG can keep them in one piece for the season, they will get us out of this mess."

Dave was at the door and held it open for us as we ran across the yard out of the rain. His arms were open to give me a big hug.

"Rache, wonderful to see you. Glad you're here. Sit down. Bet you want a coffee?"

The room looked like every other workmen's shed. There was a dirty table and half a dozen cheap plastic chairs and some mugs, which looked as if they had last been washed about 200 years ago. The sink was in the same state with three grubby plates piled on top of a greasy frying pan.

At one end, a short, tubby guy with small, sparkling eyes and a mass of curly hair sat swinging back and to, on a chair which looked as if it was on the very edge of breaking.

"Hiya. I'm MG. I keep this bloody show on the road – or should that be the water?"

Dave looked at me and smiled.

"He's always getting big ideas about how important he is but he's not too bad as an engineer.

"That's crap really. He's bloody rubbish but he's like you – he's the only one we could get."

And everyone burst out laughing and so, because I wasn't sure what I should be doing, I joined in too.

There was an older man, with a heavily lined face, at the table. He held out a massive, heavily calloused hand to shake but took mine with a gentleness which was surprising – as if he was frightened of crushing me.

"Pleased to meet you Rachel, really pleased to meet you. I'm Risto. Have you worked as a Hostie before?"

"No, this is my first job but I'm really looking forward to it – working in Greece and meeting new people. I have really been trying to find out as much about yachts as I can."

My voice trailed off because I was starting to sound as if I was making a presentation to a seminar at Uni and it felt wrong.

Risto saved me.

"You'll love the Serval – the most luxurious small yacht ever built. Have you lived on a yacht before?"

Out of the corner of my eye, I saw Dave desperately gesticulating to him.

"I'm not sure what you mean – lived on a yacht. I'm staying in a flat, aren't I Dave? That's what you said..."

Dave looked at Mike and, to be fair, they both seemed embarrassed.

"Well, if you remember, we didn't actually promise you a flat – only

34

accommodation. And there's no better place to stay in the Ionian than on a Serval 34 – there really isn't."

My mind was swimming as if I had been drinking cheap red wine at a Uni party.

"But I've never slept on a yacht before – I don't know what to do."

Mike chipped in: "Don't worry about anything. Me and MG will look after you like our little sister, won't we MG?"

"Certainly will, we certainly will. Just like my sister.

"Sort of - but probably not exactly like my sister. My Social Worker went crazy just because I put two battery leads on her pillow and pretended I was going to electrocute her in bed - the stuck up little bitch.

"Not that I did try to electrocute her, just warn her off using my deck, but you know how Social Workers get all upset over little things."

"Shut up MG." barked Mike.

Dave beamed at me again. "Hosties are the most important part of the whole team Rache, they really are. Mike does the sailing but it's you who will keep everyone happy. Most of our customers would rather have a barbie than sail.

"Can you do a barbie, Rache?"

I nodded lamely – like a sad Cabbage Patch doll now.

"And remember Rache, it's the Hostie who has the boat's mobile. She's the girl in charge – not Mike or MG. You'll be the kiddie – the one who makes the big decisions."

"But I don't know anything Dave – I'm not sure, I'm not sure that I can do what you want because I don't know what you want."

"No problem, Rache, no problem. We all had to start somewhere. You've got a degree and you can ice cats' noses so I reckon that makes you the best qualified Hostie in the Ionian. Everything else is easy.

"Let's go and have a look at the lead boat where you'll be staying."

He motioned to the others to stay where they were and we set off across the yard and out on to a concrete pier. There, bouncing up and down like plastic ducks in a bath, were three beautiful boats – their bows reaching out towards the sea and sky, their sterns tied up to the pier with thick, blue ropes.

Dave leapt on board the middle boat with the agility of a teenage lad. The boat was pitching about and I didn't fancy the jump. He held out his hand and smiled that ready smile again.

"Come on, Rache, I'll get you."

So I jumped, stumbled and Dave caught me.

I was on a yacht.

The door to the cabin folded back so neatly that it almost disappeared. Leading down to the cabin was a set of steep wooden steps, each one with a strip of black rubber so that you didn't slip.

I followed Dave below.

I had two thoughts at the same time. First, it was a tiny space to live in for seven months. 34 feet is only ten metres and our front room was six metres long.

And that was outside the boat. Inside it was much smaller. My God! I was going to have to live in a space the same length as Mum and Dad's living room and about half as wide!

At the same time, it struck me how much better organised it was than any house. There were two long seats down either side of the cabin and a table in the centre.

On one side there was a cute little stove and on the other, a table with maps and things on it.

There were cupboards everywhere and I could imagine keeping everything really neat and tidy and clean.

I smiled and so did Dave.

"And the toilet facilities…"

He opened a door on to a tiny loo with a shower head in a holder against one wall.

"Do I get washed in there too?"

"Yup, all modern conveniences – and the water gets bloody hot too.

"And now to your bedroom suite."

We wriggled our way to the front of the boat and Dave folded back another door.

I looked into a triangular space not much longer than me and about three times as wide. Wow! That was going to be snug!

"And MG will bunk down in the centre and Mike's in the dog kennel at the back, where Skippers always go."

I can remember every second of what happened next.

"You, you didn't tell me I'd be sleeping on a boat and you didn't tell me I'd be sharing with two men I don't know and, and what else haven't you told me? What else, Dave, what else don't I know?"

I felt my finger nails digging into my hands and the tears welling in my eyes. This wasn't my dream job – this was a nightmare. What had I got myself into?

I heard my Dad's €1000 calling me – and loudly too. They were in my rucksack. I could just walk out of this dump, and away from these guys who told me half-truths, or who were maybe not even that honest, and get a nice hotel and a plane back home. I could do it now, finish this and leave them to do whatever they wanted and get back to a real life with real people. I could. I could. I could.

Dave was calm. "Sit down please Rachel. Sit down. Wipe your eyes and, please, sit down just for a minute.

"You know we were in big trouble and when you arrived at the Boat Show you were just too good to be true so the bottom line is that we didn't want to risk losing you. That's why we didn't go into too much detail.

"But it's not only us who's in the shit. We're based on Tychos, the least popular of all these islands. Seventy-two people live there all year round. They've got a church, a little shop and a lady who sells gifts in the summer season. Andreas owns a taverna, and it's a very good one, but it's for tourists.

A doctor comes once a week and holds a clinic in the church. If you want to go shopping, you get on the ferry to Vasiliki or Nydri. There's no nipping out for anything.

"These people have got very little and yet when we were robbed, and we were robbed, they were the ones who were the first to offer help. We owe it to them to keep going.

"If you want to help, then we need you. If you don't, then Mike will run you back into Lefkas and we'll pay for a hotel for you.

"I'd like to say that we'd pay for your ticket home too, but I can't because we're broke – and that's the truth.

"All the early booking money has gone on getting the boats ready and now we're living from hand to mouth.

"That's all there is to say Rachel, and there are no other monsters in the cupboard. We do want you – but I'm not going to try to persuade you. Either you come willingly or we'll have to get along without you."

And with that he sat back and looked at me, not in an aggressive, staring way but just open and direct.

I paused and fidgeted under the table. I was really scared of everything – living on a boat, sharing with a guy who had tried to electrocute his sister, being a Hostie – whatever a Hostie was – but the choice was easier than I imagined it would have been.

It was as if a voice inside spoke to me and said: "Do you really want to be a teacher or write for some free paper? Do you want to be an Elf every Christmas? Is that what you really want?"

I knew the answers to all the questions.

And so, because there was no better option, I said to Dave:

"Yes, I'll do it."

We climbed up the stairs and Dave closed the neat folding door behind us. He leapt off the bouncing boat and then held his hand out to me and, again, I stumbled and, again, he caught me.

We ran through the driving rain to the shed where the other three were sitting.

Dave stood up and beamed:

"Delfini Sailing Holidays' team, I would like to introduce you to our new Senior Executive Sailing Hostess, Rachel Laaaammmmmmbbb!"

MG made a very respectable roll of drums with his hands on the table and Mike clapped.

Dave turned to me. "Say a few words, Rache."

I felt very uncomfortable and still the stranger in what was already a team. No, not a team but a family and I wasn't a member of it yet. At the same time, I wasn't going to be put off by them. I had taken control of my life. I had the €1000 in my rucksack. I could have walked out there and then and got my own hotel and bought my airfare home. I wasn't doing this out of desperation.

I felt in control and so I stood up straight and spoke – and with a lot more confidence than I used to do at Uni.

"Dave's told me everything and I know about Tychos. I want to be a Hostie and I'll do my best but you'll all to have to help me. I can learn quickly but you'll have to help.

"You'll also have to let me be me, because I can't be anyone else. So I want you to promise two things because I lived with a man before and I didn't like it. In fact, it made me ill and I don't want to go there again.

"So, you can't look at porn in front of me and you can't, well," and I hesitated because I felt myself sounding really old fashioned, "well, you can't say the 'f word' to me.

"Don't say," and I hesitated again, "don't say "fuck" to me because this other guy shouted fuck at me and I didn't like it.

"So no porn in front of me and no 'f word' and I'll be your Hostie."

Mike laughed. "It's a deal, Rache, it's a deal. Anyway, MG never looks at naked girls – he's more interested in these cute little Greek goats."

*****

We ate pasta and tomatoes with something that tasted like tinned dog food. Then Dave showed me where the toilet was, at the back of the shed, and said it would be better to use this than the one on the boat.

I was pretty well silent as the other four discussed what was needed to finish the two remaining boats and Dave noticed me yawning. It had been a long day. At 10 o'clock this morning I had been having a last hug from my Dad and, ten hours later, I was sitting in a shed with four rough looking lads I didn't know and wondering what it would be like to sleep on a boat.

The guys tried to be kind and said that I could have the boat all to myself until we moved to Tychos. Mike came with me, carrying my kit bag and rucksack as if they were two bags of sweets. He swung the bags on to the boat and then held out a hand to me, as the little yacht tugged at the stern lines holding it to the pier.

Mike was really kind. He said: "Don't worry about anything Rachel. It's all going to be good. You'll have a great time and we'll sort out everything for you.

"Dave's a good guy and MG is mad but he is a brilliant engineer.

"You have a nice sleep and we'll see you in the morning."

I brushed my teeth in the sink next to the cooker and then got undressed. It was like camping with the Guides again and I banged my knee on the table. How I was going to get dressed in the little cupboard where I was supposed to sleep I couldn't imagine.

I wriggled into the sleeping bag Dad had bought for me and scrunched up the two pillows which were in the cabin to make one.

The noise was incredible. The rain lashed down on the deck above my head like hailstones and the water banged angrily against the hull and literally shook the boat.

I began to cry. It was a horrible mixture of things. I was lonely and wanted to be in my own bed, in my own bedroom, with my Mum and Dad sleeping in the room next door.

I wanted to know that I could get in my old Ford Fiesta and drive to Tesco, on the right side of the road.

I didn't like TV but tonight I ached to switch it on and watch "Bake Off."

I wanted all the familiar things which had been my life for 22 years.

But most of all, I cried for fear of not succeeding. I had chosen this life and, more than anything else, I wanted these guys to like and respect me – to want me to work with them, not because there was no-one else but because I was good.

I wanted them to say, "Rache is a bloody good Hostie…" or something like that and for me to smile because I knew it was true.

4

Get Off My Boat You Dirty Rat!

THE sun woke me the following morning as it streamed through the plastic skylight above the cabin. I got dressed in yesterday's clothes and climbed the steps from the cabin to the cockpit. I opened the door and all above me, stretching from one side of the world to the other, was the most brilliant blue sky. It was like one of those wonderful Spring days you sometimes see in England but without the frost – as if someone had taken a pan cleaner to the sky and scrubbed it until the blue shined.

MG was on the dock with a toolbox in his hand. "Welcome to Greece, Rachel. Not bad is it?"

"It's lovely, really beautiful – and warm too." My voice trailed off because I wasn't sure what I was supposed to say or if what I had said was right or sounded too much like a Sixth Former on a school trip.

"I'm sorry for asking, but I don't know how to work the shower on the boat." This was really embarrassing – having to ask a guy I'd barely met how to get washed.

"And I wonder if you could show me. I mean - show me how to work it."

What a fantastic way this was to die of humiliation in a public place.

"No problems Rachel, except that unless you like a cold wash I really wouldn't use the shower on board because there's no hot water until the engine's been running for half an hour.

"Risto has a shower at the back of the yard and that has some hot water. Get a slosh down there and then come and have some breakfast with us."

The yard had dried out very quickly and so I walked across it without drowning in the puddles. It was really interesting that no-one took any notice. A girl with a towel and a wash bag walking through a building site in England would have drawn all sorts of attention and, well - you know, looks - but here no-one took any notice at all.

The shower was warm – for about 30 seconds – and then quickly went colder. I had a real speed wash, before I froze to death.

Wow! For a girl who liked to spend ten minutes with boiling hot water pouring over her before she could face the day, my personal hygiene habits were really going to need a re-think in Greece.

I went back to the boat, put on some clean clothes and walked across to the office. The guys were sitting round the table drinking what smelt like super strength coffee.

"Morning Rache," Dave beamed. "Sleep well?"

It was a non-question and I was about to give a non-answer – you know, yes - great, blah, blah, blah. But I hesitated - and I don't know why.

"Well, not at first. It was deafening being bombed by the rain and the waves slapping the side of the boat felt as if they were going to sink it but then - yes, I really did sleep well. The cabin is very comfortable and the rocking of the boat was so relaxing.

"So yes, I did sleep very well and then, this morning – that blue sky…"

None of the lads mocked me and it was Dave again who spoke. "Greece isn't England, Rache, and you always have to remember that – every minute of every day. Some things are worse – much worse – but there are things here which you can't ever experience in England and a lot of them are for free.

"You'll have a great time here – but not today because you're going to be working for MG. Want to know the time of the next flight home?"

I look around at the cracked chairs, the dirty table and the mugs in the sink which needed washing but mainly saw three smiling guys who wanted me to be with them, and so I didn't want to know anything about planes going home.

*****

Everything MG did was at four million miles an hour. My job was to get the boats as clean as possible so that they looked perfect for customers. MG was kind, all the guys were really, and said that I would destroy my nice jeans by working in them so the best thing was to put on shorts and a shirt and wear flip flops until my feet had got used to being out in the open air.

MG gave me a big mop and a bucket of industrial detergent and simply said: "Here you go."

And that was it. There was no checking or instructions, just get on with it.

Scrubbing decks was hardly much of job for a nice girl with four "A" levels and a degree, okay not a very good degree but still a real one, but I was feeling proud of what I was doing. I wanted the boat I was working on to be the best in the Ionian. I'd only just started with Delfini but already I was starting to feel something inside – that I was one of us instead of one of them.

I mopped like Cinderella expecting Prince Charming to arrive in the boatyard but when we took a break for coffee I wasn't happy. As we were going back to the boats, I stopped MG.

"I'm not moaning or anything MG, and I know it's none of my business and I should shut up and just do my job, but the decks aren't right. They can be cleaner than I'm getting them but I'll need a soft scrubbing brush and some proper cleaning stuff."

"Okay Rache," Rache was the only name I had now, "if that's what you want, you can have it."

So hour after hour, day after day, I shuffled down the decks on my hands and knees, scrubbing until I sweated and my knees were red raw.

*****

We worked until the sun started to set, and at the end of the day I was utterly exhausted – and very proud. Those decks were immaculate and I had scrubbed them clean. They were my decks, I had cleaned them and this felt good.

When the decks were done, MG asked me if I would go down into the cabins and make sure that there was no food or other rubbish beneath the floorboards. If you look at a yacht when it is not under maintenance, the floor in the cabin looks all polished and shining like a posh dining room. What you don't see is what's underneath the floorboards, in the bottom of the hull - the mass of pipes and cables which are the arteries and veins of the boat - and there are a lot of them.

I didn't like working down there for three reasons. First, I was inside and away from the fresh air. Second, I was in semi-darkness with only a little fluorescent light which MG had rigged up for me. Finally, there were a lot of dirty things down there!

I don't mean just spills from diesel and food which had got between the cabin floor boards and the hull. In a way, I took this in good part and so fishing out a piece of bright green bread which had probably been down there for a year didn't bother me.

No, it was the personal items. Boxer shorts and bras - well, maybe - but how they got down there was beyond me. Other bedroom items were not for me though – not without rubber gloves and a bin sack to hand!

By the fourth boat, I had a system which meant that I started at the bow and worked backwards. It was getting towards the end of the day and the light was fading. Now I was mainly relying on the fluorescent light to see what I was doing. I was just at the start of the engine compartment and, for a moment, I was certain I could see two little red eyes looking at me.

I stared back into the semi-darkness and there they were - two eyes, in the middle of a small, browny grey head – and it was staring at me. There was a rat in my boat! The cheeky thing. A rat dossing in my boat: I was furious.

I grabbed the vacuum cleaner and shook the end at the rat. He jumped up and ran through my legs and I fell over trying to get at him. He was now at the entry to the forward cabin as we looked at each other like two boxers waiting for the bell to start the fight.

I dived at him with the vacuum cleaner and he leapt on to the cabin shelf heading for the stairs. I had completely lost it by now and lunged after him.

"Get off my boat you dirty rat!" I snarled. You could see I had really lost it in terms of a full-on temper tantrum.

I had another stab at him with the vacuum cleaner. The rat must have worked out that I was not a girl to be messed with and bounded up the stairs and shot out through the cockpit and over the wooden plank to the pier.

MG was working in the cockpit of the second boat and saw the fugitive rodent leg it away down the dock.

"Well done, Rache, the little buggers love it down there – nice and warm with plenty of food – but they also chew through the piping and that's a disaster.

"Good girl. Go get 'em!"

He was rolling around laughing - and I was too. My hair was filthy, my hands were cracked and red and my knees were cut and bruised. I looked as if I had just been in a fight with a rat but I was happier than I had been since I left school. Maybe I could be a Hostie.

*****

As every day went by, I was becoming more accepted into the team. I don't want to make this sound easier than it was. The lads were polite to me, and I still had the boat to myself, but everyone knew that I was at the bottom of the tree. Delfini couldn't operate without Dave and there had to be Mike as Skipper. MG was essential too – but me? I still wasn't sure. There were plenty of other people in Lefkada who could scrub decks. Rat chasing wasn't exactly a highly skilled job either and so I still didn't feel indispensable. Liked? Yes. Wanted? Yes, probably this too. But essential? I wasn't so sure.

All five boats were on the water now and the move to Tychos was only a few days away. Mike and Dave had gone into town and MG and I were working on the last bits and pieces - any one of which can stop a yacht being ready for charter.

The front sail on a yacht is called a Genoa. It's a big sail on a modern yacht and it's the one which turns the boat when it tacks – turns round at sea that is. These days, Genoas are what's called furling. You can let them out or take them in by pulling on ropes – the sheets – and then wrap the sail round the front piece of stainless steel wire which holds the mast up.

It's a good system and it means that the Genoa can be furled from the cockpit, at the back of the yacht, which is both convenient and safe. Well, it's convenient and safe when it works!

Today, MG was struggling with the roller at the top of a Genoa which had jammed. He was raging that this was the last big job and then he was done. I had developed a lot more confidence in the last three weeks and so I asked him to explain what the problem was and how it could be fixed.

The answer was to haul someone up to the top of the mast, free the jammed roller and then the Genoa could be checked. I was now a lot fitter than when I came to Greece, and a real size 12 - yessss – but there was no way I could pull 15 stones of MG up a 12 metre high mast.

I've never been super brave or done Karate or anything really tough so I don't know why I said what came next.

"MG, get me up to the top of the mast and I'll try to free the Genoa."

"You sure?"

"Yes. Tell me what to do and I'll have a go."

So that's how I ended up with two pieces of rope under my bum looking down at a deck which, from up there, seemed a lot smaller than my Teddy Bear's toy car.

I was genuinely terrified and kept shutting my eyes. There was no wind but the deck still wobbled like crazy whenever I looked down.

MG shouted. "There's a spring loaded release. If you can free that with the screwdriver we'll be fine. Can you do it Rache?"

You know when you read those stories where they say the hero swallowed hard and it sounds really silly? Well I did swallow hard. My stomach was churning too and my hands were shaking. All that I wanted to do was get down and visit the toilet.

But I wanted MG to see that I could do the job, much more than I would give in to being scared. The two parts of my mind battled for what felt like hours but was probably only seconds. I was desperate to do something the guys would appreciate – that showed I was trying, that I was one of the team. So I wriggled about on my rope seat and dug the screwdriver into the pin which was full of salt.

I heaved and strained and then, without any warning, the pin came free – and sliced down the side of my left hand. A surprising amount of blood started to drop onto the deck below and my first thought was what a job it was going to be to get the deck clean again.

MG went crazy. "Come down, come down now Rache. Bloody well come down – now!"

My hand had gone numb for the first few seconds after the pin had sliced into it but now it was hurting like mad.

I didn't feel brave but I did feel desperate. I wanted to do this job as well as the guys could do it – to be one of them.

I shouted down to MG. "Is the Genoa free?"

"Forget the bloody Genoa, come down."

"Is the Genoa free or isn't it? Tell me!"

MG pulled at the furling sheet.

"Yes, it's free Rache. Now will you come down?"

So I did.

With no van, and the yard empty, MG called a taxi and we headed for the hospital in Lefkada with my hand wrapped up in about 10 metres of blue paper like an Egyptian Mummy.

The young Greek doctor cleaned the cut and put five stitches in it. This didn't hurt too much but then he said I had to have a tetanus vaccination in the muscle at the top of my arm: that was sore!

MG was really sympathetic and said I should have had the jab in my thigh instead and then everyone could have seen my bum when I took my shorts down!

When we got back, Dave and Mike made the right noises and were sort of supportive. I think that was what I expected. But there was something else.

MG explained exactly what had happened, and in detail too, and everyone listened without comment. There were no handshakes or hugs or cheers but just attention.

Then Mike spoke. "Thanks Rache. You did a good job today. We're proud of you."

And that was that. They were proud of me – even if I didn't get any sleep because every time I rolled onto my side the sore arm woke me up!

*****

Everyone was up at first light the next day ready to leave for Tychos. We had an early breakfast and Dave gave us the briefing.

"MG and me will take Notus and Zephyrus. Christos and Dimitri are taking Boreas and Eurus and then they'll catch the ferry to Nydri and get a lift back to Lefkas.

"Mike and Rache will take Brizo together so that Mike can show her which bit of the boat is the front and which is the back - ready for when she crashes into the harbour wall at Tychos."

I smiled because I loved them teasing me.

"We'll all motor there.

"Looking forward to your first day at sea, Rache?"

I sort of nodded. The truth was that I hadn't slept a wink because I was so excited. Forget the Year 11 skiing trip, and Tim Marsden trying to grope me in the Télécabine going down to the village, this was a real adventure.

Mike spoke. "You know Rache, you're a lucky little bunny sailing Brizo. Go on, MG, tell her the story."

"This should be a bedtime story, Rache," MG said with a grin, "because it's a true love story…

"No, it's not really. It's a true lust story.

"Hugo Brinksworth, whose Dad owns half the toll roads in Britain, fell in lust – I mean fell in love - with Charlotte Forbes, sometime South African Olympic Sailing Gold Medal winner, swimwear model and general object of desire.

"The lovely Charlotte had this dream about putting her name to the ultimate sports cruiser yacht and so Hugo's Dad thinks, well, the boy's out of trouble for a bit so what's the odd 10 mill to keep him happy, off the white powder and away from the front pages for a few months?

"Charlotte had another, what you might call friend - a bloke called Danny Marples who was a top whizzo race car designer. Danny looks at the yachts on the market and declares them all shit – sorry, Rache – piles of poo. He comes up with the Serval – named after Charlotte's favourite South African hunting cat which is super-fast, utterly beautiful and has an immense sex drive – just like Charlotte.

"He then sets the same spec for the whole bloody thing as you would for a top race car – best sails, best engine, best electronics – best everything. And the best of the best is that beautiful hull which was designed in a wind tunnel and sails like a dolphin chasing a shoal of bait fish.

"Everyone says that the Serval is the best small yacht ever made and yes we'll buy them by the thousand – and then they don't because you can get a Bavaria or Beneteau which sails perfectly well and is £50,000 cheaper.

"Only a very few were sold to real hard core sailing enthusiasts like someone we know here…"

And MG looks across to Dave.

"Now, you can't get the special parts for them and they are a total bastard to maintain but, on the right day when they're set up by a genius engineer…"

Mike did a drum roll on the table.

"They are the finest little yacht in the world – bar none. And now you're going to sail one. The only bad news is that you've got a crap skipper who'll get you lost and park the boat on a reef."

Mike smiled. "Yes, but I'll have Rache as crew while you're Billy No Mates sailing on your own."

*****

When Mike came down to the dock I was already in Brizo's cockpit, pacing up and down like a kid waiting for an Alton Towers' ride. Mike chucked his bag into the cabin and then joined me for my first ever sailing lesson.

"Okay Rache, let's get you started. Even though Brizo is a sailing yacht, a lot of the time we will be motoring. The truth is that a lot of customers prefer motoring without ever using the sails, so Brizo has a 29hp Volvo Penta diesel engine. It's not exactly a speedboat but you really don't want to be tearing along in the Ionian – it's too beautiful to miss.

"First, put the main power on. There's the power switch. See? The fuel gauge has registered so now you know there's power to start the engine."

Mike was calm and unhurried and I did as I was told.

"Now press the round button on the right-hand side, there, at the bottom."

I followed Mike's instructions again.

The engine turned over for a few seconds and then started. It was a very different sound from a car engine – quiet beneath my feet, like a bear murmuring to itself whilst it was asleep. Little coughs of water appeared from the back of the boat.

Mike spoke again – slow, easy, soothing.

"Let's cast off the mooring ropes now."

Mike showed me how to undo the "oxo" knots on the cleats and then pull the ropes on board.

"Okay Rache, you're doing great. Fancy a go at hoisting the anchor?

The answer was no, no and then no again. No, I didn't fancy hoisting the anchor for fear of making some horrendous mess of things and sinking the boat!

"The Servals were really neat in so many ways and except for being way too dear they would be the most popular small yacht in the world. They've all got a control for the anchor in the cockpit, as well as the bow of the boat so they can be managed single-handed – if you know what you are doing."

Mike was calm again. He was so unlike any other man I had ever met and was a thousand miles away from Connor. There was no trying to show how good or important he was. Instead he was simply himself, without having to pretend to be anything different.

"Don't worry about anything. There's the switch for the anchor, on the front of the console. See the two arrows?"

I nodded.

"One's for up and the other's for down. Okay, hold the switch in the up position."

I did – and then stopped immediately as the anchor chain started to clank into the boat and the bows dipped down.

"No problems, Rache. The noise is completely normal. Have another go."

I held the switch and the anchor chain climbed into the hold again. This time the boat started to creep forward.

"That's brilliant. Good girl. Keep going..." and then there was his lovely smile.

More of the chain came in.

"Now, engage forward gear."

Mike put his hand over mine and together we pushed the large chrome lever on the right hand side of the consul forward. Mike's hand was hard and confident and his reassurance passed straight to me.

There was a slight clonk as the gear engaged and the boat moved ever so slowly.

"Few more revs, Rache..."

I moved the lever a tiny bit more.

"Watch the anchor chain – you're getting to the end now."

All the time calm, encouraging and safe. You'd stake your life on this man getting you out of any mess.

The anchor came aboard with a final clonk and lodged itself neatly at the front of the boat.

"Few more revs again – I've got the wheel."

The engine note changed slightly, like the bear waking up and stretching. Very slowly, Brizo picked up speed and Mike eased away from the pier.

*****

We turned right – starboard actually because now I was a sailor – and followed the coast. Along this bit of the island, from Lefkas to Nydri, the road hugs the shore line very tightly and on each side was a long string of hotels and villas, some clinging to steep mountain sides as if they had been superglued there. A lucky few had tiny jetties or even a bit of beach, and in between there were commercial piers. Everywhere were yachts – yachts, yachts, yachts and more yachts, all getting ready for the start of the season.

We motored along with the engine almost silent. Mike showed me the instruments on the console. Some were very different from a car!

"Always keep an eye on the depth gauge, Rache. Brizo has a very deep keel for a small yacht – this is one of the reasons she sails so well – but 1.9m is one hell of a length of keel so you have to watch the depth."

I was concentrating on Mike's every word. I so wanted to do everything right, and not look like an idiot. I wanted to be able to sail and to actually know about tacking and gybing and to be able to do all these yachtie things.

"Keep the revs at about 1800. She'll bob along at about 5 ½ knots at these revs and she uses almost no fuel."

Right. 1800 gives 5½ knots. I tried to remember my self-imposed homework from England. 5½ knots – a bit over 6mph if Mike asked me.

"Ready to take the wheel, Rache?"

Of course, the answer was no. I'd only been sailing for half an hour and what I most wanted was to sit down with a cup of milky coffee and a really sticky cake with a guaranteed sugar burn!

I nodded.

"Here we go. Hold the wheel gently and feel the water over the rudder. Don't force the boat – use the wheel to guide her."

I stood in front of the great big, stainless steel steering wheel which was the size of a dustbin lid. I gripped it so tightly with both hands that my knuckles stood out white.

Mike moved directly behind me. "No, no – just relax."

I could feel him close to me – not actually touching my back but just brushing it. This was distracting!

"Here, take the wheel gently. Just with your fingertips – like this."

And those strong, honest, battered hands took mine and put my fingers so that they rested on the curve of the wheel.

"Can you feel the water on the rudder, now?"

And I could – but that wasn't all I was feeling!

"Okay, you've got control."

And he moved to the back of the cockpit and started tidying the sheets as I steered the yacht.

More than anything else, it was the lack of fuss which made the experience so special. No showing off or proving that he knew better than me. No raised voices and no criticism. No need to prove anything or brag about some tattoo he'd just had done. It was simply a man in control, teaching a woman who wasn't.

My God! And I was supposed to steer the yacht too!

*****

The coast started to turn to the right. Mike stood next to me again. In front of us there was a big electronic map which constantly changed – like the world's biggest SatNav map in a car.

Mike pointed to it. "Nydri is off to the right – starboard – and straight ahead is Sparti. We're going to port – the left - and then we'll sail down past the eastern edge of Meganisi.

"Don't go near those two islands," he pointed to a pair of smaller islands next to Meganisi.

"That's Skorpios and Skorpidi. They're owned by Ekaterina Rybolov-leva and they're strictly private. Try to land there and you'll be met by a team of ex-Special Forces guys having a serious conversation with you."

The wind had picked up now and the waves had real shape. Mike looked at the water and smiled again. Smiling was his normal state. Big, strong hands, a confident voice - and a smile.

I gave myself a firm warning. Come on Rachel, concentrate!

"I know we're supposed to motor all the way to Tychos but this wind is just too good to waste. Wanna go sailing Rache?"

I nodded and I smiled too. "Yes please."

"Okay, bring her down to tickover. Remember how to do that? Pull the control lever gently towards you."

I was focussed now - out of fear of looking silly.

"Okay, slowly bring the bows round until she is pointing directly into the wind – remember, that's called, 'Head to wind.'

"Not even this boat can sail head to wind because to sail, the wind has to be behind you or blowing at the side.

"When the boat is head to wind she will stop. The wind can't fill the sails and I'll be able to hoist them without a struggle."

Brizo very slowly came to a halt.

"I'm going to hoist the sails now. Keep her head to wind but watch what I'm going to do because you will have to know when we have clients to look after.

"Release the cleat," and Mike flicked up what looked a short, metal slug which trapped the rope and stopped it moving. "Now we can raise the Genoa."

And as he pulled the rope, I mean sheet, the Genoa unfurled and shook in the wind, like washing trying to unfasten itself from the line.

"Keep her head to wind, Rache, concentrate and keep her head to wind."

My hands went tight on the wheel again. I was desperate not to make a mess of this.

"We'll release the clutch levers for the mainsail now."

Mike flicked up the levers which lay flat against the mainsail sheets, preventing them from moving. He was smooth and effortless with his movements, as easy and fluid as an Olympic gymnast. How can a tall, long haired guy in shorts and a scruffy shirt look like a gymnast? Because they're both in total and complete control of their bodies!

Mike wanted the sail to unfurl from the mast and when he pulled the outhaul sheet, it did just that – not in a computer game but in real life. I watched him trap the sheets tightly against the levers, to secure the sail. It was a new experience for me to be this close to a real man.

The mainsail shook itself irritably as my attention wavered.

"Concentrate Rache, concentrate. Just relax and feel the wheel."

I took a deep breath and did my best.

Mike came behind me, reached over to the main power switch and flicked it off. The engine did not stop instantly but took a couple of seconds to go to sleep.

Now the rattling of the sails was so angry that it shook the boat.

"Okay Rache, just turn the wheel very, very gently to port and we'll bear away. Just gently and slowly – no rush."

I did as I was told and then something completely and utterly magical happened. As I turned the wheel the sails gave a last, truculent shake and then they filled with the wind. Now they were two graceful, white arcs like a pair of swan's wings. How could anything change so fast?

Brizo heeled over to the left and the wheel trembled in my hands. It was like being in some fairy tale. From fighting the boat as I tried to keep her head to wind, now she was alive – the wind had breathed life into her.

What was even stranger was that I felt a part of the experience. I was no longer driving the boat with the engine pushing her along, like a car on water. Without the engine, I was guiding her – it was like working with a living creature.

The speed picked up and the boat heeled over a little bit more. Now, there were small white waves forming round Brizo's bows. She was smiling – as excited as I was to be sailing. It was a wonderful, magical – and yes I need to use that word again – experience and I loved it.

Mike had stood silently behind me respectful, I think, of what I was feeling. He spoke quietly. "You're a natural, Rache, you really are.

"How do you fancy this for a job – or would you rather be icing cats' noses?"

I didn't answer.

*****

I stood behind the wheel and tried to feel the wind and the water. It was strange and yet, in a really odd way, very natural. Maybe I did have a talent for sailing – or perhaps Mike was just being kind.

I didn't have any doubts about the scenery though – it was breath-taking. Mike said that the wind was perfect for a relaxing sail and so it would be a crime to motor straight to Tychos. The speedometer showed 5 knots as we headed away from Nydri towards Kalamos, and Brizo just slid through the water as if she had been born there.

The island ahead was so beautiful that it looked like an advertisement from a tourist brochure. The mountain rose almost vertically from the sea and puffy white clouds floated round the summit like huge pieces of cotton wool.

Dark green trees reached down to the shore line of the purple tinted sea and here I was, sailing and getting a bit of pay – well, hopefully I would – rather than cleaning tables or finishing journalism assignments.

Mike stood behind me again. "Bring her closer to the wind, Rache. See how the sails lose power."

Whaaaa! They didn't so much lose power as rattle angrily and Brizo slowed down.

"You just can't sail in the direction you want to go with a yacht, you have to compromise with the wind.

"Now, bring her back and feel the sails fill again."

So I did, the sails filled and Brizo shook her head and took off - at peace with the sea, and me, once more.

Mike spoke again.

"Rachel, you are really good at this. Keep practising and keep us going more or less towards Kalamos.

"I'm going below. I've got some paperwork to do before we get to Tychos and you're doing fine without me."

I was panic stricken. "Mike, don't go and leave me. What if something goes wrong? What if I make a mess of something and we drown."

His face broke into a smile. "Nothing will go wrong and if it does, you'll sort it out. Like I said, you can do this."

And with that he jumped down into the cabin.

My first thought was what if I crash but then it dawned on me that there was a lot of space all around me and not much in it. This was very different from driving through rush hour traffic in a car.

I looked ahead to Kalamos, made myself relax and had a serious talk with myself. It all sounds very melodramatic but I really did take about ten deep breaths - and then I forced my fingers to relax on the wheel.

It was as if Brizo knew what I was doing and wanted to help. I know that sounds a bit soppy but it really did feel like that.

Now, I turned the wheel to the right and the sails started to tremble so I brought Brizo back a little bit and as they filled, we picked up speed again. It was a wonderful, involving experience which took all my concentration and yet was very relaxing at the same time.

It was a full half hour before Mike appeared from the cabin and we had moved a long way towards Kalamos in this time. I was very proud.

"Mike, tell me about MG. Why MG? That's not his real name is it?"

"Yes and no. MG is short for Mad Gary – and he really is mad – absolutely bonkers. Gary's got no Dad that he knows about and his Mum couldn't keep him under control as a kid. That's why he ended up with a Social Worker.

"They were going to put him into care but his last Social Worker really took to him and Gary respected her too.

"She was well liked and very highly regarded in Derby, so she got Gary on to an apprenticeship scheme with one of the Rolls Royce sub-contractors. Gary should never have got the place really but his Social Worker really leaned on a few people and so he was accepted.

"And you know what? He turned out to be an outright bloody genius. He'd always been fixing things right from being a kid and when he was trained up he became brilliant.

"The problem was that he couldn't see what a good thing he was on and when he started using work's machines and materials to do his own jobs, he was given the big heave ho.

"Gary reckons they were sorry to see him go, and that's probably true.

"So then he gets a job with an Aviation Services company and gets all the certification: happy days all round. Until his employers find a few bits and pieces missing from the stores and the number one suspect is Gary – although he swears he never touched a thing.

"Then it's down to the south coast, working on marine diesel engines. Same story. Great bloke is Gary – a mechanical genius who can't do enough for everyone.

"And Dorset CID love him too - because Gary works 25 hours a day through Easter to get their undercover boat back in the water so that they can spank some Irish bloke bringing in ciggies. Happy days.

"They reckon that they owe Gary a favour, which turns out to be very useful.

"Then Gary discovers hydroponics. Know what hydroponics are Rache?"

I shook my head. "No, never heard of them – or is it, "it"?"

"Well, a lot of British veggies are grown on hydroponic farms, under cover with bright lights. You feed them chemicals and they grow like mad.

"The thing is, lots of other things grow really well in hydroponic set ups too – like herbs."

"Basil and coriander and things?" I beamed.

Mike smiled. "Yes, those and other herbs – like recreational herbs."

"Oh my God! MG is a drugs dealer!"

"Well, yes - a bit - but mainly no. He started with the herbal medicine job, producing a bit for a few mates and, of course, he was as good at hydroponics as he was at everything else he touched.

"So, his mates in Dorset CID said enough was enough and it was about time he relocated and kept well out of sight - otherwise they would start noticing things.

"MG isn't stupid so he packed his case and that's why we've got the best engineer in the Ionian – even if he is mad."

*****

We sailed on for another couple of hours and Mike showed me how to tack – to turn the boat from one direction to the next. He moved around the cockpit like a dancer – graceful, effortless and knowing exactly what to do before he had done it.

As Mike floated about, I got more and more confused and tired. Mike saw what was happening, furled the sails and started the motor. In the distance, I could see the mountains which were Tychos, rising up from the afternoon sea mist.

I wish I could remember that first time we entered Tychos in every detail, but I can't. I was absolutely exhausted – with the physical effort of sailing, the emotional exhaustion of being in this wonderful place and the strain of being so close to a very special man. Together, all three left me hardly able to keep my eyes open.

I couldn't see anything which looked like a port but then the cliffs sprang apart and we entered a narrow gap, cut deep between two high ridges. Mike put Brizo into the centre and for the next ten minutes we followed a zig zag course between the sides of the mountain, which reared up higher and higher above us.

The route back to the Ionian had completely disappeared and there was nothing ahead of us but steep ridges, reaching right down to the water, but then, from nowhere and without any warning, we burst into a semi-circular bay with a small harbour wall at one end.

"Welcome to Tychos, Rache…"

5

Tychos

WE reversed towards the small harbour wall. In fact, that's rubbish. We didn't reverse at all – Mike did whilst I faffed about.

MG was waiting for us.

"Stern lines, Rache, chuck 'em hard."

So I did and MG caught them. Mike showed me how to do the essential "oxo" mooring knot - and that was that. We were moored stern to in a tiny harbour which, gift shop apart, I reckon Odysseus would have recognised 2,700 years ago – except that his island was just behind us!

All our boats had lightweight passerelles which dropped directly on to the dock so that you could walk ashore. Mike lowered the passerelle gently, and then showed me how to lock it in position so that the aluminium footway rested just above the concrete and didn't get damaged. There was just so much to learn and, day after day, I felt like I was the new kid in Year 7.

In the evening we were eating at Andreas's taverna, right next to the waterfront. When we arrived, I was absolutely dead on my feet and so I just shut up and let the guys do all the talking. Andreas had made fish stew and it was delicious but I just picked at the bowl because I had a real problem on my mind: it was the sleeping arrangements for the night!

As the evening drew on, I became more and more desperate. The first job was to visit the loo in the taverna and make sure that I stayed there until there was absolutely no chance of me having to get up in the night. I was determined that I would wet myself before I'd go past MG to use the toilet on Brizo.

I excused myself as soon as I could and walked down the harbour wall to Brizo. She was resting there, barely moving on the water. I brushed my teeth in the sink and then squeezed past the cabin table which was piled up with MG's stuff. Not that there was much of it!

In one side of the forepeak was my kit bag and on the other my big rucksack. I fitted nicely down the centre. And the Little One said: "Roll over…"

Except that I hoped both my kit bag and rucksack didn't say anything in the night!

The giant problem was what to wear. What happened if I did have to get up in the night, if I was absolutely bursting and couldn't wait, and MG looked at me? I was going to die of embarrassment. Of course, I had been with guys who had seen me without any clothes on before but this was different. I was working with MG. What was going to happen when he saw me and then the next day, well, looked at me?

I'd have to go around with a bag on my head to avoid the shame!

I dug around in my kit bag and found my third nicest T-shirt which was also quite long. Not exactly a full on nightie but long enough to cover my bum – well mainly. I'd wear the T-shirt and keep my knickers and bra on and just hoped that no-one would stare.

By now, I was quite good at getting changed on my side so I wriggled out of my shorts and shirt and put my nightie T-shirt on – and waited. And waited. And waited. But the boat was silent and eventually I was so tired that I fell asleep. The next thing I heard was MG whistling tunelessly as the sun poured in through my skylight. It was time to get up.

I slid the forepeak door back a little bit and half put my face out.

MG beamed back at me. "Morning, Rache. Sleep well? I've got the coffee on."

I didn't say anything.

"You okay, Rache? Something the matter?"

I knew that this couldn't go on.

"MG, I don't know what to do now. I need the loo and you're there and where do I get washed and things?"

It all sounded so lame.

"No worries, Rache, no worries at all. How about I go on deck and tidy up and then there will be a bit more space for you?

"You can use the shower on board - but I wouldn't. The water will be bloody freezing. Best thing is to go down to Andreas'. The water will be okay for a minute but you can have a speed wash."

I used the loo and then pushed the flushing handle up and down five times, as Mike had taught me. Then I scrambled back into the forepeak for a horizontal changing session.

In fact, MG had been lying over the water being warm for a minute. It was tepid for about 30 seconds and then sub-zero! I soaped myself all over in a flash and then danced up and down trying not to die of hypothermia. My hair could stay greasy for a day – I didn't care!

I should have got a job as a chalet girl in a skiing resort instead of as a Hostie.

*****

Everyone met inside Andreas'. There was bread, ham, cheese and a big plate of scrambled eggs along with two pots of coffee. I sat at one end of the table because I was still very unsure of myself.

Dave took control of what was clearly a quite formal meeting. "Dig in everybody. We've got a busy day ahead so get some energy inside you."

Mike, MG and Dave piled their plates high but I waited until I saw how much the middle-aged woman at the opposite end of the table had, before I spooned a bit of the scrambled egg on to my plate.

Dave was in a dynamic frame of mind. "Okay, let's do an introduction."

He looked towards the dark haired woman and the young man sitting next to her.

"Here's Rachel, our new Hostie. Say hello Rache."

I squeezed a weak smile out of my face and raised a hand limply.

"Rachel, this is Zoe," the woman beamed with a smile which went from ear to ear.

"Zoe is our fixer. Port Police. Mini-bus from Preveza to the ferry at Nydri. Lost passports – she's your man…"

Zoe giggled as she leaned across and playfully hit Dave on the head with her notes at the thought of being called a man.

"Zoe's based in Nydri but sleeps with her phone, don't you Zoe? Better than any man is her phone. She's available 24/7 and sixty seconds a minute."

"Luke is our master fixer at the base. Luke can mend anything. Good brickie too. Keeps the taverna from falling in the harbour.

"And he can sail a bit. Luke Bickerton, Mr. Fixit!"

And MG did his normal drum roll on the table.

Luke was about my age – not tall and athletic like Mike, or tubby MG style, but quite ordinary looking - except for a lovely smile. He didn't say anything but half got up and did a mock bow.

"Alissa is our cleaner and will keep the boats immaculate when she's not running the shop and I suppose we'll have to keep eating this muck which Andreas serves."

"What you bloody English want? Chips and bloody tomato sauce on everything? Fish and chips and red sauce? The English cuisine.

"Now you gonna eat real food.

57

"Hey, don't forget you gotta pay for it too. It's not a bloody refugee camp here!"

Everyone laughed and I did too, even if I was the girl in the new uniform on the first day at High School.

Dave stood up. "Okay, let's rock 'n' roll. Customers will be here in two weeks and we need to be ready for them."

Zoe came across to me and gave me a big hug. Her English was impeccable. I told her so. "Yes, it's not too bad. I lived in London for five years before I came home.

"You know, tall, handsome Greek boy with a good job in England - and we lived happily ever after. Except that we didn't, and so now I'm back in Lefkada where I was born.

"Dave says it's your first season as a Hostie. It'll be tough at first, because there's a lot to learn, especially in a small company like this, but the boys are good and please let me help you too.

"If there's anything I can do just phone me. Like Dave said, the phone stays with me everywhere. I really do sleep with it under my pillow – honestly, I do.

"Whatever you want, just ring, even if it's only for girl stuff, ring me and we can talk."

There were nearly tears in my eyes. I'd always got on well with men but being in their company all day every day was hard work. I longed for another woman to talk to – someone I could just relax with for a few minutes or even seconds.

This time I was the one doing the hugging and afterwards I felt so much better.

"Thanks Zoe. I really, really appreciate that. I will ring and thanks again."

There was another smile and then a sort of half wave.

"I'll have to go now. Luke's running me back to Nydri in the rib so I can get the paper work sorted out with the Port Police."

*****

I sat down at the table and shook the coffee pot to see if there was anything left. I got about half a cup of lukewarm sludge out of it and chucked in three sugar cubes to disguise the bitterness. It had been a long day already – and it was only 10am.

Dave came across carrying a sheaf of papers. "Everything good, Rache, ready to go when the punters arrive?"

I nodded: "I guess so - but Dave, I'm still not sure what I'm supposed to be doing. I've never been a Hostie before and you need to give me a hand."

"That's fair enough, Rache, you're right. I'll be honest with you. We're running the show on fresh air at present. If you hadn't got that £1500 cash from the Walters we'd be dead by now. Bookings are still all over the place, and they're as thin as tissue paper for July and August when we should be taking the serious money.

"Except for everyone giving us credit, we'd be sunk.

"We've just got to give these first customers the best sailing holiday they've ever had, and get some repeat bookings before they leave Tychos, otherwise we won't last the season out.

"So what do I want you to do? Give 'em a good time, Rache, give them a bloody good time and make everyone happy. If you don't, then we're dead in the water and you'll be going home by summer."

I had never felt such a weight of responsibility before. It wasn't like the things I was told were important when I was a Prefect in Sixth Form. Everyone knew that whether Years 7 and 8 went in the right or left hand queue in the canteen wasn't going to change anything. The kids still got fed and no-one went hungry.

It wasn't even the same as working in the café or the biscuit factory. There's always someone else there to protect you if things don't go right. You might get sent home early with a bag of reject biscuits but really, nothing bad happens.

Now it could.

The interesting thing was that I liked the feeling. It gave me a thrill to be in the position of being able to do something real for once - something with big consequences. I was still terrified of making a complete mess of everything - but desperate to have a go.

*****

Zoe was chatting to Luke and ready to get in the rib. A rib is a sort of big rubber dinghy but with a rigid fibreglass hull which makes them much faster than an ordinary inflatable. They are a sailing company's workhorse and can carry half a dozen people – more at a push – and are part water van and part taxi. Whenever you need to reach a boat at sea then it's the rib which does the job.

Ribs are powered by two ginormous outboard engines and can do 50mph as they skim across the water.

Our rib had seen better days, and there was a large patch on the bows from some previous collision, but it still looked impressive as it sat with its bows reaching out of the water, ready for action.

Zoe was all smiles again.

"I'm really sorry to ask but I'm still not sure what to do for the first week. I know you've got to get back to Nydri but can I just pick your brains for five minutes?"

Luke spoke first. "Yes, that's fine by me. You give Rachel a hand Zoe. I've got tons to do here and just shout me when you're ready to go."

We walked back to the Taverna and sat down. "Coffees again?" Andreas asked.

These really were nice people.

Zoe pulled a ring bound notepad out of her huge handbag. "Okay, let's get you started.

"The first thing is to make sure that everyone is settled when they arrive. They'll have been at the airport early and then gone through all the stress with security and the three hour flight to Preveza. And then there's the mini-bus to Nydri and the ferry here so expect them to be tired and irritable, because they will be.

"Get them onto their boats and settled and, for the first night, give them a simple meal at the taverna and some wine. I'm going to talk to Dave and Andreas and see if we can't make this complimentary. A free meal will get everyone off to a good start. Andreas will help us if he can and Dave can pay him later."

And she laughed, which was a bit worrying for me.

"Then one night you need a quiz. Get some questions from Google and make sure they're not all too hard."

I was both embarrassed and proud of what I said next. "Zoe, I've already done that. I did a load of quizzes at home and even prepared separate ones for the kids. Dave told me that quizzes were popular when I first got the job and so I've already got a few written out."

Zoe beamed. "Yay! Hostie of the Year! That's great. Don't let any of the Hosties on the other companies know or they'll be stealing them!

"Rachel, can you cook?"

I told her about working in the Garden Centre kitchen and there were more smiles.

"Barbecues are good. If you can do a barbie, everyone will love you."

We went on for a whole hour. Wine tastings, "The Ionian's Got Talent" competitions and which restaurants to book. Zoe truly did know everything about being Hostie.

Then she gave me one more piece of information which was vital.

"Rachel, remember that everyone wants something different from a Flotilla Holiday. Some want babysitting. They'll have you do everything for them – including real babysitting!

"Others just want to party for the week – they'll want to be social all the time.

"But some want to sail knowing that Mike and MG are always there in the background. It's really important that you leave these customers alone and let them enjoy their holidays in their own way.

"This is a tiny Flotilla with only four yachts but you've still got to give everyone what they want from the holiday – and they won't all want the same thing."

I nodded. Wow! What a tutor and what a birthday cake sized piece of luck to find her.

We walked back to the rib together.

Luke made a joke gesture of looking at his watch. "Where've you two been? Shopping?

"Come on Zoe, I'll show you to your cabin on board our luxury cruise liner..." And there was that lovely smile again.

I was faced with one giant mountain to climb but these were nice people to be with and I felt happy.

*****

As Zoe and Luke pulled away, Dave came across to me. "All sorted out?"

"Yes, it's all good. I'll get a restaurant booked for when we go to Sivota and the quiz is already done."

"Great," Dave said, with a big smile. "That's my Hostie-in-Chief.

"Rache, there's something else I need to you to do. Every holiday company has a spare skipper but you know how the situation is with us.

"I need you to do a crash course with Mike and MG – not so that you can be a skipper or anything but so that you can give them a hand if we have a whole group of clients who are new to sailing.

"You up for that?"

Was I ever? I remember at the Boat Show wondering if I would even be allowed on a yacht and now my job was to learn to sail. Could life get any better?

Except that before I could sail Mike insisted that I should master stern to mooring because this was the thing which caused Flotilla sailors the most stress.

Usually, boats are moored stern to in the Ionian. There is very little tide and so boats don't need to be moored with their sides against the harbour wall, as they are in England. Instead they are jammed in tight, right next to each other, with their rear ends to the harbour wall. Mooring like this means that you can pack a lot of boats into a very small space, a bit like a car park really, and there really are a lot of boats in the Ionian!

Stern to mooring sounds easy - but it's not when you first learn…

The Servals have 50m of anchor chain – that's half a football pitch long. The anchor chain is pulled into the boat by an electric winch which is incredibly powerful. A Serval weighs seven and a half tonnes and the winch can move the boat easily as it recovers the anchor chain.

Normally the chain comes onto the boat and drops down inside the anchor locker, where it is stored, very easily. But once in a while it jams. You never, ever, ever try to unstick the jam with your hand because if the chain moves, and your fingers are still in it, they will be cut off. No argument or discussion – the chain will just slice off your fingers and that will be that.

Every boat has a broom handle in the chain locker for poking at the chain and this is what you should always use if you need to free it up.

As I have said before, Mike is very thorough and extremely sensible over health and safety and so from the first moment I went near an anchor in Ligia he had stressed over and over again: don't touch the chain with your fingers.

You drop the anchor chain three or four boat lengths out from where you're going to moor. You need to be this far out because it's the length of chain on the harbour floor which keeps the boat in place, not the actual anchor on the end.

Experts like Mike face the mooring and hold the steering wheel in their hands behind them without even looking at it. They whizz up to the mooring, the anchor is dropped and they're having a coffee about ten seconds later. It all looks dead easy.

Down in the bottom set of sailors, where I was, there is an easier way. If you stand behind the steering wheel, everything is reversed and the boat turns in the direction you turn the wheel. Because you're back to front, the throttle is also reversed so forward pushes the boat backwards towards the mooring and back goes forward and away from wall. It's really simple. I always moor like this.

The problem is that at first, the boat doesn't like going backwards so it sort of crabs about from side to side and won't do as it is told. Then you have to release the anchor chain and work out when to throw the mooring lines. It makes doing parallel parking for your car test look like play school.

Mike was calm and patient but he made me go through the mooring stages over and over again until I really did have a screaming headache and tinnitus in my ears. I asked could we stop and take a break but he said no, we weren't on holiday, so I had to keep going until I could do the job properly. You can see how things were going…

The final time, Mike could see that I was on my last legs and then the bloody anchor chain jammed as we were pulling away from the dock. At last Mike was a bit sympathetic. He took the helm and asked me to go to the bow and see what the problem was. Remember, he is controlling the anchor chain from the cockpit.

I scrambled alongside the cabin and sure enough, the chain had just turned slightly sideways. It was nothing really – so I reached down to free it with, yes, my hand. Mike shouted something which I didn't hear properly and so I waved my hand to say wait – and the anchor chain moved.

It skidded over my fingers and I jumped back and fell over in a heap. Unfortunately, Mike saw what had happened. The next thing I knew he was standing over me looking like the Angel of Death. I remember the exact words he said.

"You idiot. You fucking moron. What do you think you were doing? You could have lost your fingers. After all the times I've told you, you're still too fucking stupid to do what you're told!"

I was shocked and I was frightened too – but not of Mike. I knew that I was in the wrong and I knew that I really had been brainless and he was right that I could have lost my fingers – but I hated the word fuck from Connor days and I wasn't being shouted at by anyone in public.

I stood up as tall as I could. "Don't you call me stupid! You're the moron!

"You're so stupid you can't even read without moving your lips. I've seen you. And you point at letters like an infant.

"You can't even read like an adult and you have to work out which letters come next when you make your cross on a bit of paper.

"I've got a degree and all that you can do is sail yachts and shout at people!"

I saw Mike's hands, the big strong ones which I had always admired, tense and get ready to hit me but I was too seething furious to be frightened.

And by this time, everyone had taken ringside seats for the argument.

Dave bounced on board. "That's enough. Now."

His face was expressionless and he was icy calm.

"Get below, both of you. I want this sorting out now."

I was panting for breath – raging angry, ashamed and wanting to kill Mike.

Dave pushed MG's stuff off the cabin seat and on to the floor. He motioned for me to sit next to him.

He turned to Mike. "What happened?"

Mike explained the whole incident – but didn't say how tired I was or that I had asked for a rest.

I just sat there in silence, my chest rising and falling as I tried to get my breath without panting.

Dave turned to me. "Is that what happened?"

I nodded.

"Right, let's sort this out now. Rachel, you were 100% wrong. Not 99% but totally. You could have lost your fingers. That's the most important thing.

"The second thing is that Mike was Master. He was in charge of Brizo - and of you. He was responsible for your safety. You follow his instructions at all times.

"Understand?"

I managed another nod.

"Don't ever put your fingers near an anchor chain again otherwise I will send you home – there and then - without any messing.

"Got it?"

I swallowed again.

He looked at Mike. "Rachel was in the wrong but you do not, and will not, call her stupid in public or private.

"She made a mistake - a bad one. But you were Master and it was up to you to help her not do the same thing again – not to be ranting and raving like some drunken amateur.

"Have you got that?"

Now it was time for Mike to look cornered. He was about to speak when Dave cut him off.

"Button it. There's nothing else to say. I don't expect you to shake hands and make up but I do expect you to work together to save this company.

"Do you both understand that?"

Neither of us said anything – but we did.

In the evening, I was sat working on a quiz – how's that for a life threatening job? – and Mike came across. The ringing in my ears started again.

"Rache, I'm sorry for losing my temper. I was wrong. I lost it because I care a lot about you. I really do."

He put his arms round me and the tinnitus started again – but this time for completely different reasons.

I said, "I'm sorry too, Mike, I'm really sorry. I shouldn't have touched the anchor chain and I shouldn't have…

And my voice trailed off.

"Shhhhh. It's all over now. Everything's fine."

And he kissed me very softly on the back of my head.

*****

Dave was a good boss and very wise. Mike took me out sailing the following day but then Dave asked Luke to give me a couple of hours of tuition whenever he could. It was a bit of a strange experience.

First, Luke was full of apologies for being with me. He said that he wasn't a real sailor and all that he could do was pass on the amateur knowledge he had gained from three seasons in the Ionian.

The conversation lasted just about until we had the anchor stowed and Brizo was pointing down the channel. Then it stopped. Absolutely full stop - nothing else to say: just stopped.

It wasn't like those contrived silences where Connor used to punish me for not wanting sex with him. It was simply that Luke didn't speak except to answer me. I would make some non-controversial comment about the sheep clambering up the sides of Tychos or something and he would say yes. Or no. Or nothing.

I suppose it was worse because Mike always gave a non-stop commentary about sailing and MG was in a permanent state of rage at something and so he never shut up either. Luke was just quiet. He was driving me mad. I was counting the minutes until we could moor again and I could go back to doing some Hostie work.

Then we reached the end of the channel. Ahead of us was Cape Ducato and an endless carpet of stiff, little, white capped waves scattered as far as we could see.

Luke smiled. "Would you like to sail, Rachel?"

His voice was rather quiet after the other guys and it was strange to be called Rachel instead of Rache but his face was open and friendly and the question was a genuine one. Would I like to sail?

After the intensity of sailing with Mike I felt like making some crazy remark like, "No, I wanna learn how to fly!" but this seemed wrong for Luke so I said, "Yes please, I would like that very much."

He smiled a little – and I did too.

"Do you want to take the helm or hoist the sails?"

Once more, this was a bit odd. Mike always had what we were doing pre-planned, right down to the last detail and he was a brilliant tutor.

MG would have shouted: "Grab the helm Rache!"

But Luke was almost respectful.

I was uneasy at this strange outbreak of good manners. "Whatever you prefer…"

And there was a deafening silence.

I was getting stressed. "Shall I bring her head to wind?"

Luke smiled: "Yes please."

Pardon? Has my hearing just gone funny? You just said "please" to me. Now that's a word I haven't heard for a long time!

He waited until I had a hold of the wheel and then went to the front of the cockpit and flicked up the cleats.

I slowed Brizo right down almost to a stop and Luke opened the Genoa.

"Want to know a little trick with the Genoa, Rachel?" and then hurriedly, as if he'd said the wrong thing, "unless you already know of course. I'm not trying to be smarty-pants."

I giggled. "Well I won't know if you are just showing off until you tell me what the trick is…"

And then he laughed out loud.

"Okay, when you hoist the Genoa, don't take it to the very end of its reach. If you leave a bit of the sail still furled it will go in a treat – easy-peasy. If you take it all the way out, it sometimes sticks and this can be a real embuggerance, sorry - I mean, nuisance, if it jams."

Then he was immediately apologetic. "Mike will have a better way of doing it than this but I just find it easier this way – and easy is always good for someone as bad as me."

He was immediately quiet again, as if he had completely exhausted everything he could say, and moved on to the mainsail.

Luke hoisted the sail effortlessly and then went to the base of the mast and flicked the control lever to ratchet.

He saw me looking quizzically at him. "If the control is set to ratchet you can always reduce the sail easily and calm everything down if it gets too blowy. It's a golden rule with me. If you to have think about whether you should be reefing the sail, it's already too late and you're asking for trouble."

And, because he sounded a bit like Mike instructing, he smiled.

"Would you like to bear away now, Rachel and let's get some way on before we tack?"

"Shall I stop the engine now?" I asked.

"Yes, if you are ready. Just take your time."

I cut the engine and then, as Mike had showed me, turned the wheel away and let Brizo's sails fill. The Genoa shook for a few seconds and then bowed out and pulled the boat round. The mainsail trembled and then filled.

We were sailing. It was mystical – like something from a fantasy film. There is no better way of describing the experience. I could see why men, and a few women, had fallen so deeply in love with sailing ever since the first dug-out canoe had a bit of deer skin for a sail.

As for Luke, I didn't know what to think. He was night and day different from the other guys – not nervous but just quiet. He was also caring. I got the feeling that he was interested in me rather than just in what I was doing or what I could do.

He was also sensitive and this was odd too. I said, "I'm going below for a minute."

We both knew this meant I was going to use the loo!

The other lads wouldn't have taken any notice at all but Luke said: "I'll bring her into the wind and keep her nice and steady for you."

What a lovely thing to do without being asked or even hinted at.

*****

It is surprising how quickly your attitudes can change. In England, I would have died rather than let a man I wasn't in a relationship with see me undressed. It's different when you're living on a boat with two guys.

I never got as far as sleeping without my knickers on but I gave up wearing a bra under my T-shirt nightie – and the guys never took any notice. We were just too tightly packed to get precious about anything.

Strangely, we all did what I used to do at sleepovers when my girlfriends were getting changed. I used to turn away so that I wasn't looking directly at them and this is what Mike and MG did too. They might have seen my naked back but that was all. They didn't look and I was discreet: that was perfect.

The guys lived in squalor – and I do mean an absolute tip. I never took much notice of what they wore but it seemed to be the same thing every day. In fact, it might have actually been the same pair of boxer pants, the same shorts and the same shirt. That was all they possessed.

I tried to do better than that and to make myself presentable. Okay, I was in shorts and a Delfini top too but I changed my shirt every day and Alissa ironed them for me so that I looked the best I could. I was never that keen on make-up and so it was a relief that I could just forget this part of being a woman – not that there was anywhere to put it on.

I was also determined to keep my forepeak different from the rest of the boat. I asked Alissa if I could have a cotton sheet to go over the cabin cushions and she was delighted to help. The guys just dossed down on the cushions but I wanted something a bit more like a bedroom.

Alissa also gave me something else. It was a little plastic Madonna, holding a serious looking baby Jesus. She said that the Madonna would look after me and that I should pray to her whenever I had a problem. If I did, the Madonna would intercede on my behalf and everything would be alright.

I was living and working in a very practical world where anchor chains had to be dropped just at the right moment and Port Police forms were completed in quadruplicate, so Alissa's Madonna meant a lot to me even though I had never thought of myself as religious. The little icon wasn't practical and, in Dave's eyes, she wasn't of any value either. But she was very important to me and so I got some zip ties from MG, looped them round and tied her and baby Jesus to the bulk head, just above where my head rested every night. It was a good feeling.

*****

I sailed a lot with Luke – more than was strictly necessary. Dave was a clever boss and knew that I had been outside of my comfort zone since the moment I left Manchester Airport in April - actually, probably since Mike had sent me behind the pin board to put on a Delfini shirt at the Boat Show! So whenever there was time, he had me and Luke out on the water with one of the boats.

Mike was right. I did have a feel for sailing and I picked it up very quickly without too much effort. Sailing with Luke was also fun and a real break. Let me give you one example which kept me smiling for a whole day afterwards.

It was blowing a top end Four when we reached the end of the channel. This time we'd taken Notus for a run. I turned her head to wind because getting the sails up was going to be hard work even though Luke was vastly stronger than me. Notus reared up and down on the waves like a warhorse getting ready to bolt. She literally shook and trembled with excitement.

We decided that half sail on the Genoa and mainsail was more than enough for the conditions - and it was! As soon as I let Notus bear away she was off like a rocket – seven knots on the speedometer as she plunged through the waves.

With a strong westerly blowing, we were running towards Vasiliki like a speed boat.

Kerrrrrrrblosh! Notus' bows dug in to the trough of the wave coming across her.

Kerrrrrrrblosh! A huge sheet of spray broke over the cockpit, soaking us both to the skin.

Kerrrrrrrblosh! Notus dived in again and shrugged off the water with a smile. I had never done anything so exciting, so involving, so all consuming in my life.

I braced my right leg against the side of the cockpit and felt my muscles tremble as Notus cut through another wave. The wheel in my hands was alive and trying to escape from my grasp. It was like having a lead on a dragon barely under control but I was ecstatic. Every part of me was working with the boat and we were one.

Luke was all smiles. "Go on Rachel, get her over. See if you can get the sea running over the gunwale!"

I giggled: "No, you daft thing. No, I'm not. If I capsize her Mike will tie me to the anchor and drown me!

"Come on Rachel – don't be a big softie. Get her over. She's a Serval, remember - uncapsizable!"

"Don't believe what you read on the web Luke Bickerton, you should know that at your age…"

"Come on Rachel, water running over the gunwale or you're a failure. Carpe Diem. Live for the day!"

And I did. I felt more alive than I had ever been in my life as I brought Notus tighter across the wind until I had her lee side just bouncing in and out of the wave crests, and the white tops were cascading over the base of the guard rails like sea snakes trying to eat the boat.

Luke leaned back on the edge of the cockpit cheering, laughing and shouting. "More! More! Come on Rachel, get her over."

And despite the intense concentration, I felt more at peace and relaxed that I had done since I left school.

Then Notus' bows dug into a particularly big wave and I sort of shrieked and gasped at the same time as water spilled into the cockpit.

That was enough for me. I brought her upright and watched Luke fall on to the cockpit floor and pretend to swim.

In a squeaky, falsetto voice he said: "Oh Mike, she's been and gone and drownded me. Mike, Mike, what shall I do? She's wet me and everything."

So I reached down and cuffed him on the ear. He stood up, shook off the water, and high-fived me. I was very happy.

*****

As I said, living with the guys had become completely normal so I wasn't concerned when I went aboard Brizo before dinner. I got to the top of the cabin stairs and there was Mike, at the bottom by the chart table, completely naked.

I knew that I should have turned away and come back five minutes later and I also knew that I shouldn't be looking at him with the thoughts I had. But I couldn't stop myself. Naked, he was even more man than when he was working in his shorts.

I really knew that I shouldn't but I saw his broad shoulders. I saw the muscles rippling along his back and down towards his waist. Then I saw the sharp dip of his bottom, tapering towards his thighs. I saw all of this as I looked.

Mike turned round and I still couldn't help myself, I really truly couldn't, but I kept on looking – at his strong arms, his broad chest, the horizontal lines across his stomach and …

I knew I shouldn't be looking there but I had to. I felt excited, embarrassed and ashamed all at the same time.

Mike saw me staring and sat on the table. He neither smiled encouragement nor showed resentment. He was naked and confident – as confident as he was in everything else he did.

"Rache, you're a wonderful girl but what you need is love, not sex - and I can't give it to you."

6

I'm Your Hostie

I had to put Mike completely out of my mind because the following day was going to be crunch time. The first clients were arriving and I would soon know if I could be a Hostie - or whether I just thought that I could.

Alissa and I had toiled at the boats to get them immaculate. I was determined to work harder than Alissa and to show her how much she was appreciated. I scrounged an old tooth brush from Dave and went all over the boats on my hands and knees, scrubbing round the edges of the cleats and guard rails. My knees were red raw at the end but there were no better presented yachts in the Ionian.

When all four boats were gleaming and Brizo was at least presentable on the outside, but heaven help us if anyone looked in the cabin where the guys lived, we put a bowl of fruit and a bottle of wine on each cabin table. Andreas' uncle made some half decent wine and even if the bottles were second hand Andreas had got some nice labels made in Lefkas so I hoped that no-one would notice.

Andreas' Auntie baked some fresh bread and a neighbour let us have a kilo of sheep's cheese, on tick as was usual with everything we did, which made the presentation something really special. Alissa cut the cheese into nice wedges, a bit tricky because it was so crumbly, and put them into little boxes with a scarlet ribbon on top. Disneyworld eat your heart out!

Zoe was right about the clients. They were tired and a bit grumpy but they were also excited about being in Tychos. Fortunately, three out of the four had sailed before so I only had one set of intensive briefings to give.

As I was crammed into the loo, explaining how incredibly important it was not to put anything in the pan except stuff which came directly out of your body because it would cause major blockages, I thought of Miss Immaculate Face at the Boat Show, with her perfume and surgically applied lipstick. If only she could see me now...

When everyone was settled in I went across to the taverna and offered to help Andreas and his Mum. The only thing we could afford, I mean Andreas could afford, was chicken and tomato pasta – lots of pasta and pretty light on the chicken and tomatoes! I had made tons of similar stuff at the garden centre but I didn't like being pushy so I offered to wash the tomatoes and then set the big table next to the harbour wall. More than anything else, I wanted to show everyone that we knew how much they were helping us and that we were grateful. For sure, we wouldn't have survived in one of the more popular ports.

*****

The following morning, everyone had a late start. Greece is two hours ahead of Britain so it was still seven o'clock in the morning as far as the clients were concerned when everyone started staggering out of their boats at nine o'clock local time.

There were a lot of bleary eyes as they lurched along to the two showers behind the taverna but I couldn't stop myself from having a giggle when I saw how much the customers livened up after a good sloshing with Andreas' cold water.

I was smart and just rinsed my face in the sink on Brizo. Us professionals know when the water's going to be hot again!

Dave was on cracking form and it was easy to see why he had done so well with the Flotilla Sailing business.

First, he introduced everyone – all the way through the chiefs like MG and Mike, to Andreas and even Luke. I waited.

At the end, he said: "And last but by no means least is Rachel Lamb who will be your Hostie for the week. Anything you want or need, just ask Rachel and she'll fix it."

I glued a happy face on to the front of my head and just hoped that no-one asked for very much.

Dave was very good at building a team and played each member beautifully. His explanation of Tychos was particularly clever, and very interesting.

"Tychos is the personal island of Tyche, the Greek Goddess of Good Fortune. The story is that she had an argument with her Mum, Aphrodite, we've never done that have we, and left Mount Olympus for a break. She nipped down here, as Gods do, found this island and lay down for a nap.

"The earth was so impressed with her beauty that it moulded itself exactly to her shape after she left.

"So if you sail west, down the Ionian with Meganisi on your right, you can see Tyche outlined against the horizon. At the top is her face, then her chest and legs and you can guess how we get into Porto Tyche, can't you?"

And of course everyone rolled around laughing.

In five minutes he had all the clients eating out of his hand, laughing at his jokes, sharing his enthusiasm and just wanting to be on holiday with him. Truly, he had the magic touch.

Mike was everything he should have been at the briefing and it was strange how quickly I accepted what he had said about us. He was drop dead gorgeous, and there's no doubt about what could have happened, but he was right, I had done sex and now I wanted something more.

Even so, it would have been a strange girl who wasn't impressed. Tall, handsome, confident, Master of the Universe and the man you really, really want to sail with – and a lot more as well!

MG was good too. He generated the feeling that nothing could go wrong, ever, with any of our boats and he even dealt with the problem of blocked toilets neatly too. Engineers hate sticking their hands into the sea drain taking out things which should never have been put down there in the first place. It was a tricky subject, and could have caused embarrassment, but MG's deftness made everyone smile.

Then there was me. After I had seen MG stand up, I did so too. For the first few words, I had that terrible, dry mouthed feeling where nothing will come out smoothly – then the ideas flowed. I wasn't the same Rachel Lamb that I had been with Connor. I was no longer just a student with a second-class degree or a Christmas Elf or even a cat biscuit icer.

I had been in the bowels of the Servals and chased a rat. I had cleared a stuck locking pin on a Genoa from 12 metres in the air. I could moor a yacht stern to first time, well mainly, and was confident enough to sail with waves breaking over the gunwales.

I had gone down a whole dress size and I felt fitter than I had ever been both mentally and physically. So yes, I am your Hostie. Come on - let's go sailing.

*****

The first week came, and went, in half a flash. We had a quiz, I did a barbecue and everyone said that they enjoyed themselves. The clients paid for the barbecue and they also paid Andreas for the meals they ate in his Taverna. At last, there was some money coming into the Tychos community. I'm surprised that the sigh of relief didn't cause a landslide.

At the end of the week, the clients came to me as a group with €500. Wow! I was suitably grateful and, as we had agreed, the four of us shared the tip. Dave hadn't been that reliable with my supposed €5 a day expenses so putting €125 in my purse was great.

Even before the ferry left, Alissa and I attacked the boats with our cleaning gear. I deliberately did the dirty jobs like cleaning the toilets. I needed to show her that I didn't think I was more important than she was but that the two of us were running these boats together.

What I did must have been quietly noticed because Andreas' Mum had washed all the bedding for us and ironed it beautifully so this saved us a lot of time. She was a big, fat, elderly woman and struggled down the stairs to the cabins, but insisted on arranging the pillows at a precise ninety degrees to the sheets, so that they looked perfect.

Andreas got stuck in as well and put the welcome pack on each boat exactly as I had specified. Everyone wanted this thing to work and it was a wonderful feeling to be part of something which was so important.

The guys were superb too – mainly. MG was so thorough it was unbelievable. It was a pity he was bonkers because he could have been brilliant in a real job. His written record keeping was mind blowing but, better still, he had every single part of all five boats in his mind. He knew exactly where a problem was coming from before it even showed itself.

As for Mike, well it's just as I have said. If you were sailing round the world in a plastic bath, you'd want Mike as Skipper. He knew just when to encourage clients to hoist the sails and when to leave them alone if they only wanted to motor. To the millimetre, he understood how far everyone wanted to sail and when they needed a break. There was no struggling with stern to mooring for them. One of the guys was always on hand to make it painless!

*****

The weeks went by and things got better and better – mainly at least! Alissa and I had a system with the washing and it worked very well. The sheets were always brilliant white and the dark coloured clothes all got washed together. My undies went in on their own and, if Alissa had the time, she even ironed them which made a big difference to me psychologically. Alissa wasn't my Mum but sometimes it was really nice to feel a bit pampered.

For some reason, MG decided that his and Mike's clothes needed washing – and that didn't happen very often! So off he goes to the Taverna. The big washing machine is there all ready for action and my knickers and bras are in a basket on the floor next to it. I've never been that fond of black or red so most of my undies were either white or light coloured.

MG throws his navy blue shorts into the machine, and Mike's, along with some dark shirts and my stuff. Then, being an engineer, he decides to go for maximum wash. Like everything else he does, the machine has got to be on full power, because this must be the cleanest and therefore the best. Kerching! He presses the button and off he goes for a coffee and one of Andreas' Mum's cakes.

An hour later he comes back and pulls the washing out of the machine. Now, the previously blue shorts are bleached to death and my stuff is all a not very fetching shade of grubby lilac blue.

I went absolutely mental. It was bad enough living with two guys in a space not much bigger than a cupboard and now one of them had invaded the last private bit of my life – there wasn't much of this to begin with!

MG was really apologetic and almost grovelly. I could understand that he was only trying to help and that he really thought he would be saving me or Alissa a job but…

Of course, the but was that I had better get used to blue knickers because for sure the nearest branch of Next was 1500 miles away in England!

*****

Because we had so few boats in the Flotilla we could be very flexible but one of our favourite trips was to Sivota. It was a nice, comfortable trip and on this day, we ambled north east with everyone under sail. The entry to Sivota can be a bit tricky to find but the key is to look for the villas on both sides of the entrance.

The clients on this particular Flotilla weren't the most confident we had ever had and very much liked to be together. They were all about the same level of sailing experience and, just as importantly, they gelled together socially. Both of these factors are important for a happy week's sailing. If you have some customers who really want to sail hard and others who are nervous even unfurling the Genoa, then this makes life difficult for the Lead Skipper.

There is a similar situation for the Hostie. If customers barely want to speak to each other there's no point in having a quiz night and if they want to swap stories at the end of every day they need to be eating at the same table.

In a light wind, we plodded across to Sivota without incident. About a mile off the entry to the harbour, I took Brizo's helm and Mike and MG zoomed round the other four boats in our small inflatable dinghy helping everyone furl their sails.

MG stayed in the inflatable and then we shepherded everyone down the passage to Sivota like two Collie dogs with a flock of sheep.

A lot of people think that Sivota is the most beautiful port in the Ionian and they're probably right. It's as if a group of talented Sixth Formers had designed a tourist brochure for the perfect sailing destination, sorted through every single perfect yacht picture for Greece and pasted them into one place.

The line of the bay is perfect. The hills behind are just absolutely right in terms of steepness and have none of the aggression of Tychos. The harbour is lined with utterly beautiful tavernas and cute little shops. In fact, you couldn't really pack any more clichés into one place!

All the restaurants in Sivota are good but our favourite was the Mount Olympus. This is at the far end of harbour, near the road out of the village which leads to Vasiliki. One of the big attractions of the Mount Olympus is that it has a row of lovely tables right along the harbour wall actually next to the sea. Across the road, the taverna has a ground floor and a big upstairs balcony too, but it is the harbour-side seats that everyone wants. The food is superb and Stavros, the owner, always made us very welcome.

I had phoned Stavros three days before we were due to arrive and asked for the tables to be put together so that everyone could eat together right next to the harbour.

The harbour was packed, because a lot of sailing companies use it as key destination. I brought Brizo in stern to - and first time, yessssss – whilst Mike and MG got the rest of the flock moored. It was an hour's job but I left them to it whilst I went down to the Mount Olympus and checked that our table was all set for later on.

When I got there, Stavros was all apologies and fidgeting hands

"I'm really, really sorry Rachel but the lady from Superior Yachting Holidays has booked all the tables and so I've put you upstairs. It's really nice up there..." and his voice tapered off because we both knew that it was a third rate option compared with sitting right next to the water.

The balcony was great but all the good tables overlooking the harbour had already been reserved by other customers. We were going to be stuck against the back wall – with no view of anything. I was disappointed and angry – and told Stavros so.

He looked embarrassed again. "Rachel, you know how it is. Give me a break Rachel. Your clients, well, they're not really big spenders and, well you know, Superior clients are and you've only got twenty people and they've got more than double that and their tips..." and his voice trailed off, "well you know how your clients tip."

I was furious. Bloody Superior bloody Yachting bloody Holidays with their bloody great big bloody posh Bavaria 51s and their bloody skippers and Hosties on every bloody one of their bloody stuck up yachts and, "Ohhh, I can't touch one of those ropey things in case I break my finger nails" and "will my plastic boobs float off if I go swimming?"

Bloody, bloody, bloody!

I went back to Brizo and it's a wonder I didn't set her alight with the flames I was breathing - I was so angry.

The guys were understanding - but not that supportive. Even MG was trying to calm things down. "Look Rache, it's not worth getting upset. There are plenty of other really nice tavernas. I'll go and see Theodore and he'll put a big table out for us at the 12 Gods. It's great there."

I was furious. My God! What a transformation I had undergone since my days with Connor.

They were trying to keep their faces straight and Mike pretended to cover his in case I smacked him.

"I don't want another restaurant. I want the Olympus. It's got the best views and I booked it. I did everything right and now I want what I've booked for my clients. If I could tip his restaurant into the harbour I would. The two faced, lying, money grabbing toad!"

MG picked up the mood sooner than Mike and he could see that I was really upset about what had happened. His face burst into a grin.

"Okay Killer Hostie, Superior Yachting get up my nose too – the stuck up bastards. I've wanted a bit of fun with them for a long time and I might just have an idea.

"Just go along with everything I say and we'll have a laugh."

*****

If you didn't know MG, you could actually believe that he was a jolly Teddy Bear, all smiles and rolls of fat, with cute curly hair – if you didn't know him.

We walked along the quay together, arm in arm, like a couple of tourists and it was easy to find the Superior Yachting Holidays lot, lounged around sipping drinks and looking as if they owned Sivota. Come to think of it, if some of the girls had sold a couple of the rings on their fingers, they probably could have owned Sivota.

They thought that it was all jolly hilarious that the peasants had been put in their place by Susannah, their Lead Hostie – yes, they actually did have a Lead Hostie – and Marcus, the boss of their ten Skippers.

The last time I had seen a woman like Susannah, it had been on the Starstriker Yacht stand at the Boat Show: same perfect lipstick, same hair, identically manicured eyebrows and a blemish free skin stretched over a perfectly proportioned head carrying hair which must have been cut about five minutes earlier.

MG was all jolly Teddy Bear smiles and, apparently, very clear about his place in the world.

"Look," and he beamed in the most benign way imaginable, "we're all on holiday. There's been a bit of a mix up," and he stood on my toe for fear of me launching into an attack, "so let's have bit of fun."

"Why don't we all have a giggle and compete for the tables?"

The Superior lot all cheered and clapped. Thoughts of the interschool rugger competitions and jolly hockey tournaments were clearly coming to mind and punishing the oiks looked to be too good an opportunity to miss.

Marcus was more suspicious. "What do you have in mind?" His accent would have made Prince William sound common.

MG the Teddy beamed again. "Just a bit of fun – nothing serious at all. Just a laugh."

More cheers and screams from the Superiors.

"Our Lead Hostie will race your Lead Hostie across the harbour and back in one of the inflatables. Winner takes all and the loser pays for the meals too. How's that sound?"

The mob in the amphitheatre best seats went bonkers.

"Yeah Marcus. Go on Marcus. Let's get 'em!" and a lot more remarks that well brought up ladies with expensive public school educations really shouldn't have been making, and I'm not going to repeat.

I took a deep breath. I was good at zooming round in the little inflatable boats we towed behind our yachts, and very confident, but if I made a mess of things then we would be in for a 3000 Euro bill and this would wipe out all our tips for a long time to come!

At the same time, I trusted MG. Mad as he might be, he also had a mind like a super computer and, underneath the curly hair and silly smile, something was happening.

Posh Susannah was horrified – literally out of her mind. I was in and out of our inflatables all the time but I was pretty sure that the only time her skinny bum sat in one was when a skipper was taking her for cocktails.

She physically blanched. "Well, I don't know…"

Her clients went crazy and started booing and jeering. Stick insect Susannah, letting the school down. They were having none of that!

Marcus had been doing some quick thinking too. All their inflatables had 5hp outboards, and were new this season, whereas ours were 2.5hp and weren't, to say the least, exactly fresh from the factory. So, even with Susannah at the helm, there was no way she could lose.

I'm sure that the other calculations he was doing were based on the mood of the clients. Superior clients were legendary for being spectacularly good tippers and he could see that Susannah's reluctance to join in the game was going to cost everyone a lot of money.

He touched Susannah's forearm, lightly of course. "Come on Suz, it'll be a bit of fun and we can enjoy the view from the taverna afterwards."

The aristos whooped and cheered and generally bayed for blood again.

MG the silly Teddy Bear smiled all round and held my hand up. "Inflatable Control Board rules then?"

And he beamed like the daft thing he clearly was. Marcus looked puzzled.

"We've got to have some rules so that when you win you'll know you've beaten us fair and square..." and another inane Teddy Bear smile.

"What do you mean?" Marcus was beginning to smell a Ligia sized rat but his patrons cheered and screamed with delight.

Instead of the normal manic shouting, MG's voice was as soft and sweet as warm honey. "We've only got one Hostie and so she's the lead Hostie 'cos we've not got anyone better."

And the aristos loved the joke...

"So Rachel against Susannah. Okay?"

Susannah looked cornered but Marcus agreed and the crowd in the posh seats whooped with joy.

"And to make it fair, we each get to choose which inflatable the other team will use." At the mention of the word "team" the nobility went hysterical, no doubt remembering all the fun at their house sports competitions. "So you choose which one of our inflatables we've got to use and we choose which one of yours Susannah has.

"You okay with that?"

It was all that Marcus could do to supress the smile. He had twelve, fresh this season, inflatables with nearly brand new motors and we had five little boats which looked as if they would have been more at home in a car boot sale.

I was just as puzzled because I still didn't have a clue what was on MG's enormous mind.

"Then we'll both bring the other's boat to the start line, just to make sure that everything's fair, the ladies board and we're good to go.

"Everybody agreed?"

The whoops shook the café walls. Bring on the gladiators and let's see some blood!

"Okay, we'll see you at eight o'clock sharp. Across the harbour, round the buoy and back – winner takes all. No re-runs or excuses."

Susannahhhh! Susannahhhh! Susannahhhh! Susannahhhh! The children really were excited.

Then MG linked my arm in his and we sauntered off down the quay.

As soon as we were out of earshot I said: "What've you done? You're mad MG. I'll be better than her in the inflatable but she's got twice the power. I'm going to lose for certain and Mike'll go crazy."

MG brought his best Teddy Bear smile out again. "Not for sure, Rache, not for absolute certain. Winning is all about crossing the finishing line first and nothing else really counts.

"Fancy a swim when it gets dark?"

*****

For once, we had a meeting in the squalor of the main cabin because MG had demanded total privacy. The Teddy Bear face had gone. Now, it was the MG I knew so well.

"Rache will get destroyed if we don't give her a hand. The Horex twin cylinder engines on their inflatables are superb motors, absolute rocket ships, and our little Hondas will never keep up."

Then he did smile. "I've worked on those engines before, you know when I was on the south coast, and they really are beautiful..."

I was getting really frustrated: "Oh come on MG, get on with it. You're killing me. You can't sabotage every single engine."

"Don't intend to, my most esteemed Hostie in Chief. I'm just going to make a tiny modification to the one the lovely Susannah will be using.

"Here's what we'll do. The Horex is a beautiful piece of engineering and just so neat – I love that engine. The two cables for reverse and forward are right next to each other, so precise: very, very Germanic. We'll take the clevis pin out of the end of one cable - and," he paused for maximum theatrical effect, "move it to the other so that when Susannah puts her elegant hand to get the motor in forward, it will neatly reverse and give you a truly flying start."

Mike shook his head. "You really are stark, raving mad – you're the genuine article. Totally cracked!"

I giggled, mainly at the thought of Susannah scratching her finger nails trying to get the motor into forward gear.

Then Mike looked serious. "Okay MG, that's the plan – but how're you going to switch the cable?"

MG was in his element. I could see why Dorset CID wanted him, and his herbal remedy business, off their patch.

"Me and Rache will swim across to their boats. Rache can hold the outboard cover up and I'll switch the cable pins. It'll be a thirty second job."

80

Mike's face went like thunder. "No, it's not happening. I'm not having Rache involved in this. I'll swim across with you and we'll both do it."

Now MG was deadly serious. "Cut the crap, Mike. I need you to be seen by the Superior lot. Buy a few drinks. Have a laugh. Keep the job calm.

"We both know what will happen if we leave Rache within smacking distance of the Superiors, don't we?"

"No, I'm not having it – Rache is not getting involved in this. I'm Lead Skipper and that's final."

I was beginning to feel like a pot plant which someone had received for Christmas and now didn't know what to do with.

"Mike, I'm going. I want to go with MG. You're not my Dad and we're not at sea. You can tell me what to do as Lead Skipper but not on shore. If I want to go for a swim with MG, then that's my business."

I was determined like I had never been before: what I did was up to me.

Inside though, my stomach was churning. I had always been such a good girl – at home, school and even university. I had never been Goody Two Shoes but I wasn't ever a bad girl either. Dad and I had sneaked an extra ride at theme parks, and I had made few dodgy sick calls to school when I was in Sixth form, but I would have died before I ever did anything criminal. Now I was – well, a bit anyway.

Mike scowled at me with a look which would have turned Sivota's harbour into an iceberg but we both knew there was nothing he could do about it.

As the sun fell behind the hills, MG gave me the brief. Woohoo! It was just like James Bond. Rachel Lamb as Jemima Bond. Who would have thought it?

"Rache, put your shirt over your bikini so that we're as dark as possible in the water" – it really was James Bond – "and tie your hair back."

"Swim nice and slowly, a gentle breast stroke. I'll have the pliers on a cord round my neck.

"We'll go for the inflatable on the end, the furthest away from the harbour.
"Okay?"

I nodded – too excited to say anything.

"When we get there, I'll flick the cover up and you hold it just clear of the motor. I know these engines so well I can do everything by touch and we'll be finished in a minute.

"Just do everything nice and slow and, for God's sake, don't splash. Just take everything super slow and swim back to Brizo."

*****

I got changed and stood in the darkness by Brizo's stern. MG was already waiting for me. I slid into the blackness silently. It should have been warm but the water sent prickles up and down my legs and arms like nettle stings. I caught a deep breath and pulled it back so that there was no noise.

Brizo was at the end of our Flotilla but we still wanted to stay as much out of sight as possible so we ducked underwater, by her anchor chain, and surfaced a few metres further into the harbour.

I began swimming. My shirt felt really heavy on me, impeding my arms, but MG was right - we were both almost invisible on the water.

He was right about my hair too. Tied back really tightly, my face was left completely clear and this was another distraction out of the way.

The fear had left me now and was replaced by intense concentration. I had been a good swimmer in England but now, being in the water almost every day, I was even more confident. I watched MG in the dark and kept pace with his slow, deliberate strokes which hardly disturbed the surface of the water.

We eased ourselves up to the enemy inflatable and MG put his finger to his lips. I ducked low down in the water so that I almost disappeared.

MG reached across the outboard and pulled at the cover release catch. It wouldn't move. He tugged again but with no better luck. The voices from the cockpit of the Bavaria showed that the victory party had already begun.

MG motioned for me to hold the propeller shaft of the motor whilst he put his legs against it for extra leverage. I slid across and did as I was told.

As MG pulled, the outboard's propeller dug into my leg. It hurt but I stayed silent.

The cover catch sprung open and MG motioned for me to hold it up for him. I leaned across the stern of the inflatable and jammed my hand under the cover, desperate to keep it in place and yet still give MG the space he needed to work.

He removed the pliers from round his neck and fumbled. A last frantic grab was all that stopped them from heading directly to the harbour floor. Everything went into slow motion for me. The fumble. His grab. The pliers - safe once more.

His hands were like a magician's. In near total darkness, he felt the "R" clips which kept the clevis pins in place. He put one "R" clip and a clevis pin in his mouth.

I felt a terrible attack of the giggles coming. Oh my God, what if he sneezes? What if he does an enormous sneeze and blows a clevis pin right across the harbour into the centre of Marcus' face?

MG put the second "R" clip in his mouth and then switched the first clevis pin.

My hand was hurting where the cover was digging into me but I didn't move a millimetre.

MG put the second clevis pin through the cable and slid the "R" clip into place – all by feel. He was a genius.

He nodded to tell me to release the cover. When I was certain, I took my hand out. MG lowered the cover and pushed the over centre fastener to lock it.

One of the girls in the Bavaria's cockpit moved right to the stern and sat just above me. I could see her long, elegant, tanned legs and I could smell her expensive perfume. I wondered what she was thinking – and what she would do if she knew what was happening just two metres away from her.

We sank low into the water, swimming with slow motion strokes. MG was almost invisible. When we got back to Brizo, Mike was at the boat. He hadn't been entertaining as MG had asked him to but had spent the time pacing up and down, worrying.

MG pulled himself out of the water onto the swimming platform and into the cockpit. Mike didn't ask him how things had gone.

I took Mike's hand and let him help me up out of the water. He saw the blood running down my thigh before I did. The propeller had clearly scratched me when MG had been wrestling with the outboard. Cuts done in water always bleed more than if you have them on land and it looked spectacular.

Mike shook his head and MG grinned – and then held his finger to his lips as I clambered into the cockpit. I sat there on the floor panting for a moment, not with physical exertion but with the thrill of what I had just done.

Mike disappeared into the cabin and came back with the first aid kit. He rubbed an antiseptic wipe over the cut. It was only a scratch but I was glad that the Greek doctor had given me that tetanus injection in Lefkas all those months ago.

The guys fished around in the kit, wiped the cut dry and stuck three big plasters over it. I wondered if they would give me a medal for being wounded in action but I already knew the answer!

I whispered to MG that I needed a shower urgently. I had to get clean and dry so there was no sign that I had been in the water.

I dropped my wet clothes into the sink and then got straight into the shower. The water was boiling hot and it washed away the tension. What an experience the last half hour had been for a Christmas Elf!

Time was getting short so I shouted to Mike to get me a towel – and one of mine too from the forepeak. I was prepared to put up with a lot of danger for this project but not enough to use one of lads' towels. Now that would be risking my life!

*****

MG walked me down the harbour to where Marcus, Susannah and the mob were waiting. Bring on the Christians and let's see some dead bodies in the amphitheatre harbour!

Susannah had clearly been given a serious pep talk because she was looking as smug as only someone who uses really posh soap in the shower every day can.

MG had his Teddy Bear face on again.

"Okay, ready to go?"

He waved towards our yachts moored further down the quay, each one with an inflatable tied to its bow.

"Choose any one – they're all the same and we want to play absolutely fair, don't we Rachel?"

I nodded with my obedient servant face, looking suitably glum.

Marcus took the inflatable belonging to Notus. It was as tired looking as the rest of our boats but the outboard started instantly, as I knew it would, having had MG look after it all season.

MG beamed. He turned to one of the Superior Skippers and said, in his best butter-wouldn't-melt-in-my-mouth voice.

"Hmmm. Don't know which one to choose. They all look perfect. What do you reckon Rachel?"

Thank goodness he didn't wait for an answer.

"That one on the end looks as if it might be a bit slower and give Rachel a slight chance. Yes, can we have that one please?

The Superior Skipper really did look superior and he and MG set off to retrieve the inflatable we had modified.

Oh yes! Bring-it-on!

I kept my beaten servant face on as MG brought Superior's inflatable to the end of the floating pontoon to rest against our little boat. He leaned across the outboard looking exhausted - and keeping the position of the gear lever well out of sight.

Sivota is only small and the word had soon spread about the competition. This was going to be the biggest, and best, sporting event the village had ever hosted.

The crowd was enormous - I mean really huge. Every single person in the tavernas and shops, as well as all the other Flotillas in port, was there to watch the spectacle and they packed the harbour wall and crowded on to anything which floated.

If this went wrong, I truly hoped that I would drown and never be found again.

Stavros had come down to the pontoon from his taverna to act as referee and starter. He had his shotgun with him – presumably to shoot anyone he found cheating!

He really was enjoying being the star act.

"Okay, here's the rules. Boats in neutral and engines on tickover. Okay?"

I nodded nervously and Susannah smiled the smile of the certain victor.

"Out to the buoy and back. When you pass the pontoon, that's the end and I'll wave my flag or something.

"No dirty driving or anything because this for fun.

"The losers don't get the best seats in my very wonderful taverna and they also pay for the winners' meals.

"All agreed?"

MG the Teddy Bear nodded and, so that there could be no doubt, added: "Yes, that's fair by me. Winners get a free meal, paid for by the losers, and they also get the harbour tables."

Marcus could not keep the smirk off his face. "Yuppie do da. That's the one. If Susannah doesn't win, we pay for everything – and we'll go and sit at the end of the harbour, in the dark, with the cats, where no-one can see us."

I made myself look the like the loser-in-waiting that I clearly was.

In reality, I was having a serious conversation with myself. I was going through MG's instructions, over and over again.

"Take it slow and easy, Rache, slow is good. Just ignore everything which is going on around you. Put the outboard in forward gear and pull away nice and easy.

"Believe me, you will be on your own. Motor out to the buoy and come back nice and steady. Nice and steady – no need to rush.

"This race is yours to lose - not hers to win."

Stavros turned to us. "Okay ladies, get into your boats. When you're ready, I'm shoot my gun and the race start."

MG was looking for an Oscar award. He shrugged his shoulders - clearly beaten and ready to accept the humiliation. I clambered into our inflatable, looking as miserable as I could.

The little Honda engine burbled away reassuringly on the stern. There was a bit of a cheer from our clients but it was pretty feeble.

Susannah was also looking for an Academy Award. She turned to face the crowd and waved like the film star, Olympic heroine she clearly was, or would soon be, and the aristos on the Superior boats went crazy, screaming and banging on the sides of the yachts.

Marcus did a low bow, and held his hand out Walter Raleigh style, to help her on board.

Our inflatables were very small, so I sat well forward of the outboard towards the centre of the boat. Over and over again, I was telling myself that the race was mine to lose. I tried to clear my head and just look across the darkened harbour to the buoy with its blinking light.

I looked up to check what Stavros was doing with his shotgun and then just concentrated on the buoy.

The noise of the gun startled me – it was immense and the crack echoed round the harbour like the most vicious peal of thunder ever. It took me so much by surprise that I was slow engaging forward gear and had plenty of time to see what was happening – and there was a lot!

Susannah was in her school sports' day, House Captain mode and slammed the outboard into forward gear at the same time as she jammed the throttle open as far as it would go. The inflatable leapt backwards like a terrified cat, slewed round on to one side and spat her into the water.

Even over the noise of the engines, I could hear the crowd cheer.

If I had been a proper all-action heroine, the story would now say that I pulled effortlessly away to victory. Except that I didn't. I was so shocked with what was going on that I snatched at the tiller and boinged our inflatable into the floating pontoon.

Now, one of the contestants was swimming for the harbour wall and the other was pointing the wrong way. Superstars or what?

As the inflatable bounced off the floating pontoon, I got a hold of myself – or MG's words did – I closed the throttle, let the little boat settle on the water and just burbled off to the buoy and back.

As I crossed the imaginary finishing line, Stavros forgot about the flag but fired his shotgun again. This time the crack was crowded out by the cheers of hundreds of spectators.

Wow! I had done it.

MG helped me out of the inflatable, with a wink and a smile. I felt like a Formula One winner with loads of people giving me hugs and congratulations. I had never won anything sporty - happiest smile at Sports Day doesn't really count - so it was overwhelming. I felt I should have a podium and a team hat or something.

Across on the harbour wall there was another lot of excitement. They had fished Susannah out of the water and she was having a full-on, screaming row with Marcus. Then she smacked him right across the cheek. I could almost hear the crack from here. I'll bet that hurt!

MG shrugged his shoulders and smiled again. For sure, you would want to be on his team in any form of competition.

*****

Stavros had set the table out for us right alongside the harbour wall, in the centre of the Taverna. Literally the best seats in the house.

MG took charge of proceedings and had me sitting next to him. He was in really high spirits and determined to make this a memorable party.

"Half a dozen bottles of your finest champagne Landlord, and then feed us everything you've got on your very wonderful menu."

And Stavros really did have the biggest smile I had seen on a taverna owner since I first came to Greece.

The champagne arrived, French too and not a Greek lookalike. MG flicked the cork off the first bottle and held it out to me.

"A victory speech from the greatest speedboat pilot in Greece."

Everyone cheered and started banging the tables and began shouting "Speech, speech, speech!"

I was really embarrassed but desperately wanted to join in the party so I got ready to stand up and make some joke about my team manager and pit crew but then Marcus appeared next to MG's shoulders.

His face was tense and there was clearly trouble coming. I felt my mouth go dry and a real rush of tension. This situation had the potential to go badly wrong.

Marcus was tall, as tall as Mike and as muscular, and he towered over MG. His voice was trembling – absolutely furious.

"You sabotaged our boat. You're a cheat and she's a cheat." He looked down at me with contempt.

MG stood up and I felt my stomach tense. His voice was flat calm, devoid of any emotion.

He had to raise his head to look up at Marcus, he was so much smaller.

He spoke slowly. "Listen to me Marcus, listen very carefully, because I'm only going to say this once. Rachel hates swearing so forgive me Rache.

"Fuck off. Fuck off now and move away from our table. If I have to leave my meal, it will be to come across to your clients and tell them that the standard of maintenance on your boats is so bad that you are risking their lives."

The tone and volume of his voice did not alter.

"After I've explained the danger you're putting them in, I'll tell them what the pictures we're going to post on Facebook will say about Superior Yachting Holidays' clients not being able to honour their bets.

"And when they've fucked you off good style – I'll kick the shit out of you.

"Okay Marcus, got that or do you need any more explanation?"

He didn't.

7

All You Can Manage

AT the start of the season, I didn't see much of Luke. I was too busy to do anything except survive and Alissa and I still had not got the cleaning absolutely right. The boats were always perfect for the clients but we sometimes duplicated each other's work and things could have been faster.

This meant I sort of bumped into Luke in Tychos, not literally of course, and I liked this because he always had a smile.

When we had a coffee and cake together, I ended up doing most of the talking because Luke was still painfully shy – or something!

When Mike had told me how he became Lead Skipper, the whole story came out in one neat, ten minute package. It was the same with MG.

Luke told me tiny bits about himself every time we met - and then always checked to see if he had said something wrong and whether I approved.

When I was getting the cleaning cloths from the taverna I found out that he was the son of two doctors. His Mum was forty-two years old when she became pregnant. Luke's Dad had told him that they were certain baby making was well and truly over and all that he had done was roll over one Sunday morning and, the next thing he knew, his wife was pregnant. How romantic was that?

The baby was Luke. He had two siblings – a sister who was eighteen years older than him and a brother who was fourteen years his elder.

During another coffee and cake break I got to know that his sister was a renowned Plastic Surgeon, who was famous as the boob improver to the stars, and the family joke was that his barrister brother represented the clients suing her. Then he added desperately, not that anyone ever has – as if I took him seriously!

One day, he was replacing the fender lines on Eurus and I was scrubbing the decks ready for the next clients. I went below and got us two glasses of squash with a load of ice.

"Why didn't you go to Uni, like the rest of your family?" I asked.

Truthfully, he actually fidgeted and started drawing patterns in the condensation on the side of the glass he was so embarrassed.

"Well, that's what should have happened. I did "A" levels but I always liked working with my hands. I could do academic work but I never enjoyed it. Give me something to do with my hands and the world was great but books and essays – well, they were a punishment.

"So, I suppose you could say that I bummed around and did nothing properly. I worked with a big house builder as a labourer and soon picked things up – a bit of plumbing, wiring, whatever. Then they let me do simple plastering and the brickwork which couldn't be seen. Like I said, if it was manual work then I could do it.

"We'd sailed in Greece as a family so I thought I would come out here for one summer and see what there was.

"I did a bit of this, a bit of that and the simple stuff on the boats which the engineers didn't have time to do.

"In winter, I'd come back to England and do a load more courses and learn more things. Getting the Job Centre to send you on a training course is easy – they'll do anything to get you into work.

"I've done a lot of courses in the last five years and so now I can do a bit of a lot of things but I'm no good at anything…"

And there was the fuddled look again.

I smiled and he smiled in return. "And I managed to get sacked too."

I laughed, "Ooooohh. You naughty boy! What did you do?"

Luke grinned and he looked lovely. "I was working as a sandwich maker on a production line. The butties came down the track and I had to put two pieces of cucumber on each one, exactly in the middle."

I didn't say a word but just half covered my face with my hand because I knew what was coming next.

"Anyway, it was driving me crazy so I started experimenting with the cucumbers – you know, turning them at an angle or arranging them vertically."

I knew exactly what he meant.

"The girl supervising the line found out and I was sacked but she was okay and said I could stay until the end of the week.

"I was grateful but at five to six, just before the shift change on the last day, I went to the head of the line, got a big handful of cucumber slices from the supply box and made sure that the last thirty sandwiches were piled high with cucumber.

"Sa-ave the Worllllddddd…" and then he did the anthem wave with his hands above his head.

I was struggling to keep my face straight.

"And did they let you keep the sandwiches you'd ruined?"

Luke immediately went shy and looked really puzzled.

"No, no, I didn't get anything."

Then I told him about my cat icing saga – but how the Manager had liked me so much that he'd given me a whole bag of reject biccies.

It sounds really silly to say this but we both laughed and I felt so much better. For a lot of the time I was under pressure – to get things right for Dave, to do my jobs properly for Mike and MG, and to please clients. Mostly I liked it, but sometimes I just wanted a break - to be able to speak without watching what I was saying, and without having Mike check the tension of the mooring lines and correct me if they weren't perfect.

I got this with Luke.

*****

By June, we were really on top of things so I was glad when Luke came over as I was having a coffee and cake at Andreas'.

"Hiya Stranger," he smiled. "I've not seen you about. Been on holiday?" And there was another open, honest grin which divided his face into two happy halves.

"I've just seen Dave and he says everything's good. Do you fancy going swimming in The Pool?

"We can take Eurus."

The Pool wasn't a swimming pool but a nearly semi-circular indentation in the rock wall about half way down the channel to the open sea. It was a spectacular place with the bluest, clearest water in the world. We didn't take clients there because there wasn't much space but for a single boat it was perfect.

I grinned. "Give me two minutes. I'll get changed and grab a towel."

I ran down the quay to Brizo. Sometimes, almost from nowhere, a voice reminded me of just how good a job this was. I could have been doing all sorts of rubbish things but here I was going swimming with a really nice guy, in a place most people would kill to visit.

The lads were not on the boat so I put my bikini on in the cabin – making sure not to sit down on the side cushions where MG slept!

I never had any problem being around the clients in my bikini but with Luke I never felt totally comfortable. I don't know why – he was always really lovely but it just didn't feel right. So I reached into my space, grabbed my towel and two t-shirts. One for wearing on the boat and the other for swimming in.

I cast off the stern mooring lines and then raised the anchor from the cockpit. Luke had the helm and we didn't need to say anything to each other. It was even better than being a team – we just knew what the other was going to do without a word being spoken.

We motored slowly out of the harbour and then pottered along to The Pool. It was breath-taking – beyond perfect - with water so brilliantly turquoise that, even with sunglasses, it was blinding.

Luke applied a touch of reverse throttle to Eurus and brought her to a full halt.

I looked at Luke and, without me saying anything, he said: "Yes, good to go. Give her a good length of chain and I'll stand her well away from the rock wall just in case the wind picks up while we're in the water."

I did, and the anchor chain rattled over Eurus' bows.

Luke took his shirt off. He was a fit man – not in a gym and health club way – but just fit from an active outdoor life. The edges of his brown hair were bleached by exposure to the sun and salt water, and his skin was tanned to a golden brown.

Briefly, I thought that I had woken up to a lot of worse looking lads than Luke when I was at Uni – then I immediately smacked the thought on the hand for popping into my head.

Luke was a superb swimmer – better than anyone in the company. He didn't bother with the swimming platform but dived straight over the rail from Eurus' cockpit. It wasn't a show-off's dive but just neat and elegant. The water was hardly disturbed as he split it apart.

His head popped up with his normal grin. "Come, on Rachel, you won't get better than this."

I turned my back to Luke, switched to my swimming t-shirt and went to the bathing platform at the back of Eurus. I could tell fibs and say that I joined Luke like a graceful girl porpoise but I didn't. I slipped a bit and so the dive, which was never going to be brilliant, collapsed into a big splosh.

Luke caught my hands and we both giggled. I felt good. Life felt good and I was really enjoying being with Luke.

We swam around for ten minutes and then Luke said we should snorkel down to see the fish because they were really tame in The Pool. Where the rock face dropped into the water it had split into a multitude of small caves and canyons so swimming there, and looking down, was like flying over a miniature world. This was tourist brochure snorkelling country.

I did want to snorkel but I was slightly unsure because my previous attempts hadn't been great! I had seen Luke surface dive before and he was the nearest thing to a dolphin you could imagine. He lay on top of the water, breathing through a snorkel, kicked his legs vertically in the air and then disappeared without making a ripple: it was beautiful to watch.

I had tried snorkelling too but I was more like a submarine diving than a dolphin. Splosh! Struggle! Then loads more splashes and bubbles just to get about 2 millimetres underwater!

I made some embarrassed waffling about not being able to snorkel properly and so he offered to show me.

I put on my mask, snorkel and fins and lay on the water with Eurus just behind me.

Luke lay alongside me, flat on the surface of the water. What happened next was so fast that it took me by surprise. He bent sharply at the waist so that his head was pointing right at the seabed. At the same time, he kicked his legs in the air and pulled his arms straight. It would be wrong to describe the three movements separately because they were just one.

Luke shot under the water like a stone and, as he dropped to the bottom, he squeezed the nose piece on his mask so that he could equal the pressure in his ears.

Now, he must have been seven or eight metres beneath me and turned on his back to wave. After what seemed to be hours, he kicked for the surface and came up right alongside me.

I have been trying to think of a really accurate way to describe what I had been watching but I'm struggling, without sounding all arty and soppy. It was a bit like gymnastics or maybe even a male ballet dancer.

I was entranced by seeing how graceful Luke was in the water, his muscles rippling and he didn't so much swim in the water but was part of it – a human dolphin.

Those thoughts whose hands I had smacked earlier on came back...

Luke lifted his mask and went through the whole routine with me. I needed to bend sharply to get my head pointing in the right direction and, at the same time, pull back with my arms to drive me towards the bottom. If I flicked my legs up, like a handstand, then their weight above the water would push me to the bottom like a rocket and, if I kept them pressed tightly together, I wouldn't even make a splash on the surface.

Well, that didn't sound too hard.

The problem was the timing because, as I have said, doing the perfect surface dive isn't so much three movements but one – well, it is when it's done properly!

Luke was endlessly patient and smiled encouragement all the time but I just couldn't get my legs to go up fast enough and at exactly the same time as I bent my waist. Finally, it went so badly wrong that I flopped over and did a sort of half backward roll ending with water up my nose!

Now I wasn't the dolphin that Luke was but more like a seal on the beach, with a bad cold and who can't stop sneezing. Luke came up alongside me and raised his mask again.

"You know Rachel, your t-shirt is getting in the way. You'd find it a lot easier without it."

He was very matter of fact and sensible but at the same time slightly diffident, as if he was intruding into my private space.

I didn't speak but just nodded in agreement and swam across to the bathing platform. I flicked out of the water, took off my mask and then pulled the t-shirt over my head.

Luke pretended to be studying the rock wall or the sheep or something, to avoid looking directly at me. I saw my body and I was pleased. I was never going to be some super stunning, film star beautiful woman but I was slim with nice, well, nice bits and I felt that the old cat biscuit muncher Rachel was gone forever.

Out of the corner of my eye, I saw that Luke was watching me now and I smiled. I was glad that he was looking and pleased that he was seeing me in a wet bikini.

I slid back in the water and swam across to Luke. He stayed right alongside me whilst I put my mask on. Then I lay on the water and tried again.

The dive wasn't perfect but it was much better than before. I bent my waist correctly and got the arm movement right but I was still slow with my legs and so I went to the bottom much more slowly than Luke had done.

But I did get there, and turned on my back to wave at Luke. He saw me there waving to him and I hoped that he saw everything he wanted to see - and was pleased. I really did.

*****

You might have heard that expression about there never being a dull moment, well there really wasn't for a Hostie. What to tell you about the next few weeks?

How about the great quiz shootout?

One week we'd got a nice group of clients on the Flotilla. They were all friends and from Surrey. One was a dentist, another an architect - then there was a barrister and a Professor of Old English Poetry who worked at Oxford.

They were all married and every one to a super, hyper-brainy woman with a mega-job.

The group were good friends and played tennis and golf together, ate at each other's houses and always went on holiday together but my God, were they competitive or what?

It wasn't sailing which was the problem. They preferred motoring in any case and were happy to be helped all the time. They ate together and paid me without a moment's hesitation for their meals. But just mention the word "quiz" and World War III started!

We were moored in the harbour at Kioni and I ordered Mike and MG off the boat – go away and don't disturb me, not even if Brizo is on fire, because I knew that I had to raise my quiz game.

I didn't show up for dinner so Mike brought a sandwich for me, as I melted the internet in Kioni to get the One Quiz to Beat Them All.

By eight o'clock, I was ready for action and headed for the taverna where everyone seemed in a very relaxed mood. There were so many smiles and the sort of belly laughs you hear after the fourth jug of wine.

I really didn't know what I had been making the fuss about. The four families sorted themselves into two teams and I appointed Mike as scorer and MG as wine waiter. The winning team would get a big box of Andreas' Auntie's baklava.

Then I asked the first question and it started snowing, or it felt like it did, because the mood changed in a moment.

They absolutely murdered the questions which had been tie breakers with every other Flotilla so far.

What is the capital of Azerbaijan? Baku. Easy, play school stuff.

Name the third highest mountain in the world. Kangchenjunga. Come on, stop messing about and give us some decent questions.

Then the tension started and the troubles really began. Someone was going to die for that box of baklava - and I was beginning to think that it was me.

What's the official, world land-speed record for cars? The barrister stood up and towered over me.

He boomed: "Do you mean the speed achieved by a rocket powered vehicle - or one using an internal combustion engine driving wheels?"

I swallowed and began to feel that I needed the toilet – and quite badly too!

MG bailed me out. "Rocket powered – the maximum speed of a vehicle with wheels touching the ground."

The barrister rattled off the answer precisely.

"763.035 mph - set by Andy Green on the 15 October 1997 in the Black Rock Desert, Nevada, USA in the Thrust SSC."

Whaaaa!!! No-one could be that good. It was impossible.

I picked up the quiz ball and served again. "What is the name of the deepest part of the ocean?" I asked in my best Quizmaster voice.

The dentist had the answer ready before my lips had finished moving. "The Mariana Trench," he said with a triumphant smile.

The barrister was on his feet again. "Objection. Objection to the Chair."

Oh no, please leave me alone. I'm really feeling sick and dizzy. Please stop beating me up...

The voice cascaded across the taverna, as it would in the High Court. "The deepest part of the ocean is the Challenger Deep!" a smile creased his face, "so no points to them and a bonus to us because they got it wrong!"

Now the dentist was on his feet, fists balled on the table. "That's arrant nonsense. The Challenger Deep is part of the Mariana Trench and not a separate entity in its own right. Therefore, we are correct in defining the Mariana Trench, and all its sub-elements, as the deepest part of the ocean."

I really thought that I was going to throw up all over the table.

Now the Oxford Professor joined in. "I think that we have a problem here in terms of what is a specific geographic entity. For example, if we consider the western boundary of East Anglia under the very able ruler Wehha in the seventh century this was not fixed in a firm, determinate way. Rather, it was a rather more flexible area. Now, are we saying the Challenger Deep is..."

Mike got up – and there was always a lot of him when he stood straight. "Whoaa. Let's call this question a "no ball" and we'll bash on. The next question please Your Majesty," and he did a low bow to me.

And so it went on for another 20 minutes until I really could have curled up in a ball and died, it was that bad.

Eventually, I had completely run out of questions and it was still a draw. I wondered what my Mum had done wrong when I was a baby to get me this much bad luck.

MG looked at me, and gave the same wink that he had in Sivota for the Superior victory.

"Rachel," he said wearing his Teddy Bear face, "may I have the honour of asking the tie breaker in what has been a truly memorable quiz?"

"Well, yes MG, of course..."

"One question to both teams. The first one to answer it correctly wins and if no-one does, it's an official draw. Here we go.

"What do the Telly Tubbies say before they go to bed?"

I would have given anything to have a video of what happened next.

There was unity from both teams. "That's not a proper question. How can we have a quiz if we don't have real questions? You're just being silly."

One of the things which was most fascinating about MG was the speed in which his character could change. Now the Teddy MG had gone and you really wouldn't want to get into an argument with the person who had replaced him.

MG spoke: "It is a proper question and I've asked it. I think that it is proper and so it is." The voice had the same flat, calm, unemotional tone which Marcus had faced.

"Okay?"

And it was.

MG got the Teddy out again. "Well, it's disappointing that no-one knows the answer but come on Rache, what would we say as we went to bed in Telly Tubby land?"

MG held my hand and we both waved like crazy to the teams and shouted "Bye, Bye…"

*****

I have praised Mike's ability to judge when to help clients and when to leave them alone because he really was brilliant. He was tall, a fantastic sailor, and sailed mainly just in his shorts and…

No - back to the story.

Very occasionally, he was forced into a corner he couldn't escape from - and it was always through no direct fault of his own.

Kath and Terry had taken early retirement when they were 55. They'd both worked in Local Government all their lives. They had three kids, went on holiday to Lanzarote most years and helped organise their village fete every summer.

They visited both their parents regularly and Terry did the garden for his Dad as his father got older. Kath was quite open with me about her life and also about what she had decided to do with her retirement.

She said that she was fed up with being sensible and wanted some adventure. Flotilla sailing was the start and they were going to do every-thing she had ever dreamed of – before it was too late.

There were two giant problems. First, neither of them was very fit and they had never done anything vaguely connected with sport since they'd left school forty years earlier. A session of Pilates in the village hall every Thursday evening wasn't going to be much training for having Boreas cranked over in a 4.

Flotilla sailing is really great for anyone because you can either motor along at four knots, and never go near hoisting a sail, or you can have a try at real sailing.

People with a sporting background usually enjoy sailing instantly. There are also a few people, like me, who just have a feel for the water. Skiers are great because they have a trained sense of balance and on one Flot we had this fat old guy who had raced motorcycles all his life. He took to sailing straight away because he had spent a lifetime balancing things, and mainly not falling over, and he was ice calm under pressure when things got sparky.

There are never any issues sailing except when clients get the wrong idea of what they want to be doing, or should be doing! Kath and Terry were perfect examples. Well, Kath was…

Things were even worse because Terry would have been quite happy to spend the whole week moored up in Tychos enjoying the sun. Kath wasn't and so almost dragged him into being the action man he was never going to be.

So, they hoisted the sail whenever they could and even when me or MG were on board they could never tack the boat without ending up in a total tangle. Kath was really quite snooty about doing everything herself and so she would put the helm about, Terry would forget which sheet did what and they would stall the boat in the eye of wind and it wouldn't get out of irons until one of us had teased it away.

Terry was an even worse helmsman and quite literally forgot what to do when he was going about. So either MG or I would hang around patiently until we were asked to sort the mess out.

Mooring was a nightmare – every time. Mike and MG were both absolutely brilliant with clients like Kath and Terry. Without the slightest hint of condescension they would subtly take control of the boats and moor them almost without clients knowing. It was all done with lots of smiles and jokes and no-one got stressed.

But Kath was having none of this, so twice a day either she or Terry crabbed towards a pontoon or harbour wall and then MG would have to pick up their anchor in Brizo's inflatable and re-site it, whilst Mike sorted out the tangle of ropes at the stern and moored the boat safely.

We were all getting very tense with this and so when we came into Tychos we thought that we would give ourselves, and Team Kath, a break. We'd moor them last and put them next to the ferry ramp where there was loads of room. When they were having a meal at Andreas', we'd re-site the boat and everyone would be happy.

The first three boats went in a treat with some quite nice mooring done by clients. Then Terry began reversing Boreas towards the dock. Right from the start, it went wrong – and then even more wrong and finally a bit more wronger than that!

Boreas slewed all over the harbour like a student leaving her first Fresher's party. The key to mooring is to go slowly. The moment you rush things, you are asking for trouble. You also need leaving alone just to work things out. Even with Mike teaching me, I needed a few seconds just to get things sorted out in my head – and you will remember what happened when I didn't!

Kath was hammering Terry with a non-stop barrage of advice / orders / comments and things were made vastly worse because Mike brought the rib alongside Boreas and he started giving instructions too.

So now, poor Terry is being bombarded with all this information and it's all got too much for him. Kath has lost it too so when she is supposed to drop the anchor she doesn't, but just lets it dangle a couple of metres underwater.

Mike sees this and shouts to Terry to bring the boat to a halt, go out and drop the anchor again. Mike's getting all wound up by now so he really starts shouting loudly to make himself understood.

Terry simply freaks out and slams the throttle into reverse instead of forward, and now he's heading for the dock flat out.

MG and I were in the inflatable and I'll not even mention the language. Smashing the stern of one of our four charter boats would have wiped us out there and then – instantly.

Luke was on the dock, re-tying one of the lines for the huge fenders the ferries use. These are just giant versions of the fenders we use on our boats to prevent them being damaged when they come alongside other yachts or pontoons.

As Boreas rushed towards the dock, Luke saw what was happening and threw the fender into the water between the yacht and the wall.

Boreas hit the fender really hard – and I do mean hard! You could almost hear the impact against the metre wide ball. As the boat bounced back off the fender Luke threw himself at the stern and caught the guard wire.

I was too scared to admire him because had he slipped he would have been killed. Bold and determined is one thing but what Luke had just done was reckless.

Boreas was now heading back, sideways on, towards the harbour wall but, this time, her fenders took the impact.

It's not like in the films where a boat reacts instantly once the hero is in charge, because yachts don't. Luke had to struggle to get Boreas under control as she bounced alongside the dock wall.

After what seemed like hours, he brought her to a halt. A large chunk had been taken out of the paint on her starboard stern but this was absolutely nothing compared with what could have happened. Luke was even good with the clients. He calmed them down and then brought Boreas alongside the dock so that we could moor her side to, and get everyone sorted out.

The other guys were just as good. No-one raised a voice or even a hint of criticism. Everything was just calm and re-assuring. The truth was that there was no point in getting wound up and shouty with the clients. Mike was responsible for their safety and he should have just taken the boat out of their control. That was that: it was the Lead Skipper's responsibility.

Later on, we had coffees in Andreas' and Dave said the same thing. Cut the crap, Mike, you've just screwed up and don't do it again.

There were no excuses from Mike or MG. We had been lucky and sometimes you need luck to survive. Goodness, had I grown up!

The Dave threw something in which really brought the conversation to a complete halt.

"We've been lucky and got away with it so a big, big thanks to Luke."

Of course, Luke was sat as far away as he could from everyone and just hung his head and mumbled something incomprehensible.

"Luke has really got us out of the shit because the boats aren't insured for damage. We've got third party liability insurance, so we're all personally protected, but nothing for accidental damage. We're living day to day and so the insurance had to go and I just had to pray that a client wouldn't try to ram the harbour wall and write off a boat."

There were a few embarrassed half laughs and MG just buried his head in his hands.

"If Luke hadn't got that fender between Boreas and the wall, the job would have been over. End of.

"Good job. Luke."

I was still the junior member of the team but I knew that I was more than pulling my weight so I wasn't uneasy about what happened next.

"Can I say something, Dave?"

He nodded.

"Luke doesn't work for Defini full time but he is part of the team. We all know that we couldn't do without him – and not just with the big things like today.

"But he doesn't get a share of the tips at the end of each week and I don't think that's fair. From now on, we should split the tips five ways, not four, because that's right."

Mike nodded in agreement and MG said, "Good with me. Luke can have all my bloody tips after the mess he's saved me today!"

Dave did hesitate for a moment, probably because none of us really knew how bad things were financially, but he smiled and said: "If that's what we all want then I'm good with it."

And he held up his coffee cup, "Cheers Luke."

I was walking back to Brizo to get my wash bag for a shower before dinner and Luke came trotting up behind me.

"Rachel, you shouldn't have done that. I didn't do much and..."

"Oh, shut up Luke and stop talking crap!" And then I thought that my Mum would go mad if she'd heard me speak like that.

"You've saved everyone today – the company and me, so just accept that you've been wonderful and enjoy it – and I might even let you sit next to me at dinner tonight."

He smiled: "That'll be a real treat – better than a share of the tips."

*****

Kath and Terry came to see me before dinner. I think that they chose me in case one of the guys shouted at them - which wouldn't have happened but could have done! Causing £50,000 of damage to a yacht might well have caused anyone to get tense!

They were all apologies so I sat them in Brizo's cockpit and told them about the row Mike and I had, but clearly a heavily edited version, when I was learning stern to mooring and how bad I had been. Everyone relaxed and, in a funny sort of way, it actually did the couple good because for the last two days they took things really carefully, motored a lot and let the guys moor them. That's how a holiday should be – not stressed out of your mind all the time

*****

As Kath and Terry were getting ready to leave Brizo, Kath gave me a packet she had made from notepaper. It was very pale pink, almost white, and had Luke's name written on it, in the centre, very carefully in extremely neat handwriting. It was sealed with a little piece of the black plastic tape we keep on all the boats.

"Could you give this to Luke, please, because we don't want to make a fuss?"

I smiled and said I would.

The packet had been upside down on the table throughout dinner and no-one took any notice of it. When everyone was having coffees at the end of the meal I said: "Your two greatest fans have sent you something."

I passed the letter to Luke and he peeled back the tape and opened the package. First, there was a short note, written in the same immaculate handwriting as was on the front of the envelope.

Luke read it silently.

"They've said thank you."

I reached across. "Come on, let me see it."

He didn't smile but replied in a quite serious voice, which I rarely heard him use.

"No, please, I'd prefer you not to. It's, well, it's sort of personal, so please let me show it to you another time."

I suddenly felt quite protective of this strange man and wondered what actually went on inside his head. He could be playful and pretend to swim in the cockpit of Brizo when I filled her with water. He dived like a dolphin but never laughed at my clumsiness. He did incredibly brave things and yet went into corner when he was thanked. Truly, I had never met anyone like him before.

Luke held the package open for me to see inside. There were two, unused, 100 Euro notes.

"I'll be back in a minute. I've got to give this money back to them. It would be wrong to take it."

I took his hand. "No Luke, don't do that. What you did for them today was incredible – not just good but amazing. You were amazing and they want to show you that.

"Say thanks, but then leave it. You'll upset them if you reject their present. You did a wonderful thing today and you've got to let them show you that they appreciate it."

So he did.

Luke came back for another coffee. We talked for quite a long time about nothing really and when he stretched out under the table I felt his leg against mine – and I didn't move.

*****

When I had first met the guys at the Boat Show, and Dave had been teasing me about bringing a load of knickers, I thought that he was a bit weird. On Tychos I realised that although he had been winding me up, he was also completely serious and it was very good advice.

Alissa did sell essentials at her little shop, and there was a bit better range of stuff at Vasiliki and even more at Nydri, but it was never like going shopping in Chester where you were always spoilt for choice. If you wanted anything particular you really needed to have brought it to Tychos with you.

It was difficult to stay fully human living with the guys but one of the ways I did it was with minty gel toothpaste. No matter how busy we were, or what had happened during the day, I always, but always, brushed my teeth first thing in the morning and before I went to bed at night – and always with mint flavoured, gel toothpaste.

I would brush my teeth, shut my ears to the noise coming from Mike's cabin and whatever lucky lady had booked in that night, try not to trip over MG's rubbish and then crawl into my own, personal, private space with my mouth tasting clean - just as it had all my life. In short, minty gel was a big thing for me.

The problem was that the last three weeks had been bonkers mad. Alissa didn't stock minty gel, but said that she would try to order some from her wholesaler who would have to get it from Athens – and I would probably be in a Care Home and have no teeth at all by the time it arrived!

There was none at Vasiliki and we had only visited Nydri once in the three weeks and then I was in maximum baby-sitting mode. By the time I had got everyone else sorted out, there was no time to go toothpaste hunting even though I had bought minty gel in the town before.

After squeezing the last molecule out of the tube with a pair of MG's pliers, really I did, I was desperate.

Luke and I were sat together for dinner again, and everyone was starting to expect this by now. I told him about the minty gel crisis.

As normal, he was all smiles. "It's no problem. I've got to take a passerelle bracket to be welded in Nydri tomorrow. I'm taking the rib first thing in the morning and I can nip into town while Evangelos is doing the welding and get you some."

I offered him €5 but he just waved it away and said: "I'll take it from the tips you got for me."

The following day, we were off for an overnight stay in Mitikas and I had to go to bed with unwashed teeth. My God! I was becoming a guy!

After Mitikas it was another overnighter at Little Vathi and I gave in and used some ordinary toothpaste. Now my teeth were clean but they felt as if Alissa had attacked them with the deck cleaner.

By the time we moored in Tychos again I was desperate to see Luke - and for more than the normal reasons this time.

Brizo was the last to moor. The guys were doing their sheepdog impersonations in the inflatable so I brought her to the wall, dropped the anchor well out and then just tightened her very gently against the chain until I could throw the mooring lines to Luke.

What I did next was completely wrong – totally and utterly out of order and later, I was really ashamed of myself.

There was no greeting, no asking how things had been. Just a desperate: "Have you got my toothpaste?"

Luke jumped on board before I had even lowered the passerelle, dug around in his rucksack and brought out three tubes. "And I know where to get it next time you run low."

I left him to stop the engine and bounded down to the cabin, got my tooth brush and began brushing.

It was like the best possible warm shower when you're really cold or super grubby. I squashed the gel down between my gums and the mint flavour rushed round my mouth, hoovering up all the nasties. It was wonderful.

I rinsed my teeth for a long time, climbed up the stairs into the cockpit and gave Luke a big hug.

"Ooohhh. Thanks for that, you're a star!"

He looked at me with that unsure face he always had when he wasn't absolutely certain if he was going to say the right thing, so I helped him out.

"Did you find the shop in Nydri? That one just before you turn left down to the harbour road, opposite the sandwich place?"

"I did look there, and a lot of other places in Nydri but no-one had any mint gel toothpaste. I guess the Greeks don't like it and perhaps it's not popular with the tourists. Anyway, it was good fun jogging up and down the main street and trying not to get run over by quad bikes."

I was bit puzzled. "Where did you get it from, then?"

"Well, the rib was there so I nipped along to Lefkas Town and had a look there. They're not keen on your toothpaste either!

"Eventually, I found some in that posh pharmacy, you know the one on the pedestrianised street which runs through the town from the quay? Well, they sell it so I bought all they had and then the lady said they would get some more from Athens so that you'll be okay in the future and I don't mind going back again – for you."

I felt my eyes going wet and the only thing I could say was a really feeble, "Thank you."

"And I got something else for you…"

He reached down into his bag again and got out a small black and white box. He passed it over the table to me.

On the long side was written, in a very ordinary print, "No 5."

Then, on the next line, "Chanel" with "Paris" underneath.

In smaller writing it said, "Le Savon - the Bath Soap."

Luke had only bought me a bar of Chanel soap – for nothing, not for my birthday or for Christmas but just for absolutely nothing.

Now my eyes were a bit more than just wet.

My mind was racing. He shouldn't be buying me gifts like this for no reason, and I was about to say something but he spoke first.

"I wanted to share a bit of the €200 with you and I thought you might like a treat – something you didn't need but might like?"

It was as much a question as a statement.

Then I remembered what I had told Luke about acknowledging the gift he had been given and accepting it with good grace so I said nothing but "Thank you" – but I felt an awful lot more.

8

Rachel, I Need You

BEING a Hostie really changed me – and in such a short time too. After five months, I was completely used to customers turning to me as a one stop fixer of everything.

"Rachel, which is the engine lever thing?"

"Rachel, what do I do with the anchor?"

"Rachel, I've got a tummy problem."

"Rachel, I can't find Clare's teddy. Do you know where it is?"

"Rachel, I'm fed up with him and I want to go home."

The key thing is to smile, sort things out the best you can and most people will be happy. It's also really important to share yourself out so that no-one gets a lot more attention than anyone else. But, like everything, there are exceptions – and this one was a bit strange.

From the moment I met Sophie, I really liked her. She was a tiny thing, with long, curly, very black hair and a nervous smile which constantly flickered on and off like trying to watch a video with a dodgy internet connection. She clung on to Dan as if he was about to disappear at any minute.

As soon as she got off the ferry, she wanted a lot of reassurance – and I do mean a lot! This made things a bit difficult because she treated me like an older sister and best mate, rather than a Hostie. I was actually two years younger than her so it was all a bit odd.

Sophie was a receptionist at a big IT company in Reading – one of those which served Intel and Microsoft. She was very quiet but dead reliable and so everyone liked her. She didn't actually say that they liked her, because every time we got talking about her she started blushing, but I bet they did because she was so keen to please.

Her parents had a thing about boys and sex so she never had a boyfriend at school – not even for a cuddle or a snog. When she started work, the lads just disappeared. So, she settled into a routine of work and a bit of shopping with her girlfriends and helping her Mum round the house and slowly even the thought of a boyfriend started to disappear into the distance.

Just before I started my incredible career as a Christmas Elf, Sophie had decided that she would take a trip to Berlin with a couple of her girlfriends. With not a lot else to do, she signed up for a beginner's German course so that she could get into the German culture a bit.

On the same course was Dan who worked as an admin guy in Reading Council or somewhere. It's difficult to describe Dan, except that if you ever had to help the Police make an identity picture of him you'd have a hard time because he was just so average. In fact, he was the most average guy I have ever seen. He was average height with blackish hair, but not properly black, which was a bit curly but not much. He had a sort of, well, ordinary face and…

Well, there was just nothing about him.

He spoke quietly - not exactly nervous but not confident either. You wouldn't actually ignore Dan but you'd also need to a good reason to listen to him.

And Sophie worshipped him – I mean actually treated him like some God.

And what was better was that Dan adored her too. If they had joined every dating site in the Universe, none could have done better than the coffee break at their German course.

Sophie had been sitting on her own and Dan had asked her if all the other five seats at the table were taken – well no, he wouldn't have said that because it would have been too pushy – so, Sophie says no and Dan says would she mind if he sat opposite her and Sophie says no she wouldn't and then little streams of stars come out of their eyes, just like a Disney film, and Dan says perhaps they can have coffee together again next week - and they do.

Then Dan says would Sophie like another coffee after the course has finished and Sophie says yes please, but only if I can pay, and so they go to Costa and she buys the coffee and he gets them two muffins - and by Christmas, things have got so serious that he sends her a Christmas card with three kisses on the bottom. Hot or what?

On New Year's Eve, they go to the Firework Display at Henley. They sing Auld Lang Syne and, at the end, Dan kisses Sophie – on the lips – and they fall so heavily in love it's a wonder they don't crash all the way to the centre of the earth.

Now, Dan has really got the hot and heavies for a passionate love affair and wants to show Sophie some adventure so he books a holiday with Delfini. Sophie really only goes along with the idea because if Dan was in a Roman amphitheatre surrounded by fifty lions and a load of gladiators, she would want to be alongside him. She is in love with a capital L.

But she is also carrying 24 years of baggage round with her – and so is he. They have little bits of tiny snogs – are these snoggettes? – but he doesn't do anything rude, or even a bit rude, and so the first time they actually spend a night together is when they board Zephyrus.

And of course, what she sees, and he sees, is all a bit of shock – for both of them!

Sophie also finds the sailing part of the holiday physically hard work. She's not much bigger than a large doll, and has hands that you can see through, like my Mum's best bone china plates, so she can't do much in the way of pulling or dragging things around.

Dan thinks that this is all very lovely and makes cooing noises all the time. Sophie blushes and beams back but things are going so incredibly well that she even takes off her top and sits on the cabin roof in her bikini. Woohoo! Cheeky thing!

The first three days of a holiday are either rubbish or great – depending on how much you like sailing. For Dan and Sophie, there is an irregular, light wind of not much more than a couple of miles an hour so we mainly motor around having late breakfasts and long lunches and don't do much with the sails.

Sophie and Dan are now really into this yachting business and Sophie actually asks if she can have a go at steering the boat. Dan is really proud and can't wait to tell everyone about his super athlete girlfriend when we have dinner in the evening. Round the World Racing here we come!

The problem is that the three Jimmies – yes, they really were all called Jimmy - on Eurus, are getting a bit fed up and so Mike decides that we will spend the night in Palairos and then, in the morning, try to catch some of the wind which nearly always blows down from the Lefkas Canal.

Palairos has a really nice little harbour with easy mooring, so Mike and MG got everyone nicely settled in without any trouble.

It was a lovely hot summer's evening but the clouds were building so I checked the weather forecast on the Poseidon website. We all absolutely swear by Poseidon. It's a specialist sailing forecast, provided free of charge by the Greek Government, and gives wind speed and wave height as well as the usual weather things like temperature, rainfall and wind direction. Sure enough, the weather was predicted to be turning. First off there was a 3 or 4 southerly going to be blowing up in the morning and then the wind would swing round to a northerly in the afternoon. By this time we would be close enough to base to motor in before it got choppy.

I briefed Mike and MG and they were happy. Sailing in the morning to keep the boys in Eurus happy and then everyone tucked up safe and sound before the northerly picks up and the ride gets bumpy: perfect all round!

*****

One of the best things about Palairos is the New Mill Tavern right at the top of the village. It's a good hike from the harbour to the New Mill but everyone was in a really relaxed mood, so it was no effort. I'd spoken to Cathy the day before and I knew that she would have a big table set out for us so that we could all sit at together in the restaurant's little garden.

Cathy runs the New Mill along with her daughter Mahi, and husband in support. The restaurant is right at the back of Palairos, actually in a housing estate, and you wouldn't think much of it from the outside. What makes it special is the food – and Cathy of course, who is a complete show on her own.

The restaurant gets manically busy with Neilson customers from Club Vounaki, which is just down the road, but Cathy and Mahi always have a special welcome for us.

This was a lovely group of clients so they had all paid me easily for the evening meal. We never ordered anything specifically – just put the money on the counter and then sat back whilst Mahi piled up the plates with Cathy's own idea of traditional Greek food - and filled up the pitchers with gallons of wine.

The three Jimmies got a bit gobby, but in a nice, slightly drunk lad way, and after half a glass of wine, Sophie put her head on Dan's shoulder and cuddled up to him. Watching them was lovely.

What made Mike special was that he never lost his enthusiasm for being in the Ionian and always wanted to share what made the place special for him. So, after the meal, instead of going back directly through the town Mike took us along the top road and we stood and looked down over the bay, with the moonlight flickering off the waves. If this was work, well it wasn't too bad!

We turned back to the town, just before Club Vounaki, and walked along the sea front to the harbour, gossiping a bit more loudly than we would have done before eating and drinking at Cathy's - but in the best of moods.

It was one of those evenings which made me glad to be in Greece and grateful for being a Hostie. Ian and Sue walked as close together as only two people in love can, with their twins running round and hiding behind the grown-ups in a game of chase. Their daughter Lucy had her 18 year old mind very much on a game of chase too – but with the Jimmies!

When we reached the end of the little stony beach, Mike played skimming stones with the little ones and made his rocks crash into the water so that they won. He truly was a special man and despite what had happened between us I admired him – and I knew that he had been right.

Gill and Paul were the two retirees. Quiet and slightly distant but enjoying themselves in their own way.

But best of all were the star struck lovers Dan and Sophie walking hand in hand in the soft, warm summer evening and, without a doubt, the two happiest people in the world.

Dan put his arm around Sophie's shoulder and every couple of minutes sneaked a little kiss on to the top of her head. She beamed up at him with a smile which would have melted the heart of an iceberg.

Like I said, if this was work then it had my vote.

Mike said goodnight on the dock - but not before he reminded everyone that we were having an early start in the morning. This was the other side of him: the complete sailing professional with everything sorted out in his mind well before it happened.

*****

Brizo was at the end of the quay, barely moving on the water. She was utterly and completely beautiful. If you could love an inanimate object it would be that boat.

I threaded my way through MG's junk, wriggled into the forepeak, took off my clothes - and was asleep in seconds. It had been a good day.

I was normally the first up of the three of us but, this time, Mike was well ahead of me. He had re-checked Poseidon and the forecast was still sound but now giving a lot more changeable weather with the chance of a thunderstorm in the afternoon. A Force 3 on the Beaufort Scale is 8 to 12 miles per hour – a nice breeze and perfect for Flotilla sailing.

Mike was sure that the 3 would become a 4, at which point the sea gets a bit rougher and the sailing lively. This would be great for the Jimmies but not so good for Ian and Sue with the kids, and probably not for Team Deeply-in-Love, Dan and Sophie either.

But, as I have said, what makes Mike an amazing Skipper is that he always thinks ahead.

Everyone gathered round Brizo's stern and Mike started his briefing.

"Good morning campers. Everyone had a good night's sleep?"

There were appreciative murmurings.

"We're going to have a fantastic day's sailing – couldn't be better really – and MG, Rachel and me want you to get the best from the weather.

"There'll be a nice southerly breeze as we leave Palairos and we can tack out towards Church Bay and then tack back again towards Kalamos.

"Everyone happy with tacking?"

There was another ripple of agreement.

"Motor out of the harbour, just like normal, and then bring your boat head to wind and you can hoist the sails with no problem.

"We're going to sail all day, if that's okay with everyone, so that we can be back at Tychos nice and early and have a break before dinner. Everyone good with that?"

More nods.

"It's going to be a great day for sailing but the wind will pick up in the afternoon so I want you to just use half sail."

The Jimmies pulled a face – and this is where Mike was brilliant with customers because he loved sailing.

"Don't worry boys, the Servals sail faster when they're upright. Lucy might like to see you all on your sides," giggles and those sorts of looks from the three Jimmies and Lucy, "but Notus will sail better if she's upright.

It's why I admired Mike so much. What a way to give a briefing. Smiles and total control all in the same breath. Have a great time but I'm here to cover your back. No wonder he was so popular.

"Ian and Sue, can you pop the lifejackets on the twins please and keep them well inside the cockpit all the time? Everything will be easy but we don't want you kids jumping off the boat and leaving your Mum and Dad all their own, do we?"

The twins shrieked and giggled.

Like I said, Mike really did have the magic touch.

"Sue, are you okay with Lucy travelling back with the Jimmies?"

Lucy pulled a mock sad face and Sue smiled. Lucy might need some lip balm by the time we got back to Tychos but the Jimmies were three good boys and all four of them were going to enjoy the day.

"One final thing. We'll be tacking past Club Vounaki. We'll be outside their sailing area but you never know where you might find a windsurfer because the wind's perfect for them.

"Try to avoid running one down - the paper work takes Rachel ages."

Cheers from the three Jimmies and rolled eyes from retirees Gill and Paul who never wanted to see another form ever again.

"Give your skipper a hand, by keeping a really close watch out until we're well down towards Kalamos."

Then Mike addressed the kids directly, "Can you two do that for your Mum and Dad?"

And again the kids were involved. They nodded in unison and clapped their little hands furiously.

Without ever having to raise his voice or repeat anything, everyone was happy to work with Mike. He should have been Prime Minister instead of Lead Skipper!

*****

MG and I went along the harbour wall, cast off the mooring lines and our little fleet turned left at the end of the jetty and out into the bay.

Mike had the passerelle in the vertical position when I got to Brizo. I jumped the gap easily. I was fit and confident now, a very different person from the Rachel who had struggled aboard in Ligia just five months ago.

"Do you fancy taking the helm, Rache, or are you on coffee duties?"

This is what teamwork meant. Everyone working together for each other. I loved it.

MG was locked into his paper work on the chart table. He was obsessively thorough about record keeping and when he was wearing his focussed look we didn't go near him.

The boats waddled round and came head to wind. The three Jimmies had their sails hoisted in a couple of minutes whilst Lucy did her essential job of sitting on the gunwale with her legs dangling over the side, wearing a bikini which hadn't taken very much material to make!

I got the binoculars out and watched Dan and Sophie making hard work of the job. Dan held the boat head to wind, under power, but Sophie wasn't strong enough to raise the sail by hand and so had to use the winch handle. Half a turn then stop. Half a turn and another rest. Poor mite. My heart went out to her.

Mike came up with two coffees and I asked him to take the helm whilst I hoisted the sail. I loved feeling my muscles work as I pulled at the outhaul sheet. It was hard work but good – natural and satisfying.

The last job, and in some ways the most important, was to go forward to the mast base and flick the furling control over to the ratchet setting. This was always hard for me. The retaining spring was stiff and you had to really tug it out and back to get the ratchet engaged.

Even though it was a tough job, it had to be done. With in-mast furling, the ratchet has to be engaged after the sail is first hoisted because, if you don't do this, the wind can blow the sail out when you want it in! If things are already getting lively, the last thing you want is the wind pulling out more sail when you actually want less.

*****

Mike scanned round with the binoculars and everyone was good. The wind was a lovely, warm southerly at the top end of a 3. Brizo sailed like a dream in these conditions. We were all together for the first tack and mainly together for the second as we turned towards Kalamos - but then the Jimmies started to pull away. When they could take their eyes off Lucy, which wasn't very often, they were three good sailors. Dan and Sophie came almost to a stop before they persuaded Zephyrus to go towards Meganisi.

Mike said: "Phone Dan, please Rache, and just make sure that they are okay."

"Yes, no probs."

We always used the mobile phone because Channel 16, the RT channel, was just a constant babble of conversation so when we needed to speak to clients the mobile was always more reliable and certain.

Dan answered the phone.

"Hi, it's Rachel. Everything good?"

The pause was only for a few seconds – but it was too long for me. "Yes, it's all good Rachel. We're really good and…"

The "and" was a long one – too long. I made a decision.

"Do you want MG to come and sail with you for a bit, while you and Sophie enjoy the scenery? It's no problem if you do. It'll give MG something to do."

Dan was immediately defensive. "No! No thanks. We're okay. No need for MG – I can look after Sophie myself, and I can sail just fine."

This was tricky. Mike had heard the conversation and he shrugged his shoulders.

"I know what you're thinking, Rache, but they've chartered the boat and they're sailing it so all that we can do is back off. The last thing we want is a complaint to Dave and then a crap review on TripAdvisor. Just keep an eye on them but we'll leave them alone for now."

*****

I'd like to say that I was the great sailor girl and noticed what happened next – but I didn't. Mike did – but I didn't.

We had been tacking backwards and forwards between Kalamos and

Meganisi in what was now the bottom-end of a 4 and Brizo was flying along at six knots.

Then, in what seemed like two seconds, the wind veered to the north and the sky turned grey black. We were still a good two hours from Tychos and now things were getting sparky for holiday sailors.

"Rache, text everyone and tell them to get their sails in now and start motoring. Tell the Jimmies that this means them too – and now!

"Ask Sue to get the kids into the cabin and keep them there. It's going to get bumpy."

Mike was now in the most difficult position possible for a Lead Skipper. We were almost exactly equidistant between Vasiliki, Frikes and Porto Tyche. Neither Frikes nor Vasiliki were straightforward options in these conditions whereas our base was the safest anchorage in the area – if we could get everyone to it.

"I'm going to bring her into the wind. Get the sails in Rache. MG, give her hand, mate."

Mike gently eased Brizo round until her bows were directly into the wind and MG and I hauled on the reefing sheets. The Genoa slapped about as if it was possessed but we got it furled and out of the way.

As we brought in the mainsail, I heard the reassuring ratchet click preventing the wind ripping the sail back out of the mast. As Mike always said, never solve a problem – just make sure that it's not there in the first place.

The wind and rain arrived almost, but not quite, simultaneously and I wasn't enjoying myself. From the rolling, metre and a half high waves which had been exciting, the seas now almost doubled in size and broke as they cascaded one on top of the other. I'd never been in these conditions before and I didn't like them.

It was also as if someone had turned the lights off. From the brilliant, blue summer's day of the morning now it looked like mid-winter in England. Then the rain came.

There is nothing I can think of which describes how much water fell out of that black sky – it simply poured down as if we were in the world's biggest car wash. Sheets of rain marched across the sea and battered into Brizo's sides like alien sea monsters. I had never seen the raw aggression of the sea before and although I was scared, I was awestruck by the power which was all around me.

Now we couldn't see any of the other boats.

Mike said: "Send another text to everyone, Rache. Just make sure they're all okay. Tell them to motor in really slowly and everything'll be good."

I did as Mike said but the text wouldn't send. Maybe it was the storm – perhaps we were just a bit too far away from a transmitter but now we had no way of reaching the other boats – and they had disappeared from sight in the rain too.

I had never seen a serious amount of water in Brizo's cockpit before. She was still elegant and graceful but as we turned across the wind, she buried her beautiful bow deep into the waves throwing huge sheets of water up and over the gunwales and into the cockpit.

Mike told me to get lifejackets for the three of us. I struggled into mine in the cockpit and I was so proud when Mike asked me to take the wheel whilst he zipped his up and then clipped the straps across his chest.

I expected Mike to take the wheel from me immediately – but he didn't. "Don't fight her, Rache, just feel the wheel in your hands and guide her."

Whump! Brizo's bows dug into a wave and the cloud of spray swept back and soaked me - over and over again. Whump – followed by the whoosh of the waves tearing past the hull as we corkscrewed into the sea.

The force was immense as first one side of the rudder and then the other was squeezed by the waves. But Brizo was as loyal as ever and let me guide her towards Porto Tyche.

My arms were starting to ache as Mike instinctively took the wheel from me – gently, courteously, naturally. He knew just when I needed a break. We three were a real team now and there was no need for anyone to pretend.

*****

I saw Tychos first. A flash of lightning – yes, we even had the full special effects by now – lit up the sky and there was Tyche's face, unmistakable even in the torrential rain. We were within sight of home and I was glad.

I shouted down for MG to come up and look and I still feel regret for what happened next. Brizo pitched violently down into the trough of a particularly nasty wave and MG was flung off the cabin steps and fell backwards with a sickening thud on to the floor of the cabin. He didn't move.

I didn't scream, I really didn't, but Mike later said I looked as if I had been electrocuted. "Mike, MG's on the cabin floor and…"

"Rache, take the wheel…"

I slid down the opposite side of the cockpit to stand by Mike. He was clearly focussed but completely calm.

"Everything'll be fine. Take the wheel Rache and keep her heading for Tychos. Nice and steady Rache, nice and steady. Good girl."

I spread my legs wide so that I had a stable position behind the wheel.

Brizo corkscrewed into the waves and I heard the note of the diesel engine change as it worked hard to drive us up the face of one enormous wave and down the other. This wasn't recreational sailing.

My mind was in turmoil and I was frightened. Frightened that I wouldn't be able to handle the boat and we would drown and terrified that MG was dead.

A couple of minutes later, Mike climbed up over the cabin partition and smiled.

"It's all good Rache. He's got one hell of a bruise on the back of his head but he was already coming round when I got down there. He's lucky bugger though. If he had caught his head on the edge of the chart table we'd have had a real problem.

"Ever organised a burial at sea, Rache?"

I laughed but it really wasn't much more than a feeble squeak. This was properly scary and I didn't like being here at all.

Mike wouldn't take the wheel when he could, maybe should, have done so. Instead, he acted as pilot and I eased Brizo down the centre of the channel.

The passage was much more difficult than normal with the wind managing to find its way through even Tychos' protective ridges and the rain hammering down in great, grey blankets.

We entered the harbour and Luke was already out in the rib, shepherding everyone to the moorings. I felt an immense sense of relief and I could let out the breath that I had been holding in for hours.

I was also really weepy. I had been severely frightened by the storm and so worried about MG. Now, I was home safe and still alive. I wanted coffee, a shower, dry clothes and all the good things which ordinary girls want and need - and I did feel very, very ordinary.

I glanced around the moorings. Eurus, with the three Jimmies and Lucy, was there. Ian and Sue with the twins in Notus' cockpit, still in their life jackets. Gill and Paul had been watching out for everyone as they arrived and then helping them moor. Wow! I'm hope that I'm half that fit when I'm 65.

But no Zephyrus. I looked again. Where the bloody hell had Dan and Sophie gone?

Luke came alongside in the rib. I shouted down.

"Have you seen Dan and Sophie?"

"No, they're not here."

I told Mike and, for the first time since we had met at the Boat Show, he looked worried.

"Try 'em on the phone, Rache, we might be able to reach them now."

I rang and after what seemed like hours Dan answered.

"We're in a mess. I don't where we are and the boat is crashing on its side and we're going to drown…"

Then I heard Sophie. "I want Rachel. I want Rachel. Rachel, come and save us. We're drowning. Rachel, come and save us. Please Rachel. Please. Please, please, please come and save us."

"Don't worry, Sophie, we'll come – I'll come, just wait a little bit and everything will be fine. Really, Sophie, just give me a few minutes. Stay on the phone and just wait a few minutes. Everything's going to be fine."

I turned to Mike. "I've got to go with you Mike, she needs me. I've got to go."

Mike's face was blank and expressionless. He paused.

"Okay, we can do this. The thing is just to think this through."

Luke spoke – quietly. "If we go out in the rib, and can find them, I'll get them in and you can bring the rib back."

Mike nodded. "Sounds like a plan. MG is in no fit state to go anywhere. We got plenty of fuel?"

Luke nodded.

"Let's get on with it then."

"I'm coming too. Sophie is in a real mess and unless I'm there with her she's going to go mad. Luke will have enough on his plate getting Zephyrus sorted out without Sophie throwing a fit."

In the films, there is a long argument at this point, where the heroine insists on being brave and the guys won't let her. There wasn't any discussion with Mike, which was a good thing, because I think that if he had said a single word I would have run for the shore. I had already been very badly frightened and I couldn't stand the thought of being out in those seas again. I wasn't so much scared as absolutely shaking petrified. I wasn't Super Girl or GI Jane or that girl who got into the Marines. I was Rachel Lamb with a second class degree and a Brownie Hostess Badge. This wasn't what I had thought a Hostie was supposed to do.

But it was. Sophie was out there feeling God knows what and I had it in my power to help her. I was her Hostie and I owed it to her and that was all there was to it. If I didn't go, I would spend the rest of my life knowing that I had left her out in the Ionian to be frightened on her own - and I couldn't do that.

I half climbed and half fell into the bottom of the rib and Luke scooped me up.

"Good start Rache. What are you going to do now? Jump overboard?"

His smile made feel good - and a bit less frightened.

Mike slammed the throttle open and the rib reared up out of the water as it came on to the plane and skimmed across the waves.

Luke stood right next to Mike and they held a shouted conversation.

"Where do you reckon they'll be?" Luke screamed.

"I've been trying to work that out. We lost sight of everyone south of Vasiliki. This northerly will be blowing them down towards Tychos but I just hope that they're not too close otherwise we're really in the shit.

"I'm going to head north out towards Vasiliki and Cape Ducato and hope that we pick them up somewhere.

"Rache, keep phoning and texting and tell them we're on the way. Try to keep them calm and tell them we'll be with them soon."

I did – but there was no signal.

We turned left from the channel and headed parallel with the coast. Mike was as clear thinking as ever and his idea was to put the rib between Zephyrus and the cliffs – and as soon as possible!

Even in these huge waves, the rib was flying along and in ten minutes we could see Cape Ducato's lighthouse on the cliffs marking the start of the Outer Ionian.

Luke shouted across. "They're not here. Let's go towards Vasiliki and then run back again."

Mike nodded.

I was battling to stay on my feet in the rib. Every few seconds, the boat smacked into the water, my legs buckled under me and my back felt as if it had been in a crusher.

Neither Mike nor Luke took any notice of me. I had insisted on being here and no-one had forced me. Tea, sympathy and a support group? Not here.

It was Luke who saw Zephyrus. In fact, we must have passed her in rain on the first run. She was pitching wildly with the boom carrying full sail and dipping in and out of the waves. It must have been horrendous on board.

Mike didn't slam the rib around but eased it gently across the waves and then back on the plane to accelerate towards the yacht.

Dan was in the cockpit, clinging to the wheel and Sophie was hanging on to him like a tiny bedraggled doll. Neither of them had their life jackets on and this was looking like a full five star mess.

Mike took charge.

"Wait until she's at the bottom of a roll and then jump."

As Zephyrus waddled sloppily over towards us, Mike brought the rib alongside and Luke jumped, grabbing the cockpit rail and hauling himself on board. It looked smooth and easy but I had just seen someone risk their life – for real and not on a video game.

Sophie had seen me in the rib and was screaming my name now.

Mike said. "It's tough Rache but leave it. Leave it to Luke and he'll sort them out."

I was relieved. I couldn't do this. I wasn't a hero and I was frightened – but then Sophie came to the cockpit rail and held out her arms, like you see those acolytes doing at religious festivals.

"Rachel, Rachel!" she screamed.

"Bring the rib alongside, Mike. I can do it." He didn't say a word.

The key was timing. Mike had to bring the rib as close as possible to Zephyrus just as she rolled towards us - but then avoid getting me crushed between the boat's hull and the rib.

Luke had made it look easy – I didn't.

I sort of half jumped and half fell off the rib and grabbed the wire guard rail round the cockpit. So far, so good. Then Zephyrus rolled away. Whilst Luke had already been inside the cockpit when the boat reared up, I was left dangling on the outside and hanging on to that steel wire as if my life depended on it – which it did.

It felt a lot longer, an awful lot longer, but it can't have been more than a couple of seconds. Luke's hands reached down and hauled at the shoulders of my life-jacket. He dragged me over the guard rail and head first into the cockpit.

I was hurting everywhere – from banging against Zephyrus' hull, hanging on to the wires and being thrown into the cockpit upside down.

I lay there panting, exhausted and thanking every God in the Multiverse that I wasn't dead.

Then Sophie knelt alongside me, cuddling me and saying thank you, over and over again. I said a few soothing words but I had bigger things on my mind.

I knew she needed the reassurance I was supposed to give – but didn't feel.

"Everything's fine – everything's going to be okay. We're here now – it's all going to be good."

All this, whilst I was wondering if it was going to be good - or if Zephyrus would capsize and all four of us would drown.

"Sophie, can you do something for me please?"

She nodded, sobbing. Every time Zephyrus rolled, Sophie gave a little mew, like an injured animal. This was really stressing me.

"Can you go into the cabin and get everything tidied up please? There's stuff all over the place and the boat will sail a lot better if everything is off the floor."

"Will it, Rachel?"

"Yes, definitely, getting everything tidy will help me and Luke a lot.

"Do you think Dan could you give you hand?"

It was the best news she'd had for a long time. Her and Dan out of the wet and someone else taking charge.

Dan had started the engine when things had begun to go wrong so that was one Godsend.

Luke gently brought Zephyrus into the wind. Now she was just pitching into the waves but the boom was swinging dangerously. If we weren't careful, there would be the Grandmother of all gybes and the boom would snap off at the mast – or worse!

I turned to Luke to see what the plan was. He was focussed. Not as calm as Mike would have been but working out what to do as he went along.

"Rache, can you take the helm and ease her towards the wind just until the pressure's off the boom? I'm going to try to centre the boom bit by bit and bring the sail in."

Seven months ago I was cleaning tables and now he was expecting me to take control of a boat in conditions that scared me stupid.

Luke smiled. "Nice and steady Rachel, just coax her round."

I braced myself again. That would be all. Fall over, let the wheel fly out of my hands and decapitate Luke - all in one go! It would make getting sacked for putting funny noses on cats' faces look a bit like getting a bad conduct mark in my jotter at school!

I eased Zephyrus ever so slowly into the wind and watched the boom like a hawk. As the pressure came off the sail, Luke cranked the winch like mad and got the mainsail in and the boom nearer to the centre line of the boat. The Genoa was jammed so we just let it fly and lash about.

"Okay, with the wind behind us, we can motor into base. There'll be a lot of racket from the Genoa but nothing's going to come to any harm.

"You're a special girl Rachel, a very, very special girl." Then he kissed me briefly on the left cheek and looked at me - and I did feel special.

*****

Mike had circled us constantly and when he saw that we had got the boom centred and the mainsail in, he powered away in the rib.

There's not a lot else to say. We motored in and moored the boat. I was too exhausted to reverse, so Luke eased Zephyrus into her berth and I dropped the anchor. Andreas caught the mooring lines first time and Luke cut the engine.

It's difficult to describe how I felt. I was shattered and shivering now. I had been soaking wet for four hours and the cold was getting to me.

Maybe I was also shaking with emotion. In the modern world, very few people come close to real danger. Those poor people in wars in the Middle East do but in warm, comfortable, support group England no-one really does.

We also don't have to push ourselves to the limit at anything – to give absolutely everything we have mentally, physically and emotionally. There's just no need to try this hard.

Now, I had just missed drowning and I could have killed three other people if I hadn't been good enough to keep the boat where Luke wanted it. This was what made it such a strange experience. I hadn't been playing a video game. I was actually hanging off a boat in three metre high seas with a real chance of drowning – unless Luke had fished me out of the water!

The whole experience was more real than anything I had ever done in my life before and it was so tiring.

But there was also a sense of duty and this was different too. You can't really have much commitment when your lecturer doesn't turn up, and no-one's going to die if Santa is short of a few kids. Now Sophie needed me.

I shouted down.

"Come on Sophie, let's get you warm. Have you any dry clothes in the locker?"

She nodded again with her sad, porcelain doll face.

"Come on, let's get you washed and warm again."

I held her hand as she staggered off the boat and then I linked my arm through hers and guided her to the showers behind the taverna.

"Will you be okay getting washed yourself?"

The nod came. "Yes thanks, Rachel."

She went into the cubicle. I heard her clothes drop on to the floor and the shower start.

I was incredibly, achingly tired but propped myself up against the wall until I heard the shower stop and Sophie start towelling herself. She was moored and now I could get myself sorted out.

*****

That night, we met before dinner. Mike needed to know what had happened and why. I had the answer.

The trouble began with the ratchet lever, which had been too stiff for Sophie to move from the moment they first hoisted the sails. But the weather was great, and she didn't want to seem a wimp, so she didn't tell Dan. That was the start of the mess.

Sophie was already frightened with tacking in the morning and she was probably tired too. Stage two.

Then Dan wanted MG to sail the boat for them – but didn't like asking. He was Sophie's man and wanted, and needed, to show it.

When we sent the text to bring the sails in completely and motor, they both tried to do what they were told but instead of the mainsail being reefed it had exploded back out of the mast and the troubles really kicked off.

The wind picked up, the rain came down and they had both thought that they were going to die – really die - as in never make it back to land, ever.

Everyone listened in silence, then Mike spoke.

"Good job Luke and Rache. Well done and thanks."

It was a serious moment.

"And as for you," Mike looked at MG, "you lazy bastard, faking injury just so that you could get an early coffee.

"Don't make him one again, Rache, he doesn't deserve anything."

And the tension flowed away. We were a team, a family, working with and for each other and it felt good.

*****

We had a surprisingly good meal with a lot of wine. The Jimmies had risen even higher in Lucy's estimation so everyone was happy there.

The twins told us about flying around the cabin like Harry Potter. Gill and Paul were just quiet. They had reefed the sails when we told them to, motored Boreas through the storm and into Porto Tyche. Gill was already tidying up the cabin before everyone else had arrived. I guess that's what you get when you've been married for forty years.

As for Dan and Sophie, they took centre stage with the rescue and at the end made a formal thanks to Luke and me. They gave us a big box of loukoumi from the gift shop.

They also announced their official retirement from sailing – ever again – and said that they were spending the last two days of the holiday in a nice hotel in Nydri – but they hoped everyone else would have a wonderful time.

I had a couple of big tears but gave Sophie a big, long, tight hug and told her how much I loved her and that she must stay in touch when she returned to England.

The party broke up late but we weren't going anywhere in the morning so I wasn't thinking of getting any sleep.

I stood at the counter, sorting out the bill with Andreas and Luke alongside me.

"Fancy a walk round the harbour? It's very beautiful."

He was right. The storm had left as quickly as it had arrived and now, the sky was washed spotlessly clean and there was an immense scattering of silver stardust stretching across in a huge arc.

I was still a bit chilled and Luke saw me shiver.

"Here, take my jacket. I'm warm."

He put it gently round my shoulders and I could smell him on it.

"You're a very wonderful woman, Rachel, you really are. Special and wonderful. I like you a lot."

And then he kissed me on the lips. And I kissed him…

9

You Can't Hurry Love

LUKE and I didn't fall in love like, "Oooohhhh. You're the man of my dreams. Let's get married tomorrow morning."

We didn't drift into love either just because we couldn't think of anything else better to do.

The best way I can describe what happened was that we became like two Servals, running very close parallel courses and every so often they touch. Except when they did, the two boats exchanged a little bit of each other until very slowly they became more and more alike. Does this sound strange?

One time, I was sitting in Andreas' and realised that I had put two lumps of sugar in Luke's coffee with just the amount of milk he liked, and stirred it. I did all this, without thinking, whilst I was talking to Alissa because I just knew.

He'd see me on the quay and either stop for a chat and a hug or let me get on with what I was doing because I was under pressure. I didn't have to justify that I couldn't talk – he understood without a word being spoken.

Bit by bit we got more and more like this.

Of course, I did fancy him. He was a good looking guy and brave too. I also admired his patience with clients and his brain so yes, he was a real catch. But what made me love him was his smile and his kindness. If ever he could do anything for anyone he would – and without making a fuss or claiming credit.

When I thought about the guys at Uni or, even worse, Connor, I knew that Luke was amazing.

But things were changing between Luke and I and the Harvest Festival at Karya showed just how much.

*****

124

Nydri gets incredibly busy in July and August - absolutely unbelievable. Restaurants are open way into the early hours of the morning and the shops on the main street never seem to close - not ever during 24 hours.

In some ways, Nydri is a strange town – it's almost like three big villages in one. Along the harbour wall, it's all rather posh. This is yachtie country and everyone is either a yachtie or wanting to be a yachtie. For almost a mile, it's jammed with yachts and mooring spaces are like gold dust unless you've got everything pre-booked, as we always did.

We had an arrangement with Kostas at the Three Palms Hotel. He was always lovely, always smiling down the phone at me and full of encouragement. Kostas owned the hotel which was built on the site of his grandmother's little farm and that's how he could afford such a prime site.

The Three Palms was really lovely and Kostas and his wife cared for the hotel as if they lived there themselves – which they actually did!

Kostas had built an excellent floating pontoon out into the bay, with mooring for forty yachts and this was good business for him at €15 a night during peak times.

The Three Palms was in the perfect place, just outside the main town, down towards the Ionian Boat Assistance place. In fact, it was liked so much by clients that quite a lot of them took a room in the hotel when we moored there and enjoyed Kostas' big beds and showers which ran boiling hot for as long as you wanted them.

In the evening we would all walk along the front, look at the Captain Aristidis or one of the other little ferries which kept the islands supplied, have a meal and a drink and enjoy what has to be one of the best places in the world for a sailing holiday.

Mike was always, and I do mean always, a bit naughty. When a client would look at one of the tour boats which take the zillions of visitors a day out to the islands for snorkelling or visiting secret caves – the ones which no-one in the world had seen since yesterday – he would pretend to be horrified. "No, no, no! Don't go near them – they're for tourists. We've all got our own personal yachts."

And then MG would stand up straight, pull his tummy in, do a smart salute and say something like, "Aye, aye Sir, Your Admiralship." It was the same joke every time but I always smiled.

Behind the harbour road is the main street in Nydri and this couldn't have been more different. It's a pure, 100% tourist avenue but in a very Greek way. There are loads of little cafes, more shops selling beachwear than you can imagine, bike, quad and mo-ped hire shops and even pedicure places where you can have little fish eat the dead skin on your feet. Uggghhh! Not for me!

There are also tiny supermarkets every 100 metres and these are what keep Nydri authentically Greek and not Blackpool, Skegness or even Orlando. You can buy real Greek things like kitchen spoons made from olive wood and the local Lefkada honey which can be so dark brown that it is almost black in colour, and I liked this. Somehow, a jar of honey made in the mountains kept the plastic tourist rubbish from overwhelming the town.

The third Nydri is behind the tourist street. There's almost nothing left of the really old Nydri but new Nydri shows the face of a lot of Greece. The houses and apartments aren't freshly painted for tourist holiday lets and the gardens aren't immaculate either. Here, people depend on the seven golden months of the tourist season to keep them alive through the cold winters when everything is boarded up. Money is short for the Greeks who live in Nydri throughout the year and once you are away from the postcards, fridge magnets, inflatable whales and hire shops it shows.

By the second week in September, the kids had gone back to school, the Italians were all back at work and Nydri could breathe again!

The money had been coming in very well with clients booking with us again and Dave was beginning to relax and not look so permanently tense. At the start of the week, he announced that everyone was going to the Harvest Festival celebrations in Karya, where there was a giant street party with Greek music and dancing – the full thing. He phoned Zoe to get a minibus booked and we'd take the clients up to Karya and have a great time.

I sat in silence and then, in my best little girl voice, I said: "And can Luke come too?"

Dave smiled. "Can't think why you'd want him there but yes, he can come across in the rib with me. It's your bonus for not drowning anyone last week…"

*****

Everything was working out really well. I went round the boats and got the clients' €30 for the mini-bus and the party, and there was nothing but smiles all round.

I'd also got an idea for me. I was becoming fonder of Luke every day and so for the Karya party I wanted to do something a bit special for him – and for me.

First, I phoned Kostas at the Three Palms and begged the emergency room from him. They hardly ever used this room because it was really too small to let, and it was next to the water pumping system for the swimming pool, but it did have a tiny bed, a shower – and a mirror!

I dug out my best Asos long dress, and some undies which were still their original colour instead of MG blue, and Alissa washed and pressed everything for me.

Behind the till, she had some Estée Lauder mascara which she had ordered for a client who then never turned up to pay for it: typical! She also had a nice leather barette with an olive wood pin. It was really cute, with a yacht embossed on it.

I folded everything very neatly and then packed a clean towel – and my box of Chanel No. 5 which I still hadn't opened.

Luke was on the quay, fixing something as usual, and I gave him an outline of the plan. He was really pleased – and then I said that he was sleeping in my forepeak and that he'd better take care of it – or else!

No-one was ever allowed in there, for any reason, and so it was a sign of how things were between Luke and me now: I really was letting him into the absolute centre of my life. If he had ever laughed at my space, or told the guys what was in there, I would have died. But I knew he never would and so I was actually very happy to let him get this close to me.

*****

Sometimes we got a really perfect group of clients and this trip was one of them. Sally and Anthony, who had baled us out with the £1500 advance payment all those months ago at the Boat Show, had come back for a second trip. There were Jenny and Sam, and their mates Suzie and Rod, sharing Boreas and getting on really well.

Julia and Amy worked in the same leisure centre and were such good friends that they always went on holiday together.

Finally, there was Marc and Estelle who were in their early 30s. They both worked in a posh London bank and I think that they were seeing if they liked sailing before Estelle bought a yacht with the loose change which was littering the bottom of her Louis Vuitton handbag!

You can never rely on the weather in the Ionian and for the last two days it had been windless – literally not enough breeze to move a hanky - so we motored across from Kalamos and got to the 'Three Palms' pontoon nice and early.

Everyone moored first time. It was interesting to watch how carefully Estelle checked Marc's oxo knots. Woohoo! You could see who was the boss there. I wouldn't like to be the one who gave her any bad news!

We wandered along the harbour front and settled in front of the Lemon Tree, at the end of road. Their ice-creams are great and there's always a nice atmosphere.

Suzie and Rod were on the one of the big couches with their mates. All four of them clearly had something on their mind.

It was Suzie who spoke. "Mike, we've been talking and we've had an idea."

She giggled like the naughty girl at the party who won't sit down for the birthday cake to be cut.

She chuckled again and Rod's face was nearly split in two it had such a big grin.

"And Jenny and Sam are up for it too."

There were more giggles and by now my Hostie's antennae were getting really twitchy.

"Well, because the weather's like it is, can we go skinny dipping tomorrow, like - all together - and have a party and a bit of fun?"

And she nearly fell off the couch laughing.

I was in shock. This big rock had really dropped out of the sky and straight on to my head. I had always been a bit shy, well modest any way, and the idea of being naked in front of people I didn't know was horrendous.

By now, Mike and I had become really close colleagues. The blazing row, and the other incident which neither of us ever mentioned, were long forgotten. Mike sensed I wasn't smiling and that skinny dipping wasn't going to be on my Bucket List – ever.

"I think that's a great idea. We know just the place, right at the southern tip of Meganisi," he said.

My face was frozen in horror…

"We can motor out there in the morning, moor up and have a great swim."

I was horrified.

"Rache can take Sally and Anthony to that little bay, just off Thilia at the back of the channel, and then we can all meet up in Sivota in the evening.

"How's that sound?"

I went all saggy and breathed out. Yes! Mike had got me out of this one – and as neatly as he gybed Brizo in a 4.

If the first idea felt like a rock dropping on my head, the next bit was like standing at the bottom of an avalanche.

Sally said: "Why can't we go skinny dipping too?

"Are we too old for you young ones?"

Now the avalanche had been upgraded to a complete mountain.

This is absolutely, completely and totally, the worst situation for a Flotilla crew to be in. You never leave anyone out of anything they want to do because they are too old, too young, too fat, too thin – too anything. Flotilla sailing is for everyone. Every client has paid the same amount to be on the Flotilla and everyone has to have the same chance to enjoy it.

If two - let's say, not exactly anorexic - customers, who were getting ready to apply for their bus passes, wanted to go skinny dipping with the young ones - then that's just what they were going to do.

The situation was made far worse because Anthony and Sally were really popular. They had joined in with everything all week, got a bit drunk and sung Beatles' songs for us and then been on the losing team of the quiz with good grace. You couldn't have got two more sociable people and so Suzie chirped up.

"Yeaaahhhh. Sally and Anthony skinny dipping. Yeaaahhhh!" and a round of applause broke out.

Anthony laughed and then said. "Just one thing. We're two fat, old wrinklies and we're new to this. So, no cameras or phones. No pictures or video or anything. We want to join in the fun but what happens in Meganisi stays in Meganisi. All agreed?"

Everyone muttered in agreement

I prayed for a big hole to open up and swallow me – but none appeared.

With everything decided, Sally and Anthony went back to the hotel for a nap – well they would at their age, wouldn't they – and the rest went for a wander around Nydri. Mike and I were left on our own. He could see that I wasn't the happiest fairy who has ever perched on top of a Christmas tree.

"Sorry Rache. You could see how things were going but it just happened. I've been skinny dipping loads of times before. Nobody looks at anything and it's great. We'll all have a swim, get changed, have a glass of wine and then motor into Sivota for dinner. It's nothing really."

"Well it is to me." I said.

"Mike, is Luke coming?"

He laughed. "What's up, hasn't he had a full tour yet?"

"No he hasn't! And I'm serious. Is Luke coming?"

Mike laughed again. "Well, I'll just have to try to remember..."

"Mike, listen to me. If Luke we will be there - I won't! Believe me Mike - I really won't. I'll go back on the ferry first thing in the morning and I won't be there when you get back to base."

Mike saw that I wasn't playing about. "Sorry Rache. I knew that you were fond of Luke but I didn't realise how things were exactly."

I didn't say a word.

"No, Luke won't be there. First thing in the morning, he's going to pick up some stuff from Risto at the boatyard and them him and Dave are going back to Tychos.

"Luke won't see you – and me and MG won't either. I promise.

"I'll let MG know exactly how things are and everything will be good.

"You know Rachel, we both admire you and we like you too. You're an amazing Hostie and you've got a bigger set of marriage tackle than any bloke. Nothing bad will happen tomorrow - it won't."

*****

I wasn't at all happy about the whole idea but I couldn't think of any way out except dropping a huge rock on my foot and spending the night in the hospital in Lefkas. I really did get as far as looking at the big concrete blocks at the end of harbour and thinking seriously about this – that's how bad it was! Then I thought how worried Luke would be and how much he had been looking forward to going to Karya.

Mike left but I needed another coffee. Flotilla crews always have complimentary drinks and food from tavernas and cafes, providing you're not silly, wherever we stay so I could have sat there all day drinking coffee – except that I couldn't because I had a lot to do.

I'm proud of what I did next. My first job was to phone Zoe and make sure that the mini-bus was booked and that we had guaranteed seats at the party. I had no need to do this because Zoe was always perfect, but I did it anyway. Hostie first – Rachel second.

Then I set off down the main street to find some really nice sandals. I had hardly ever worn my trainers once the weather had become warm but spent most of my time in flip flops and then, increasingly, just bare feet.

Shorts, Delfini shirt and flip flops – seven days a week. Dave was right when he said the most important item of clothing I should bring was knickers!

But this was different. I wanted to look the best I could for Luke. For the first time in my life, I was with a man who really meant something to me and I wanted to show that I cared.

Twenty shops later I came back to the second one I had visited. I bought a pair of really nice sandals made from very fine rope, with a lacquered sea shell where the strands crossed over. They were pale brown, with a small raised heel, and I did hope that Luke would like them - I really did.

I went back to the Three Palms and tried to have a nap before Luke came at half past six. In fact, it was a complete waste of time. I lay on the bed, tossed and turned and watched the minutes tick by. If the idea of being with Luke and not looking my best was bad, the thought of skinny dipping was freaking me out.

At five o'clock, I got undressed and stood completely naked in front of the mirror. I studied myself. I couldn't believe it. This was what everyone was going to look at tomorrow: me - not wearing any clothes.

My tummy was flat through exercise. That was better than England. But then there were my boobs. Oh God, my boobs! I looked hard. Were they too big or not large enough? Were they the right shape? Should they be further up or further down? In the end, there they were, stuck on my chest, and there was nothing I could do about them.

I turned round to examine my bum. It had two spots on it, one on each cheek, where I had been sat down for too long on Brizo. No, there were three spots! The third one had been hiding where it thought I wouldn't see it.

I'll bet everyone would look at me and say: "Oooohhh look, Rachel's got spots on her bum."

My legs were too short, my collar bone stuck out too much and my arms now had biceps like a guy's - and I don't know what else.

I looked at the girl in the mirror and couldn't believe that she was going to have the nerve to get undressed in public.

But I was a small size twelve, and nothing wobbled when I ran, so maybe it wouldn't be a total disaster – and I had won a prize at my school sports day for the happiest smile.

*****

Time was running out. My imagination started going crazy.

The knock at the door. It was Luke.

I answered it with no clothes on. "Ready for the party, Rachel?"

"Actually no, Luke. If you just give me ten minutes to check for any more spots on my bum I'll be fine."

I made myself calm down. The Chanel soap was in my bag. I was going to get a shower and wash myself with the Chanel, Luke's Chanel, I would have the scent of his soap all over me. That would help.

Chanel boxes are really, really good quality and made from thick, shiny paper which is beautifully printed. I'm surprised that they don't just sell the boxes on their own without anything in them.

I carefully opened the packet and there was Luke's soap inside. But it wasn't just the soap – there was the thickest, strongest cling film ever, anywhere in the world, wrapping the soap. I tried to tear it open with my finger nails but it was like armour.

My imagination kicked in again.

The Mighty Wizard of the Bath Soap said: "Only the most worthy maidens who can break through the magic film barrier of Chanelfulness are permitted to bathe with the Holy Pink Soap."

It was like being on the finishing line of the Olympics and not being able to move the last millimetre to get the medal.

In the end, I bit into the cling film and tore it back. I can tell you two things. First, Chanel Number 5 smells really nice - and second it tastes horrible!

I turned on the shower – Kostas' wonderful, hot, endless shower. The soap felt silky smooth on my skin. It slid over me in a way which made every other bar of soap feel sticky. And the scent – oh, the scent! The perfume wrapped itself around the water, and flowed over me until I was one big, wet, pink Chanel statue. I could see why the rich people got washed in soap like this every day.

I rubbed my hair dry with my towel and combed it. I looked my undies and thanked every God in the Multiverse that MG had not attacked these too. Now at least I could get half dressed.

Luke was really strange in some ways. He was always telling me how lovely I looked, which made me feel very special inside, but he was also almost obsessive about me looking, as he said, just as God made me. He'd see me all hot and sweaty after cleaning a boat, with my hair stuck to the front of my face, and tell me how lovely I was.

This made me very cautious about make up. I didn't think that Luke would welcome lipstick and the rest of what he called "war paint" but my eyelashes were very pale, almost transparent, and so I wanted to wear mascara. The truth is I wanted to wear it for me. I didn't want to be a Hostie in shorts and a shirt and flip flops - but a woman. A woman for Luke and, more importantly, a woman for me.

I looked in the mirror and a nice face looked back at me. There were a few, tiny wrinkles but it was generally a nice face. It had soft grey eyes framed with light brown hair.

The teeth were okay too. Thanks Mum, for making me have the braces!

And I liked the smile. It was a nice, open smile – a smile that was happy to be on the face – not strained or artificial but one which said, "I like being here."

I pulled a face, stuck my head out, carefully applied the mascara and then removed the excess with a tiny comb which Alissa had put in the Estée Lauder box. This was a serious business!

Alissa had pressed my dress beautifully – a zillion times better than I could have done. My Mum had bought the dress for me from Asos before I went to University and it had cost £75 - a fortune! I think that, secretly, she thought I would go to posh garden parties and meet some really handsome millionaire's son, get married and live in a big mansion and have a house keeper. You can imagine what she thought of Connor and a one bedroomed flat in Stoke-on-Trent!

The dress had just fitted me in the summer before I left for University but by Christmas it didn't. A comfort diet of crisps, cheese burgers and chocolate Hobnobs meant that when I came home and tried the dress on, it barely got past my bum and there would have been no chance of ever sitting down in it!

Now, it slid on and looked lovely. It was a very pale, gentle brown with soft Autumn flowers printed on it.

I stood in front of the mirror again. My hair looked shiny and natural and, after fifty goes, the barette was in just the right position. My grey eyes looked bigger with the mascara and the dress fitted perfectly, as if it had been hand made just for me.

I looked for a long time and I was happy with me, happy with who I was and ecstatic about being with Luke.

I was so pleased that I sent a picture of me in the dress, reflected in the mirror, to Mum along with a smiley face and got three kisses back almost instantly along with: "You look lovely. The best looking girl in Greece. Your Dad will be thrilled. Enjoy the party."

*****

The knock on the door was not long in coming. I wanted to hesitate, to delay Luke seeing me in case he was disappointed. At the same time, I was desperate to throw open the door and hug him and be kissed.

When I did, we both stared at each other and said nothing. Luke stood there looking, well - looking like everything I had ever dreamed of in a man. He was smiling, as always, and was wearing a really smart white shirt which had been pressed so well that I was sure Alissa had done this job too!

His shorts were new, nothing like either of us wore for sailing, and he had new sports sandals too. He was utterly lovely and he was mine. I could have cried with joy.

He looked at me for what seemed like a long time and then spoke in a soft voice. "Rachel, you are beautiful, the most lovely, beautiful woman in the world and I love you."

He took me in his arms and I rested my head in the nape of his neck.

"You smell lovely too. Is that Chanel?"

We both giggled.

Then he took my hand and we walked in silence to the car park.

*****

The mini-bus and Zoe were already there. Anthony and Sally were chatting to Zoe and Estelle was looking as if she had just come off a Vogue photoshoot in her skin tight mini-dress, high heels and Burberry clutch bag – naturally, label side out. Marc shuffled from foot to foot like her manservant awaiting orders.

The young ones were nowhere to be seen so I went down to the pontoon and shouted into Boreas for them to get a move on. Judging from the reply, they had already been sampling Lefkada's best wine!

I was in full Hostie mode when we left and so I sat at the front of the bus with Zoe and didn't take any notice of Luke being squashed up next to Suzie and Rod. Well, not much anyway.

We headed out of Nydri, on the coast road, towards Lefkas and turned left to climb up into mountains. It wasn't far in terms of miles but the bus was well loaded and it took us half an hour to wheeze up to the village.

It was packed and so we had to park at the top, past the church. The party was right in the town centre, under the plane trees, and as we passed I could see the long lines of tables set out for the party. Karya tries to be a tourist village, with shops selling local lace and ladies parading round in traditional Greek dresses, but somehow it still feels like a real place and not a theme park imitation.

I am not very religious, even though the Madonna in the forepeak had done a good job of looking after me so far, but the parade through the village was very moving. It was led by the bearded, Greek Orthodox priests, in their long black robes and tall hats. The singing and the incense gave me a strong sense that something spiritual was happening. It touched something deep inside me and at that moment, I knew that I was coming up to an important crossroads in my life.

Parishioners followed the priests carrying the church's icon, and its emblem, and at the back was the very grandly named Philharmonic Marching Band of Lefkada in their dark blue uniforms and shiny helmets.

I would have liked to share all this with Luke but I was still Hostie and so I talked to the clients, took pictures of them with the parade in the background, and did my best to make sure that they enjoyed every second of the experience.

There was a party atmosphere, but not a rowdy one, as everyone went down to eat. The food was very Greek - some really traditional, and other things modernised. There was tons of Lamb Kleftiko, which had been cooking all day, and probably most of last night too, and Souvlaki - which are Greek kebabs - but these had pieces of chicken wrapped in bacon. On every table was a big bowl of salad with lumps of the crumbly sheep's cheese I had become so fond of from Tychos. There was so much that even MG looked slightly fazed – but then tucked his napkin under his chin and attacked!

At one end of the square was a little improvised stage for two young guitarists and an elderly bouzouki player. The guitarists almost provided a platform for the bouzouki to perform. The sharp, almost metallic, bouzouki soared above the guitars' middle notes and then fell below them, dancing around like a house martin chasing flies in our back garden, in England.

Sometimes, a middle-aged lady in a deep red dress and an avalanche of black hair, would join the musicians and sing in a thin, mournful voice which, although I couldn't understand a word of what she was saying, opened some emotional doors deep inside me. Yes, this was one of those times…

Underneath the table Luke rested his hand on my thigh and, when I could, I touched it.

The bouzouki straining for heaven, the singer's stretched, mournful voice and Luke's touch brought me to the edge of tears despite all the noise, the laughing and wine fuelled conversation around me.

I don't know how things were organised, if they were at all, but a few Greeks got up and started to dance the Sirtaki – that dance we call Zorba the Greek, where everyone puts their hands on the next person's shoulders and moves in and out.

I like dancing, so I pulled up Luke up to join me in the line. He resisted, insisting that he couldn't dance and I thought that he just being modest as usual: he wasn't!

The Sirtaki starts off really slowly, going back and to in very simple steps. I put my hand on the shoulder of the Greek guy next to me and he looked down and encouraged me to follow his feet. The bouzouki drove the beat on and I soon felt myself dipping and rising to the music.

A tall Greek girl was next to Luke and she tried, she really did try, to get him to do anything nearly like the steps but he couldn't follow the music and got one leg crossed over the other. This was weird. On a boat, Luke was really athletic and the way he had jumped onto Boreas in Tychos when she was about to hit the harbour wall was like Superman. But here, where he had to do something to a pattern someone else had decided, he was a disaster.

Although I was really enjoying myself I felt sorry for Luke and so, when there was a break, I dropped out of the line and took him back to the table. The truth was that I wanted him to be happy more than I wanted to enjoy myself so the decision was easy.

Estelle came back with us but Marc carried on dancing. He was very good, and managed the dips properly - even the short backwards kicks. He was dancing next to a Greek girl, wearing a traditional dress with a little apron, and he looked at her with an affection he never showed to Estelle. It was very sad and made me even more grateful to have Luke.

*****

The party went on until late but we were having a slow start the following day so no-one was concerned.

On the way back to the bus, Luke first held my hand and then my waist. Gently, he lowered his hand on to my bottom. He rested it there and ever so tenderly stroked and caressed me. The feeling was electric. It's easy to say this but the tingles ran right through me and deep inside.

Loads of lads had touched my bum before. I had punched George Ratcliffe in the face for touching me when we were getting changed for PE in Primary School, and things had sort of gone on from there – parties, the Télécabine and then Uni.

But Luke didn't grope my bum, he gently, subtlety, patiently touched and caressed me and it was the most erotic thing which had ever happened to me.

Anthony and Sally really were a wonderful couple. They walked alongside us through the village and I think that Sally could see that Luke and I weren't just marching back to the bus like two colleagues!

She said: "Rachel, do you mind if we sit at the front on the way back and you and Luke swap with our seats at the back? We'd like to see Nydri at night as we drive down the mountain."

I think that the two of them must have shared one mind because Anthony was instantly on board.

"Yes, do you mind swapping, if that's okay, so we can see the view?"

I giggled. "Yes, just for you…"

Luke sat next to the window and I cuddled up alongside him, holding his left-hand in both of mine. We didn't say a single word on the way back: there was no need.

When we got back to the Three Palms, there were lots of hugs, a few kisses and laughs about the following day's skinny dipping.

Luke said: "May I walk you back to your room?" What a formal way to speak to me.

My voice was very quiet when I replied. "Yes please, I would like that very much."

We walked alongside the swimming pool and through the outside restaurant area. Luke had his hand on my bottom again and my mouth was dry with anticipation. I was sure that I loved Luke – certain that he was the one man for me.

We reached my room. I fiddled around in my bag and finally found the room key. I turned the lock and the door opened. I switched on the light and there was the bed.

I turned to Luke. He held my head, ever so tenderly, in both hands and kissed me on the lips.

"I love you Rachel, I love you more than…"

And his voice tapered off.

"Will you have time for breakfast with me in the morning?"

I didn't know what to say. This was the moment, the right time, when we should have been one – two people who loved each being together but this strange, confusing, wonderful man wasn't ready. My head was spinning.

He gave me another kiss and then I shut the door.

Love was hard work – exhausting and confusing but I had to learn the rules - and they were completely different from the sordid, grubby things I had experienced with men before.

Now, I had spent an evening with the most wonderful man in the world who touched me with such tenderness that I ached for his love – a man who could make me feel like the most wanted woman in the world and yet who was prepared to wait for the perfect moment.

Yes, love was difficult.

10

Spiders and Skinny Dipping

EVERYONE met in The Three Palms for breakfast. It was a relaxed start after what had been a wonderful evening and spirits were quietly high. The two receptionists, Julia and Amy, were deep in conversation and clearly excited about what was going to happen next. I was glad, on many levels, that Anthony had spoken up so strongly against films and pictures – and not just for my sake. The ladies worked together, in the same village on the outskirts of Hereford, and I could just imagine the fun and games if a video of them jumping off a boat with no clothes on ever got out. For sure, Hereford was not Inner London and there were very different social standards.

Mike gave us the briefing – even for skinny dipping he was still the ultimate professional sailor.

"Okay folks. First, when you slip the lazy lines give them plenty of time to sink - and then motor out very slowly, otherwise MG will be going diving. If he's cutting a rope from round your propeller you won't be going anywhere today."

On cue, like the professional double act they were, MG pulled a comic, sad face.

"Keep well to port, the left, of the church, because it gets shallow very quickly near the point and keep an eye out for any ferries or tour boats coming from behind you because they will be using the same bit of Meganisi Channel as us - and they're a bit bigger!"

And of course, everyone smiled like the well-behaved audience that we were.

"We'll just motor gently up the Channel and if you can keep a good distance between you and the boat in front of you this will make for a relaxing trip.

"When we get to the western tip of Meganisi, we will be turning left.

Watch out for the big cave. It's where the famous Greek submarine *Papanikolis* used to hide during the war, when it was on patrol against the Germans.

"We'll go between Meganisi and Kithros."

Mike pointed to the chart he had taped to the wall again.

"There's plenty of depth there but stay in the centre of the channel. Follow our course and you'll be fine.

"The most beautiful swimming spot in the world, and I really do mean the best, is right at the very tip of Meganisi. If you follow Brizo out to sea a little bit, me and MG will come round in our inflatable and give everyone a hand with anchoring.

"Then the party can begin.

"Everyone ready?"

And judging from the cheers, everyone was – except me.

There were a lot of giggles, and nice cheeky comments, as everyone went back to their boats.

*****

Luke and I had hardly spoken over breakfast. There was no tension – just unease. I had to get things right between us before I left.

"How do you feel about, you know, well…

I was really embarrassed at even saying the words after what had happened the night before.

Luke smiled and held my hands inside his. I could have cried, he was so gentle.

"It's no problem Rachel, it's really not. Everyone will just see the outside of you and if you're good with this then I'm okay too.

"But what they won't see is what's on the inside. This is only for us - so let them look and enjoy the most beautiful girl in Ionian."

I relaxed and smiled too. His words of support had swept away the pressure and doubt.

"Just the Ionian? Is that all you think of me? What about those three girls in the tiny bikinis who came down from Corfu yesterday? I suppose you fancy them more than me!"

And I made mock grimace and folded my arms.

"Course I do. You were the only thing available on Tychos - well you and a few sheep."

I chased him out of the Three Palms and he ran down the steps.

Then I was worried. No, don't go now Luke – don't run off, not even playing.

He didn't, because he must have had the same thoughts as me and turned back to the steps. "I love you Rachel, I love you more than anything in the world.

"I'll be alongside you all day so don't be worried about anything."

Then Dave honked the horn on the van. Luke gave me the briefest of kisses and ran across the road.

*****

That conversation with Luke was the last piece I needed to put me in total Hostie mode with the skinny dipping. My head was clear and, during what had been a really restless night, I had more or less decided what I was going to do. Luke's words just confirmed the plan.

First, I was going to do the skinny dipping absolutely and completely because I'd been in a similar situation once before. At one time, I was frightened of spiders and so my Dad showed me that they were really harmless creatures – not exactly cuddly but nothing to be scared of either.

First, he taught me how to get a spider on to a piece of paper and help it out of the window. Then he had one crawl on his hand and let it escape. Nothing happened. He didn't get bitten or attacked or anything.

One day, when he and Mum were out shopping, I went spider hunting and found the great big one I had seen in the greenhouse loads of times. It was so big that it could have been a pet spider with its own kennel and spider toys to play with. I knew that my Dad wasn't there to help me and that there was only me and the enormous spider: just the two of us.

I trapped it in a corner of the window and then coaxed it on to my hand. I let it sit there so there could be no doubt that a massive hairy spider was really sitting on my hand. No cheating or it being nearly on my hand: it was there and I could feel it. Then I put it into the garden.

The spider lived in the greenhouse so it was probably pretty fed up at being evicted and then having to walk all the way back home but it had done a good job for me because I could never be frightened of spiders again: I was a changed person.

Actually, after this I did put them out on paper but I could have had them on my hand and I wouldn't have been scared.

I was going to do the same thing with skinny dipping.

First, I was going to make sure that everyone could see everything – and I do mean absolutely everything, with nothing hidden. This was going to be putting the spider on my hand.

I would stand on the swimming deck of Brizo completely naked, put my hands above my head and then wave to everyone.

In the morning, before breakfast, I looked in the bedroom mirror and worked out the minimum time it would take to do this. There had to be enough time for everyone to see whatever they wanted to see - and then I could escape into the water.

I reckoned that ten seconds would be enough. If I counted "one and two and three" up to ten in my head this would take me to ten seconds and then the job would be done. The spider would have been on my hand and by the time I dived into the water it would be in the garden.

At the same time as I wanted to stand on Brizo's stern with no protection, I didn't want a striptease. The truth is that I would have died of embarrassment – even with Luke's support – so I came up with a plan.

I would wear my Delfini shirt, with nothing underneath it, and my elasticated bikini bottom. Then I could stand on the swimming platform pull my shirt up and over my head, my bikini bottom down, put my hands above my head to wave for ten seconds - and then into the water and it would be over.

I could do this.

*****

We motored out past Skorpios and by the time we'd reached Thilia Suzie, Jenny and their guys were in high spirits. How could I tell? Well, first the lads had already mooned as we sailed past Skorpios. I thought this was a bit bold in case the security guys there were in a bad mood and decided to put a bullet up their bums! Then the girls' bikini tops came off and the party had really started.

I did a terrible thing and I'm embarrassed to admit it even now. I dug around in the centre console and got out our marine binos. I did a quick check on the girls and thought that maybe my figure wasn't too bad after all, compared with what else was going to be on show.

The end of the channel is spectacular with the sheer cliff faces below Poros on the right-hand side and the softer coastline of Meganisi on the left. There is an incredible depth of water just 100m from shore so the five boats could spread out, running parallel with each other, down towards the southern tip of the island.

You hear people who don't sail say that the sea is flat calm and they think it is absolutely still, like a big sheet of glass. It is like this sometimes, but very rarely. Even on a day with no wind, where the sails wouldn't move a millimetre, the sea is endlessly restless.

It was like that then. If you can imagine the biggest jelly in the galaxy just wobbling back and to very slowly and gently, this was the sea as we turned south east. There was no ripple on the surface, just a vast bending of the water as far as I could see – reaching right out of sight to Arkoudi.

This is why what happened next took my breath away. Of course, it was Mike who saw them first – and thought the quickest.

"Dolphins, Rache" and he pointed down towards Arkoudi.

Swimming across us was a pod of six dolphins.

"Text everyone. Tell them to cut their engines now." And almost before he had finished the words Mike had stopped our engine.

Everyone else was just as quick. Now, the five boats glided slowly to a halt as the dolphins swam lazily through us.

They were in perfect rapport with the conditions. They didn't so much dive as simply bend the water apart and submerge without disturbing the surface. I had never seen any animal in such harmony with its environment.

The largest male passed to our starboard, on the far side of Notus, and another pair of what I guess were younger dolphins glided to port and out of sight next to Zephyrus.

A mother and her small calf swam casually towards Brizo, a couple of metres to our port, perfectly clear in the water.

Mike held his finger to his lips, for us to be absolutely silent and still.

The mother slowed down, almost to a stop, and the calf rolled on to its side. It looked at me with knowing eyes and I was desperate to reach out and touch it – to show that I understood, that dolphins and humans could, and should, live together.

The calf continued to study us and then cuddled right up against her Mum, snuggling just as I used to do with my Mum. There was no mistaking what was happening and no need for any imagination. A little one had been on a tiny adventure and now wanted to share what she had seen with her Mum.

Once more, the thought that I was being paid – well, sort of – to do this was incredible and I said a silent prayer of thanks to the Madonna in my forepeak.

No-one started their engines, or asked to, until the last tip of the dolphins' fins had disappeared as they swam towards Lefkada.

When they were completely out of sight, Mike said: "Okay, let's go skinny dipping. Text everyone, Rache."

I did – and snapped out of my nature watching mind and back into being a Hostie.

*****

I have said many times how close Mike and I had become as we worked together. I couldn't imagine ever looking at him now and having the same thoughts as when I'd seen him with no clothes on in Tychos!

The fact that there were very few days where Mike's cabin was not entertaining guests was also, in a funny sort of way, relaxing. He was getting what he wanted and this meant that we could stay really good friends and work together closely, without any of the tensions which could have been there if he had been less popular with the ladies!

I was also sure that Mike would now never have lost his temper with me either. We both did our jobs, and covered each other's backs, and he was grateful that I could sail and handle a boat as well as I did. Just having one Lead Skipper was always going to be a problem and Dave had been really smart in getting me to a level where I could help clients.

As I had this thought, I had another one too – and not a very professional one. Dave had really given me a special bonus by putting me in a boat on my own with Luke!

Because the cove where we were going to swim was so small, Mike was going to moor the boats in a loose semi-circle which would keep other yachts away and make the party private. This plan had my vote every time!

After four windless days, the water had settled to a clarity which was as pure as a frosty winter's morning in England. If anyone had written this cove into a tourist brochure, it would have sounded silly because it was just too perfect.

I reversed Brizo very slowly and when I saw 15 metres on the depth gauge, I dropped the anchor. She settled calmly and quietly, like a big Labrador sailing puppy getting ready for a nap.

The lads had very little to do except position the boats either side of Brizo because this was the easiest anchorage ever. Plenty of depth, no obstructions or wind – even a Hostie whose previous career had been as a cat nose icer could do this!

As the guys toured the boats, they explained that I would lead the skinny dipping party and when I dived in off Brizo's stern the fun could start. That's sort of what I had asked them to say. What I was thinking was very different.

Mike did just what he had promised. He and MG were very sensitive and stood behind me on the swimming platform. Round me was a nice arc of boats – all of which were going to have a great view.

Not that there was going to be a long wait because, almost before the anchors had dropped, Suzie and Jenny had got rid of their bikini bottoms and the guys were dancing around behind them in a state of real excitement.

Estelle was out of her bikini too and stood on the swimming platform of Notus looking immensely proud and almost daring anyone not to look at her admiringly. Much as I tried not to stare, I just couldn't stop myself because I was having one those terrible thoughts which sometimes invade my brain, making me giggle uncontrollably. Then I look like a baby with a bad attack of wind my face is so screwed up.

Estelle was tanned, and toned, to absolute perfection. I think that she must have even had her hair dresser look after those bits which you don't normally see in the salon - everything was so neat.

But what was making me giggle were her immaculate, perfectly formed breasts – far better than nature could ever have given to her. I couldn't help thinking that Luke's sister might have done her boobs and now there I was, on the stern of a yacht in the Ionian staring at the craftsmanship. What would Luke think of me?

Poor Marc sat on the stern looking crushed and still wearing his trunks. He was a nice guy – pleasant and good looking – and I couldn't understand what he saw in Estelle or what she found attractive in him.

Julia and Amy were really cute. They did a version of one those Calendar Girls pictures, where the Women's Institute ladies all got undressed but never showed anything. They had their backs to us with one hand covering their top bits and the other lower down – very discreet.

I stood on Brizo's stern, still with my clothes on. Rod and Sam started the chanting.

"Raaa- chell! Raaa- chell! Raaa- chell!"

Soon the others had joined in. Anthony had flung off his shorts and Sally had climbed out of her flowery, blue bathing costume and was sitting on the stern looking all floppy and cuddly.

"Raaa- chell! Raaa- chell! Raaa- chell!"

I don't know who it was, but someone shouted. "Come on Rachel, let's get the party going."

I pulled my shirt over my head and let my bikini bottom fall to the deck. Then, I stepped right to the edge of the swimming platform and held my hands above my head, just like you see Olympic Gold medallists do when they have won.

I manufactured the biggest smile I could, turned to the left and paused, and then to the right and waited for a moment there. Finally, I stood up as straight as I could in the centre and forced myself to grin as if this was the best fun ever.

Nothing was hidden from view. My hands stayed above my head as I counted - one and two and three - ticking off the seconds. I had to let the spider sit on my hand until there was no doubt that he had been there – no hint of compromise, cheating or escaping too easily.

Then, at the count of eleven, not ten because I had to be certain I had conquered this, I dived off Brizo's stern and into the Ionian.

*****

Instead of the self-discipline of standing without clothes in front of clients, I was embraced by the sea in a wonderful, warm blanket of intimacy. I was shocked, quite literally amazed, at how all enveloping it was and how completely different from swimming in a bikini.

I came up for a breath and all around me everyone was in the water, having a great time. I swam to Brizo's bows, not from any sense of embarrassment at being naked with the others but because I wanted Luke with me.

I took four or five deep breaths to clear my lungs and then lay on the surface, remembering how Luke had taught me to surface dive. I bent at the waist and thrust my bottom and legs hard and fast into the air. The water rushed over my naked legs as they drove me towards the seabed and my hair streamed out behind me.

Five metres down, I twisted and turned and felt the water over and through and in every part me. Perhaps it was the memory of the baby dolphin but I felt at home, as if I had returned to the sea we had left all those millions of years ago. It was an intensely moving and spiritual experience which, in the middle of all of the embarrassment and stress I had felt, came as a total surprise.

Something else happened too – something quite remarkable. I came up from the dive and I was a new woman – changed forever in those 45 seconds. I dived down as the old Rachel, cluttered up with the baggage from years of trying desperately to fit in where I didn't belong, and I came up to the surface transformed - like a snake getting rid of its outgrown, useless skin.

I was in love, confident and happy with myself. Skinny dipping had been a good thing!

*****

I dived a few more times, just to enjoy the intensity of the experience, and then swam breast stroke, very slowly, back to the group. They were all having a great time and I splashed around being as silly as everyone else. Mike was right, skinny dipping was nothing to be worried about and was really good fun – especially for the new Rachel.

When I was ready, I climbed up the swimming ladder and out of the water. Mike was also right when he promised that neither he nor MG would see me. MG held the deck shower and I turned round and round sloshing the sea water from my skin. He was looking at me and smiling – but saw nothing. That was good and kind too.

I dried myself and put my bikini back on because this felt right. I could have sat in the cockpit with no clothes on but I preferred not to: it was no more complex than that and the freedom and power I now had was wonderful.

Anthony, thoughtful as ever, had brought half a dozen bottles of wine and a load of Pringles. Yeaaahh. Pringles and Greek red wine. What skinny dipping party could be without them?

He and Sally were dressed, as were Julia and Amy. The party girls had put their bikini bottoms back on and that was nice.

Estelle covered her perfect, plastic boobs with a transparent rose coloured top but no-one took any notice. Supreme elegance didn't score many points on a Flot skinny dipping party.

We sat and laughed, drank wine and crunched Pringles until Mike, as always our Lead Skipper, declared that we should be motoring to Sivota before all the moorings were taken.

It hadn't been the perfect day, because Luke wasn't with me, but it had been the most important moment in my life.

The old Rachel had left Nydri this morning and the new Rachel would be motoring into Sivota six hours later.

I didn't know how I was going to explain what had happened to Luke but I knew that he would walk alongside me, hold my hand and understand.

But I didn't know what was waiting for me…

May You Live in Interesting Times

(It's a Chinese Curse!)

BEING a Hostie had taught me one giant lesson above everything else: you never know what's going to happen next!

The week started off on a bit of a low - but nothing traumatic. An elderly couple had asked Luke if he would sail their boat down from Corfu so that Risto could give it a full service over the winter. Dave was good with the idea so Luke was going to scrounge a lift to Corfu and then bring the boat back to the yard.

I was doubly fed up because this week's Flot was leaving Tychos on Sunday and Luke wasn't going to Corfu until Tuesday so I wouldn't even see him whizz past in our rib. Sad face!

Some weeks you get clients on a Flot who are, well - just ordinary, and that's not being bad mannered to them. They're just ordinary in a really nice way, not super brainy like the killer quiz teams, or perfect Estelle looking but folk just like my Mum and Dad, who work hard and have saved up for a wonderful week's holiday. This Flot was like that.

We sailed a bit on Monday but to be honest, the group weren't the three Jimmies in for a white knuckle reach in a top end 4. Mike read the mood perfectly – when didn't he? – and so we stayed overnight at Vathi which has loads of space for learner moorers and some nice restaurants.

The following day, the Poseidon weather forecast was giving almost windless so Mike said we could motor round to Kalamos, moor between the island and Kastos and enjoy some swimming – but no-one mentioned skinny dipping!

In the evening, I was going to do a barbecue on the beach and have a quiz. With the right clients, barbecues and quizzes went together like twin sisters and I always enjoyed them.

Everything looked so stress free and easy that I couldn't imagine what could go wrong...

All the clients were comfortable with their boats so I motored across in Brizo with the guys. Actually, I didn't. I lay under the Bimini sun shade and had a long nap. Either Mike or MG were at the helm – but I didn't care who because I just wanted to doss about for an hour.

It was MG who woke me up, "Come on Sleeping Beauty – here's something worth seeing."

In fact, I had been asleep for a lot longer than an hour and we were well into the wide channel between Kastos and Kalamos: that's why I was bit shocked by the enormous Superyacht moored about a mile away from us. There were plenty of these yachts in the Ionian but the one off our starboard bow was something special.

For a start, she was painted in the most stunning midnight blue – the sort of colour the posher footballers have for their Bentleys. She was also elegant in a way that few Superyachts ever are, with a bow which swept into the water and a raked stern almost flowing into the sea rather than cutting through it.

"Ooohh, she's beautiful," I said, "just like a Serval but slightly bigger…"

"And a bit more expensive too," added MG. "The word is that Bloss and Vohm took $250 million off Mr. Bianchi for her - and that makes even a Serval look like loose change."

"Want to know the story, Rache?" The ship was clearly anorak territory and there is no bigger fan of gossipy stories than MG.

"No she doesn't, and I don't either. One bloody billionaire is the same as the next one to me. They've all got too much money," Mike wasn't really fed up but he just wanted to wind MG up a bit.

"Go on then, tell her, but only if I can be first for the barbie. There's nothing left when you've filled your dustbin lid!"

There was a lovely atmosphere on Brizo and I couldn't help thinking what a nice place it was to work with two really good guys.

"Go on MG, tell me about her."

"Okay, if you insist. It's actually a good story."

And Mike buried his head in his hands…

"It's 1992 or something about that time, I always get the dates mixed up. There's a young Italian Civil Engineer doing a Postgraduate degree at Durham University and he's feeling a bit left out of things, being foreign and everything.

"So he gets talking to this Asian girl who is studying English Literature – she must have wanted to become a cat nose icer, Rache…"

Obviously, I gave him a good cuff for that one! The cheeky thing!

"And they get on very well.

"She says: 'I'm from Kushan, and if you fancy coming to visit me during the summer break, I can find you somewhere to stay and it won't cost you anything.'

"Of course, he's never heard of Kushan because it's one of those Central Asian republics which have just got their freedom from the Soviets, but he likes the girl and he's short of money for a holiday so he thinks why not?

"After flying on Crapistan Air, or whatever they were called in those days, he eventually arrives in the capital Ariana and there is his friend Ruthinna, or Ruth as she likes to be called, but she's not got a knackered old Lada taxi, or a donkey and cart, but a bloody big Zil limousine just like the Soviet big wigs used to have.

"Piero, that's his name, thinks: 'Bugger me' – or whatever that is in Italian – 'What have I got myself into?'

"Anyway, they set off and the first thing Piero thinks, because he is pretty well obsessed with roads, is that all these need a good seeing to but he doesn't say anything out of politeness.

"After a bit, they turn in through a set of gold painted gates and Ruth says: 'Welcome to my house,' or something like that, 'my Dad's the President of Kushan.'

"Fast forward a bit now. Dad gets on really well with Piero and recognises that the boy is super bright and keen to help. So, with what bit of money the country has from the sales of copper ore and woolly hats he puts Piero on to the job of getting at least a few roads fixed.

"And Piero does, but everything is done with almost no money and mainly just with grants from the Western countries because funny hats don't make much money.

"Then oil is discovered in Kushan and the Americans want some really, really good roads to service their shiny new pipeline running all the way to India. Money no object!

"So our Piero does a brilliant job, aided by a load of ex-American Special Forces blokes who are now working for the CIA and don't take kindly to anyone even putting camel droppings on their lovely new roads.

"But he's smarter than just taking the Yanks' money and blowing it. He makes some very clever property investments, mainly in London and Geneva, and ends up being worth something around $5 billion – or that's what the papers say, anyway.

"The downside is that he, his wife and their young daughter are now target for tonight for every religious nutter and upwardly mobile criminal in the world so he writes a cheque for $250 million and gets himself not only the most beautiful Superyacht in the world but also the safest.

"She's not the biggest Superyacht ever but she is probably the best – 20 knots flat out and a cruising range of 6,000 miles with so much high tech stabilisation stuff that you could sail through a hurricane and probably not even notice it was rough.

"But what makes her really special is the stuff no-one knows about. Because Mr. Bianchi is really important to the Americans they have stuffed the ship full of defensive systems so there are forty something crew to sail her plus another load of security staff.

"Our Piero prefers ex-Russian Spetsnaz Special Forces blokes because they aren't bothered about who they kill, whereas Western mercenaries tend to be a bit careful when they're working for civilians.

"And see those big ribs?"

MG waved towards a pair of enormous ribs, each with a radar dome and a large, covered cockpit, carrying half a dozen very serious looking guys.

I nod.

"Go within half a mile of The Appian Way and you'll be looking down the nasty end of an Uzi and they really won't be at all concerned about pulling the trigger."

I said, "MG, why's she called The Appian Way? That's a strange name."

"It's sort of an in joke. Piero's a road engineer and the Appian Way was the main road into Rome 2,000 years ago. It brought all the money into Rome so Piero thought it would be quite funny to name his ship after a money making road."

Whoooaaa. I couldn't imagine how much five billion was. One billion was a thousand million, so this guy had five thousand, million dollars in his purse! And I'd been stressed taking £1500 from Anthony and Sally!

"He does have one weakness though. Being Italian, he loves fast things and he's got a couple of 1960s vintage speedboats – polished mahogany and bloody great American V8 engines. They drink race fuel like a drunk at a wedding but they are bloody fast – 50mph and no mistake.

"He'll have one out to play before long and you can work out how you're going to get $250,000 in tips to buy one!"

*****

There's a lovely beach just off the ruins of the old olive oil mills – the perfect spot for our barbecue. As always, we put Brizo at the back of the Flot so that we could keep any eye on everyone.

We got everyone moored easily and I was starting to feel really good about the evening to come. I thought what a useful thing it was to have learnt catering at the Garden Centre. The guys were ferrying my stuff from Brizo to the beach so I was left to do all the interesting bits, which was great.

A few clients were swimming but most of them were watching this fantastic wooden speedboat tearing up and down. It was gorgeous, all gleaming brown wood with the two American car engines roaring away like wild animals as it planed across the water.

There was a young guy driving and a little girl sat on the top of the front seat with her hair streaming out behind her like some supermodel. Wow! She was really having a good time!

They made three or four passes each way and I was surprised how close they came to us. Okay, Brizo was stood well out from the beach but how about a bit of good manners with their bow wave?

I remember every second of what happened next as if it was a very, very, very slow motion film. The speedboat was heading past us at a ridiculous speed. The little girl was sat on the back of the seat laughing. Then there was an explosion. Not like Stavros' gun going off at Sivota but more muffled. The boat turned towards Brizo still flat out with the engines screaming. My first thought was that we were going to be rammed. Then there was a second explosion. It sort of went whuuumphh! And the little girl was thrown high into the air as the speedboat flicked on to its side.

I saw her rise up, maybe two whole metres or perhaps a bit more, with her little arms flung out like a doll, and then she hit the water and lay still – very still.

I pulled off my top, grabbed our yellow horseshoe lifebuoy and jumped. The lifebuoy was hooked round my neck and I swam a desperate breast-stroke, harder than I had ever swum in my life. The child was not moving and the forty metres to her looked as if it stretched away forever.

Please God, don't let her sink. Madonna, look after her for just a few more seconds.

Now I could see that she was wearing a buoyancy vest – not a life-jacket which would have flipped her on to her back and kept her head out of the water but a little foam vest, like you see kids wearing at the beach. This was keeping her afloat.

Three more strokes and I was there. I turned her over, put her arms through the horseshoe and pushed her along - kicking with my legs and one arm until my lungs were bursting.

It seemed as if Brizo was twenty miles away, even though I had only been in the water for a couple of minutes. I climbed up the swimming ladder and dragged the lifeless little girl on to the bathing platform.

I was desperate. I had learned CPR at Guides but now this was a real child and she wasn't breathing. I pulled the Velcro on her vest open and pressed thirty times on her chest, just as we had been taught. Then I did my three breaths into her mouth. Another thirty presses and still nothing.

Please, please, please Madonna, don't let her die.

I breathed again into her mouth and, just as I was going to start pressing again, she coughed – and then choked. I didn't know whether it was the correct thing to do but I turned her on to her side and she coughed again, and then some more, and water came out each time.

Her breathing was erratic but she was alive. I remember thanking Madonna, and my Mum for making me go to Guides when I wanted to quit, and God and everyone else.

I was on my knees bent over the little girl but when she began breathing, I sat up and my hands flopped down at my sides. I wasn't a heroine and doing brave things was exhausting and all too much for me.

I heard the scream of the rib's engines before I actually saw the boat. It bounced alongside Brizo and a guy leapt off and on to the bathing platform.

I don't think that I will ever forget his face. It was mainly furious, raging angry but it was frightened too. Then I felt the boot in my stomach and I had never been in so much pain – I couldn't imagine it was possible to hurt so much and not be dead.

The force of the kick lifted me off my knees and my head hit the bottom of passerelle, where it was attached to Brizo's stern. I felt as if a bomb had gone off inside me and don't remember a thing for a long time afterwards.

*****

I didn't wake up like you do normally - you know, rub your sleepy eyes, stretch a bit, yawn, check the time and get ready for the day. This time, it was the soreness which poked me into life. Later, Luke and I laughed about how each part of the pain had to wait in line to be recognised – to see who had won the, "Let's Hurt Rachel the Most" competition.

My neck won. Wow, my neck was in agony, as if someone had shaken me until my head was about to fall off!

My stomach was pretty good too. That guy had given me a really good kick and the ribs on my right-hand side were really joining in the pain game.

And my head... Wow again! My head! I could feel a lump on it like an ostrich egg.

For a minute, the three competitors in the pain competition stopped me from actually noticing where I was. When I did, I felt even worse – because I was completely certain that I had died and was now in some really weird place where dead people go until they are graded for Heaven or Hell or something.

I am trying to think what I saw first but I can't actually remember. It was the feeling on my skin which told me that things weren't right. I was wearing a top with some pyjama bottoms but the material was so incredibly light and smooth that it felt as if it wasn't there.

You know the expression, such and such a thing feels like silk? Well, it really doesn't. I was wearing pyjamas which fitted me perfectly and yet were so delicate that they didn't seem to touch my skin. It was a scary experience.

I was lying on a bed – not a normal bed but a huge thing which was big enough to take about ten people. It must have been the biggest bed in the world. The sheets were relatives of the pyjamas – thin, smooth and almost non-existent. At the end of the bed, sat on very pale, strawberry coloured chair, was a nurse.

For sure, I was dead and she was the lady responsible for sending the bits of me which were left to the right places.

The nurse was tiny and Asian with a re-assuring smile. Perhaps this is what angels all looked like. The angel spoke: "Good morning, Miss Lamb. I won't ask how you feel because I have a pretty good idea…"

Her English was perfect but with just a hint of some Far Eastern Country. Perhaps Heaven only had contract staff from Thailand or the Philippines.

My head started to clear. "Where am I? Who's put me in this bed?" I wasn't so much frightened as confused.

Then I realised that I wasn't wearing any underclothes.

"Who undressed me? Who took my clothes off and put me in this bed?"

Now I was tearful – but with anger. Someone had taken off all my clothes and put me in this bed and without my permission.

I sat up straight and my God, the pain! I didn't think that it was possible to hurt this much and still be alive. I was about to try to get out but my stomach hurt so much that I couldn't straighten my legs.

The angel nurse stood up and I noticed that she had what looked like a small, plastic egg with buttons on it in her right hand. One finger was pressing it.

I had another go at getting out of bed and the nurse said: "Please Miss Lamb, please let me help you. Dr. Sweeney will be here in a moment but please let me help you to sit up."

I went crazy with anger and fear, "Dr. Sweeney? Where am I? What's happening to me? I want to go back to Brizo now!"

I was so furious that I forgot the pain and scrambled to the edge of the bed. I swung my legs out and my feet touched the floor. Even with all my rage and soreness and fear, I was shocked at just how far my feet sank into the carpet before they reached solid ground.

I stood up – and then my legs gave way. The nurse held my arm gently, but very firmly, as I clonked down on to the edge of the bed. I sat there, dizzy, confused, scared and unable to stand up. It wasn't a good time.

I had my head in my hands and so didn't see that a chubby, silver haired man had come into the room. He had the look of Santa from my days as an Elf - but in civilian clothes.

"Hiya Rachel. You look really rough. Bet you're feeling a bit knocked about too."

The nurse interjected. "This is Dr. Sweeney, Miss Lamb. Dr. Sweeney put the staples in your head wound and gave you a sedative to help you rest."

Santa beamed reassuringly. "You were a bit lucky yesterday. Good job that you're a fit young lady. A kick that hard could have been nasty but the scan shows there's no concussion. You'll have a cracking headache though!" And he smiled again.

I remember looking round the room. It was huge, almost the size of a classroom. Opposite the mega bed was an equally enormous dressing table and then an opaque glass door, leading to what looked like a bathroom. More glass doors, clear ones this time, opened out on to a massive sundeck, set out with loungers and a table with fresh flowers on it. There, in the distance, was Kastos. I went dizzy again. At least I knew where I was.

The doctor took my hand. He had a very unusual attitude. You could have called it intrusive, taking my hand and speaking to me as if he was my Dad, but his confidence pushed these ideas out of the way. I got the feeling that there was no pretending with this man, he knew just what he was doing and he couldn't care less about the politically correct way of going about his job.

His accent helped too. It was the same northern Lancashire burr that I used to hear when we visited my Dad's auntie in Rawtenstall when I was a kid. The rolling rs were there and the same relaxed, unhurried pace. It was a good accent to have if you were going to speak to someone who was confused and more than a bit frightened.

He sat on the edge of the bed, still holding my hand and said: "Would you like to know what happened?"

I nodded and felt very tearful.

"Well, you know the first part. You saved Margaret's life, Mr. and Mrs. Bianchi's only child."

I was about to open my mouth but he put his finger to his lips. "Sshhh. Just take things easy. You saved her life and we're all very grateful.

"Security didn't see what happened except for a big explosion. So, they screamed across ready for serious action and found the girl they're supposed to be guarding unconscious on the back of a strange boat. Leaning over her is someone they don't know and so bang, they took things into their own hands and you got kicked.

"Believe me, they don't normally work like this but they were stressed – really stressed.

"You hit the side of your boat and cut your head. Then they threw you in the bottom of the rib so that they could work out which terrorist organisation you were working for once you were on The Appian Way - and then give you a proper kicking.

"Of course everyone soon realised what had happened and we were all very grateful. You wouldn't believe how grateful…

"We've got excellent medical facilities on board – really world class – so I had good check over you and patched up the cut.

"Mr. Bianchi is very relieved because killing the lady who has just saved his daughter's life wasn't in the script. I agreed - but reminded him that you were still going to be as sore as bloody hell and it's lucky that you're not dead.

"So Lamai, undressed you, and got you into pyjamas, and then one of the female crew helped her to get you into bed and tucked up for the night.

"Now you've woken up with the Mummy and Daddy of all headaches and feeling bloody furious, upset and probably a lot more things too.

"Sound about right?"

I didn't say anything because my head was hurting so much that my vision was actually fuzzy.

Santa nodded to the nurse who brought a couple of pink tablets across to him. "Take these. They'll not make you feel any better but the headache will go away and you can be angry with us without feeling as bad as you do now."

I swallowed the tablets without argument. Then I felt utterly weary and so I lay back on the bed and I sort of remember the nurse pulling the sheets over me – or maybe she didn't because everything went very fuzzy again.

*****

I don't know how long I was asleep but the sun was bright and so it must have been the following morning. I woke up with a raging thirst. The nurse was on her feet instantly with one of those mugs you give to babies, with a spout on, in one hand.

"Please Miss Lamb, try to take some water."

I did and it was unbelievably delicious. My throat felt as if it was covered in a thick layer of fur and the water didn't move any of it for the first sip, the second or even the third. But I carried on raising the drinking mug and let it gently pour water down my throat. Little by little, my body came back to life.

The nurse gave me a second mug of water which was neither hot nor cold but just ever so slightly warm so that I could almost not feel it. I drank this too.

The doctor had been right. I wasn't hurting any more - but I did feel terrible.

I raised myself out of the bed and in a thick, sticky voice said: "I need the toilet."

The nurse smiled and helped me out of bed. She indicated the opaque glass door to the right of the bed. I was determined to get there on my own and refused the little nurse's hand but she walked alongside me until we reached the door.

I sat on the toilet for a long time. It was as if all the bits of my brain had been scattered in a Force 10 storm and now they were all slowly coming back to base inside my head. One by one they moored and I could start to make sense of what had happened.

After ages, I stood up, flushed the toilet and opened the door. The nurse was standing there with a white dressing gown. She held it out for me and without thinking, I slipped my arms into it.

The nurse spoke. "If you were able to see them, Mr. and Mrs. Bianchi would like to express their thanks for your bravery yesterday."

It was such a strange, formal, prize giving way to speak that all that I could do was nod.

The nurse offered me a pair of slippers, in a matching material to the dressing gown.

"This way please…" and directed me towards the table on the sundeck.

Now that my brain was back in port, my strength was building by the second. You can forget any gym membership in the world, if you want to get really fit – become a Hostie!

Even so, I was savagely sore - and when I had walked the twenty-five metres to the table I was dead on my feet.

I remember Mr. and Mrs. Bianchi very well for their ordinariness. That sounds really strange because the couple were worth $5 billion but we had sat next to loads of forty something couples having meals who looked a lot richer than these two.

Mr. Bianchi was a bit overweight – not hugely fat, but slightly chubby –

and had waves of greying hair. Mrs. Bianchi was medium build, with a face which was lined through a lot of smiling, and had blonde highlights in naturally dark hair. Estelle would have been appalled!

They stood up when I arrived and motioned me to a chair but before I could sit down I saw the lovely little girl I had dragged out of the water.

I just held out my arms out and I cried – with relief and happiness. She ran to me and I kissed the top of her head over and over and over again with the utter joy that she was alive.

When I eventually released her, she looked up and said, in perfect, accent free English, "Thank you for saving me, Miss Lamb."

And then, "Miss Lamb, I have drawn a picture for you - if you would like it?"

The drawing wasn't very good. It showed us in the water, without the lifebuoy, but with me holding her up clear of the sea.

I said: "That's the most wonderful picture I have ever seen. Thank you..."

And then I realised that I had forgotten her name. I asked her. "Margaret," she said, "my name is Margaret but you can call me Maggie because my Mum and Dad call me Maggie and I like it."

"Thank you Maggie. This is the best present I have ever had in my life."

Then, realising that the situation was becoming just too emotional for everyone, I said: "We'll have to go swimming again together - but this time when you are awake."

It was a good call and the tension flowed away.

Dr. Sweeney held out a chair for me. I sat down and didn't know what to do, or say next. It was a terribly awkward situation and I felt very uncomfortable.

There was a long pause, a really long one, before Mr. Bianchi spoke.

He was as correct as the nurse. "First, thank you from the bottom of our hearts for what you did. There is nothing we can say which will ever express how grateful we are – nothing."

His wife joined in. "Miss Lamb, what you did saved two lives, not one, because without Margaret my life would have been over. Thank you."

And she tried to choke back a tear – but failed.

Mr. Bianchi nodded in agreement. "Miss Lamb, there is no way of expressing our gratitude for what you did. Margaret is our only child and is incredibly precious to us. Without your actions, she would have died."

I didn't know what to say so I sat there, looking all embarrassed and stupid because I actually did feel embarrassed and stupid!

His wife added, "What you did was incredibly brave and then to get attacked by one of our own staff...

"I can't imagine how you must feel."

Mr. Bianchi spoke again: "Miss Lamb, there is nothing in the world which can express our thanks sufficiently but if you would accept this gift as a token of our gratitude, my wife and I would be so very pleased."

He slid a long, black leather case across towards me and Maggie stood alongside me, keen to see what was in it.

"Please…"

I opened the case and inside was the most breathtakingly beautiful necklace I had ever seen. Beautiful wasn't even a good description – it was far more than this.

At the end of the necklace was a five petalled flower outlined in diamonds. In the centre was a single brilliant gem which seemed to be on fire, it was so bright. Three smaller flowers nestled above the large one, each with their own array of brilliant stones and another smaller flower sat further up the chain with its own cascade of diamonds.

Mr. Bianchi saw my reaction. "Boodles do some really nice things for me. Do you like it?

"Please try it on."

I took the necklace from the case and let it rest against my open hand. No matter how I looked at it, the workmanship was perfect. I let it stay on my hand, feeling the weight and the metallic softness of the gold.

It was the most utterly beautiful thing I had ever seen in my life and I could never have dreamed of owning anything like it.

Then the special part of me, which is always there when things are at their worst, spoke to me. I really wished it hadn't – but it did.

"Mr. Bianchi, this is the most wonderful, beautiful, incredible necklace I have ever seen. I don't even know how to say how wonderful it is, I really don't, but I can't accept it from you.

"I did jump in the water but your security guys would have been there in a few seconds and saved Margaret without me.

"I didn't do it because she was your daughter. I saw someone who needed my help so I just did it. It wouldn't have mattered who it was because I would still have done the same thing."

I remembered what I had said to Luke about being gracious when someone had shown their gratitude but this was different. I didn't know how much it had cost but I did know that it was a fortune. For sure, the jewellery shops I looked in never had necklaces like this on show.

So, although I wanted the necklace desperately, achingly badly, and I could actually see and feel it on me, I returned it to the box, closed the clasp and pushed the case back across the table.

Mr. Bianchi just nodded. "Thank you Miss Lamb, may I call you Rachel, because Miss Lamb sounds so proper and rigid?

"Thank you for taking the time to explain how you feel. I do understand - and I respect your feelings.

"Is there anything else my wife can help you with – anything at all?"

I paused for a moment to think - and there really wasn't. I was healthy, well mainly except for the sore bits, and happy with the guys I worked with but overwhelmingly I had Luke to love and to be loved by. Nothing else was as important.

"Well, I'm a bit sticky because I haven't had a wash since yesterday so if you didn't mind me using your bathroom for a minute, and borrowing a towel, I would be really grateful. And if one of your crew could lend a top to me, so I don't have to go back without a shirt, then I'd be really happy.

"Then I can get back to Tychos and look after the clients."

It was the Santa doctor who spoke. "Rachel, in another life, I was a Major in the Royal Army Medical Corps mainly attached to the Parachute Regiment. If you'd been a twenty-two year old Para, with the same injuries, I would have had you casevaced out of operations and into a field hospital.

"You're not as strong and fit as a Para, and you are hurt. Is that clear?

"I want to keep an eye on you here, where I have the staff and facilities to look after you if anything unsuspected occurs.

"I want to do that not because you have saved Mr. Bianchi's daughter but because I am a doctor caring for an injured patient. Do you understand that too?"

I didn't like the way things were going and I didn't like the way Dr. Sweeney was speaking to me.

"But I've got to get back, Mike will need me…"

My voice trailed off weakly and unconvincingly.

Mr. Bianchi spoke. "If Mike is happy for you to stay, will you please join us for dinner this evening and we can all relax?"

From nowhere a grey haired, middle aged lady appeared. Mr. Bianchi held out his hand for the iPhone which was offered to him. "Rachel this is Avril who, when she wants my opinion she gives it to me."

Everyone on their side of the table laughed at this in joke.

The phone was already ringing and Mr. Bianchi passed it to me.

After what seemed like a long time, Mike answered it with one word. "Yes."

"It's me Mike, Rache. I want to come back to Tychos and help and they want me to stay here because of the bang on my head and the kick I've had and…"

I was getting embarrassed and upset at having everyone listen to what should have been a private conversation.

Mike's voice was hard and business like. I was shocked that he didn't ask how I was or anything about me.

"Rachel," that was strange because I had been Rache since the Boat Show in January, "stay on The Appian Way and get better."

"But Mike, what about the clients and everything?"

"Rachel, I've just told you what's best for you and best for us - so just do it.

"Get better and we'll see you soon.

"I've got to go now – Dave's calling me."

And with that, the phone went dead. I just looked at it hoping that it would ring again and Mike would talk to me. It didn't.

I was in such a state that I remember actually biting the inside of my lip. This was all too much for me. I was an ordinary girl who iced cats' noses and took kids to see Santa and now I was here on a billionaire's yacht and I felt as if I was drowning in an avalanche of new things.

The next thing I said was really lame. "I would stay, but I've not got anything to wear."

Avril smiled the smile of someone who God really did text for advice. "We've got a few things here which you might consider.

"I guessed at the sizes and I hope that there is something which you might feel is appropriate."

She turned to the Bianchis.

"If you would excuse us girls for a moment…"

We went back into the bedroom and there was what looked like a shop full of clothes laid out, all of fantastic quality and with labels I'd only ever seen in the magazines I read in the dentist's waiting room! Fleur of England, La Perla and Myla. Oh yes! Myla. I'd already seen that label on the pyjamas they'd given to me!

Avril looked really pleased with herself.

I desperately wanted to not to say the next thing, but I just couldn't keep the words in my mouth.

"How did you get all them all so quickly? I mean, you can't even get minty gel toothpaste in Nydri."

Avril had the same patient look you see when someone is trying to be nice to a not very bright puppy.

"Working for Mr. Bianchi, there are certain things we can do which might not be familiar to you because they are just a little bit different.

"When we have The Appian Way in the Ionian, Mr. Bianchi likes to have our Gulfstream jet at Preveza, in case it's needed. The Gulfstream is very fast, much faster than a commercial plane, and so it was able to be in Luton two and half hours after it left Preveza.

"We have an account with J. Featherstone in London and I know Alison Crowton, the head of their Private Shopping Department, extremely well.

"She was very kind and came into the store from home. The poor mite must have been dreadfully tired but she was so helpful and we sorted out some things for you.

"I was terribly rude and looked at the size of your clothing and then we made a few guesses together.

"Alison got everything nicely packaged and sent to Luton by courier ready for the Gulfstream. An hour after it had landed at Luton, the plane was on its way back to Preveza."

I was silent. What sort of mad world was this where someone could spend thousands and thousands of pounds on designer clothes without even trying them on? Everything was just crazy. One of the world's poshest stores opens up in the middle of the night because they've been asked to and then a private jet is sent to collect the stuff. And I always waited until after 3pm to shop in Chester because I got free parking!

"They're fantastic Avril, unbelievably wonderful but they're not my clothes. Can you take them back and get a refund?"

Avril listened to what I had said with a quiet smile and didn't raise any argument.

"Would that make you happy, Rachel?"

"Can one of your guys get my clothes from Tychos, but tell Alissa not the blue things please, and she'll know what you mean, and please can I have the soap which Luke gave to me and my nice dress with the Asos label?"

Avril smiled. "Yes, of course. I'll arrange everything.

"Rachel, you are looking very tired. It's not easy – what you've been through. Perhaps you might like a rest before dinner?"

I nodded with my Cabbage Patch doll head. I was using this a lot today.

I flopped on the bed still in the dressing gown and I was asleep in half a second.

Walking The Appian Way

THIS time, I woke up in the right order: eyes, yawn, stretch a bit. Ow! That was my ribs telling me that they still hurt – and a lot too!

My clothes, not the things which Avril had got for me from London, were all neatly laid out and I was a bit embarrassed about this. Goodness only knows what they thought of my stuff from Next and Asos, when it seemed that everyone on this ship wore tops worth more than my car!

I don't know how they knew I was awake – perhaps there were spy cameras or little drones or something – but there was a knock at the door.

I limped across and stood there feeling really, really stupid because there was no handle. A voice came through the wall from some hidden intercom.

"Hello Rachel, it's Avril."

I think she only ever had one voice in her head: calm, controlled, Mistress of the Universe.

"There's a button, just to your left, if you would like to open the door."

Or, translated, "Come on thickie, have you never been on a Superyacht before where all the doors open with buttons?"

There was a discreet, polished, stainless steel button. After a season on yachts, at least I was really good at recognising stainless steel by now!

The door glided nearly silently back and there was Avril, along with a girl a bit older than me. She was averagely pretty and wearing a very short, tan coloured skirt and super smart blouse in the same colour and with all the creases ironed in like razor blades.

"This is Lynda."

The girl smiled and nearly curtsied – but fortunately didn't.

"If you need anything, Lynda is here to help.

"Mr. and Mrs. Bianchi suggest dinner in a couple of hours, if this is okay with you.

"They're two lovely people and very informal. In fact, Mrs Bianchi insists on all our visitors calling her Ruth so it would be nice if you could too."

One of my mad thoughts galloped into my brain. "Sorry Mr and Mrs Bianchi. I'm starving and I fancy my tea a bit earlier so can Ruth nip down to the galley and put some pasta and a tin of tomatoes on – quick!"

You could just imagine it…

I did my best Cabbage Patch doll nod and said: "Yes, that would be wonderful. Thank you very much."

Avril melted silently away and I was left with Lynda – and an embarrassed silence. She cracked first.

"Is there anything I can help with, Madam?"

What? Who's Madam?

"No. No, thanks very much. I'm going to get a shower."

Arrgghhh! She walked across to the bathroom. Oh God! Is this what happened with posh people? Someone watched whilst you got undressed and had a shower. This was 50 million times worse than skinny dipping.

The bathroom door opened and Lynda stood to one side – which was a good job because I was feeling very dizzy and a bit sick at the thought of what might happen next.

"I hope that you have everything you need, Madam, but if there is anything I can help with please phone 06 and I'll be here to help."

I am surprised that I didn't cause a tidal wave with the sigh of relief. At least she wasn't going to undress, wash and dry me!

*****

The bathroom was huge, with a shower about the same size as my room at Uni and a bath which the baby porpoise would have loved. I took off my purple pyjamas and walked into the shower. On one side was a little, gold metal table sticking out from the wall and there was a line of bottles on it with posh names but which meant shower gel and shampoo in ordinary language. There was also my Chanel box and I was sure that it contained Luke's soap.

In front of me was what looked like a yacht control panel except that there was no SatNav. Apparently, I could have the water coming from the top, the bottom, the sides, all around and goodness knows where else too. I moved the switch to the central position and set the heat control to the centre too.

Showers always take forever to warm up so I got right up against the wall until the water was comfortable but this one was instantly at the right temperature. It was like being under a waterfall and I stood for ages, letting the torrent wash away the sea salt stickiness and the stress of the last 24 hours.

Luke's soap was lovely and, as the Chanel perfume wrapped round me I felt him with me.

Last of all, I opened one of the shampoo bottles and ever so carefully washed round the lump on my head.

I put the dressing gown on in the bathroom, because I wasn't sure whether Lynda or Avril or some big security guy with a machine gun was going to be in the bedroom when I opened the door. No-one was there but during the time it had taken me to have a shower someone had been in, changed the sheets and laid out a new set of pyjamas on the couch next to the dressing table. This was freaking me out!

The shower had cleaned my body and my mind too. I was desperately, achingly longing to have Luke with me – to kiss me and stroke my head and tell me that he loved me and that everything was fine - but I was determined not to mention him to Mr. Bianchi.

No-one on The Appian Way knew about Luke and so I decided that I would leave him to sail down from Corfu and then be back at Porto Tyche ready for him when he arrived. This way, he wouldn't have to worry about getting to me - or if I was hurt.

It was the hardest, and bravest, thing I had ever done.

There were tons of perfumes and things – even a bottle in the shape of an owl made from what looked like hundreds of tiny bits of crystal - but I decided that I was fine as I was. I didn't want to be here and either Mr. Bianchi took me as I was, in my Asos dress and Nydri rope sandals, or I would go home - there and then. As you can see, I was feeling much better.

The phone rang and a very polite voice, I think it was Lynda, asked if I could be so kind as to join Mr and Mrs Bianchi for dinner? Well - yes I can, because I could eat an MG sized helping at a barbie now. Unfortunately, I had to sound like a Flot Hostie thickie and say I didn't know where to go.

It was Lynda on the phone and an instant later she was there, buzzing at the bedroom door. Just outside was a spiral staircase made entirely of different coloured woods, some which were such a dark brown that they were almost black and others of the palest, lightest fawn.

She respectfully indicated the way and I started to climb.

I wasn't nervous, not in the way you get tense when you're turning across the wind in a 5, but more apprehensive. I had never been on a Superyacht before and I didn't know what you were supposed to do before a meal. I mean, did you have to go through some sort of Superyacht ritual, like pat your head and rub your tummy at the same time - or something else really weird?

Half way up the stairs I stopped. I didn't want to show myself up but I was happy with who I was and I was proud too. A year ago, I would have been terrified but not now. I could moor stern to, my colleagues trusted me with any boat in our little fleet and I had looked after my clients when they needed me most.

I could even do a quiz with eight psychopaths and yes, I could skinny dip too so I was going to be Rachel and they could either take me as I was or not at all – because I wasn't going to pretend to be something I wasn't.

The covered dining area, with the far end open and looking out over the stern, was very similar to the one outside my bedroom. Woohoo. "My bedroom" – that was a bit cheeky! Mr. Bianchi stood up as I walked towards the table and Dr. Sweeney did too.

Avril was there, along with Mr and Mrs Bianchi, Ruth I remembered, and Margaret. Maggie ran to me and wrapped her arms round me in the biggest hug ever.

Mr Bianchi was all smiles. "Thank you for joining us Rachel, it's a great pleasure."

Ruth had a lovely, gentle, welcoming smile. "Rachel, I'm so pleased that you can share our meal tonight. I'm still lost for words with…"

Her voice trailed off and she choked back tears.

"With you saving Margaret. My, our, life would have been over if we had lost her. We owe you a debt which can never be re-paid."

I was in a real emotional corner. If this had been one of the guys, I could have made some silly comment to get things back to normal - but it wasn't. A mother was speaking from the heart and although I was incredibly moved by what she had to say, it was also very stressful. I wasn't a paramedic or a firewoman who rescued people for a living – I was Rachel Lamb, a Hostie who could moor your boat, or make a decent barbecue, but saving a life was something vastly different.

So, I didn't do a very good job of responding. "Thank you so much, Mrs Bianchi, I mean Ruth, but I only did what anyone would have done. If the guys had seen Maggie in the water they would have got her out even quicker than me but thank you for what you've said and the most important thing is that Maggie drew that lovely picture for me."

And I gave her another big hug.

Maggie got us all back on to the right tack: "Papà, posso sedermi accanto a Rachel per favore?"

"No, my love, in English please. Rachel is our guest and her language is English. So not Italian or Kushan but English."

Margaret pulled a face. "Ooohhh, Dad. Okay. Dad, please may I sit next to Rachel at dinner?"

"No, you can't – because she probably wants some peace and quiet and she won't get it with you there."

I was holding Margaret now. "I would love to have Maggie's company please."

As you can see it was all super relaxed. I don't know what the atmosphere is like on every Superyacht but this was more like having dinner with clients at Andreas' Taverna on Tychos. Nothing was formal or stiff and the only thing which made it different was the food: it was unbelieveable!

Mr. Bianchi was all smiles again. "I'm sorry Rachel, we weren't sure what you would like so Daniele has done his own version of a Greek Mezze and I hope there are a few things which you might enjoy..."

And then a couple of other Lyndas – unless she was one of triplets – loaded the table up with hummus, kebabs, smoked aubergines, grilled fish and about twenty other things. I was careful, but still starting to get worried about the stitching on my dress!

I took care with the wine too. I liked a glass of wine but because there was so much of it always available, and for free, on sailing holidays I was less interested in alcohol than I was at Uni where I used to drink for all the wrong reasons.

Being a Hostie helped too. There was no point in me being staggering drunk and then a client needing my help, so on The Appian Way I took a glass of a fantastic Greek red wine and just sipped at it throughout the meal.

After the desserts, coffee appeared and everyone was becoming really relaxed.

It was fascinating watching Mr. Bianchi. The other adults made most of the conversation and I was carefully manoeuvred into whatever was being discussed. Margaret was too, but not in the way you see spoilt British kids being allowed to dominate what was going on. Instead, she was allowed her turn but then listened quietly as others spoke.

Meanwhile, Mr. Bianchi smiled and made the occasional comment to show that he was taking part but mainly he watched and listened. In a funny sort of way, he reminded me of Mike looking at the wind indicator on Brizo's masthead, feeling the weather second by second.

Ruth was a good Mum and sensed that Maggie was getting tired, "Come on Miss Rescue, time for your bed."

Margaret pulled a face and then said: "Rachel, you will be here tomorrow morning, you will - won't you?"

"I couldn't leave without a big hug so yes, if your Mum and Dad will let me stay, I'll be here tomorrow."

The Bianchis smiled like two parents who have just agreed to a sleepover.

Ruth said: "Come on then, last big hug for Rachel and then off to bed."

A Lynda appeared and I am certain that Margaret would have been tucked up to perfection but Ruth turned to me and said: "Would you please excuse me for a moment? I've got many roles but nothing is more important to me than being a Mum."

I smiled and she left with a Lynda.

Dr. Sweeney also excused himself, along with Avril and another Lynda. There must have been dozens of them all cloned from one master copy buried deep inside the hull somewhere!

Now, I was left just with Mr. Bianchi. He spoke very softly, in English which had just a hint of an Italian accent and also the occasional bit of Geordie which was really funny.

"Rachel, is there nothing we can do to show our appreciation? I know that you don't want the gift we got for you but would you like Luke to join us here, whilst you get your strength back?"

I felt as if my head was going to explode.

"Luke? Luke, you know about Luke? How do you know about me and Luke?"

I was scared and tears were instantly welling in my eyes.

Mr. Bianchi looked genuinely concerned. "Rachel, please forgive me. There was no intention to intrude into your private life. Things have moved very quickly in the last 24 hours and we became aware of your friendship with Luke.

"He is currently anchored at Paxos and I promise you that we haven't disturbed him – and wouldn't without your permission."

I relaxed but not before two great big, fat tears had rolled down my cheeks and a sniffle had started. I wiped them both away with my napkin.

"No. Please don't contact Luke, please Mr. Bianchi, I want him here with me so much but I don't want him to be worried. Luke is, well, Luke..."

I couldn't find the correct, sophisticated, English literature words to say what I wanted to say so what did come out was really clumsy.

"I love Luke and I know that he loves me and because I love him so much I don't want to see him upset – I can't have him upset and he will be and he would leave the boat straightaway and come here and love me and that's what I want too. But I love him too much for that to happen."

And two more tears and another sniffle appeared.

"I understand Rachel. Love is a powerful motivator and your love for Luke is a wonderful thing. None of my staff will interfere, I can promise you that."

I napkined the second lot of tears away, made some lame apology for sniffling and thanked Mr. Bianchi for his understanding.

He waited patiently for me to dry my eyes.

"Rachel, you are a very unusal person – I don't think that the word unique is too strong. You saved my child's life..."

I started to object but he held up his hand to silence me.

"You saved my child's life and yet will accept nothing. You know how wealthy I am but you want nothing. This is unusual.

"Is there anything we can do to show our appreciation – anything at all?"

It was an incredible question. To someone who could send his private jet to London to bring a load of clothes back for me, money meant something different than it did to me. What could I ask for?

I was silent for what felt like hours and hours. If he could help me get started with a mortgage I could get a little flat in Northwich, or somewhere else nice but not too expensive, and never have to worry about sharing with a total bastard like Connor ever again.

And my Fiesta. It was a good little car, and had never let me down, but it was ten years old so maybe I could have a better second-hand car or something.

Or perhaps I could take Luke somewhere nice for week's holiday.

I was very conscious of being near immense power. The idea of the clothes arriving from London still melted my brain but it was more than that. A private jet was easy to understand but I was beginning to get a sense of the power which throbbed through Mr. Bianchi's life in a way which I was struggling to understand.

He knew about Luke and me but what else did he know – that I had been a cat nose icer or maybe even the deeply intimate things about Connor? $5 billion bought you a personal shopper at midnight but what else could it buy? The thought worried me and so I thought that absolute honesty would be the only way for me to handle the situation – and still stay sane.

"Mr. Bianchi..."

"No. Please Rachel, Piero."

"I'm sorry, Piero. I'm not stuck up or ungrateful or anything – I'm really not. If I had done something really clever, like keeping The Appian Way off a reef or something, then I would have been really grateful for a present. My car is ten years old, and help with a deposit on a little flat would have been wonderful and you can't imagine how much I want to wear the necklace.

"But what I did to help Margaret is completely different. If you believe I actually did save her life then it's beyond value. You know that you would have given all your money to save her because she is so precious to you and Ruth.

"So, because she is worth this much to me too I can't take anything from you.

"If she had been the child of an illegal immigrant I would have saved her just the same – and I would have been prepared to get kicked too.

"I'm not an angel or anything, it's just what I believe.

"Please don't take offence, because I really would have liked the necklace especially, but I didn't want it enough for me not to like myself for doing something which I think wasn't right."

Piero nodded, smiled and, after a pause, spoke. "I said that you were an unusual person Rachel, and maybe even that's not the right description. Probably unique is more accurate.

"In Kushan culture it's believed that once in a generation there is wolf born with a pure white tail and this has the ability to see things other wolves can't. Maybe you're a white tailed wolf."

He smiled and I had a little giggle at the thought of being a wolf, when last year I don't think I would have qualified as a nervous hamster!

Piero spoke again, "I know you have great difficulty accepting praise but let me tell you what happened after you saved Margaret's life. You might find it interesting.

"I value privacy and discretion very highly so it wasn't only clothes on the Gulfstream coming back from Preveza. Avril contacted my London lawyers and they sent three of their staff, plus another lawyer from a company we have no connection with, to fly back to Preveza.

"I don't know how much they charged me but I would guess that it was something in the region of £5,000 an hour – from the moment they got the phone call from Avril.

"Do you know what their job was?"

I was back in Cabbage Patch doll mode again. "No, I can't imagine."

Piero smiled the same gentle smile he had so often.

"I'll tell you. They offered every one of your clients £10,000 for any images or video they had – plus their signature on a confidentiality clause which forbade them from contacting the media. We even gave £10,000 each to the two children on the Johnstone's yacht so the family had £40,000 in total.

"The independent lawyer we brought along was there to ensure that the people agreeing to the confidentiality clause knew what they were signing and its status in law. One can't be too careful in these cases.

"As it happens, everything happened so quickly that there was no video or pictures but, as I said, it was better to be careful.

"We made payments to Mike and MG too – and they were accepted.

We made a considerably larger payment to Dave and he didn't hesitate – not even for a moment.

"Yet, all you have is a picture from Margaret.

"Does this change your mind?"

The car, the flat and the holiday I wanted with Luke all screamed at me. Wow! £10,000 was a fortune and I could have done so much with it. Maybe Piero might have even given me a bit more than £10,000 and that would have been incredible.

At the same time, I had to get up every day and look at the person I saw in the mirror and be happy with her. So, again, I said no. Politely, very reluctantly - but for certain. A life wasn't mine to give, or take away, and the fact that I just happened to be in the right place at the right time didn't change anything.

*****

I can say one thing about living on a Superyacht with a team of Lyndas – it's great! I ate all my meals with the Bianchis – sometimes just with Piero, Ruth and Maggie and sometimes with Avril, Dr. Sweeney and the business people who seemed to come and go as if they were in one of those big revolving doors at Marks and Spencers.

Mainly, Piero listened to what others had to say and then made a comment, a decision really, and everyone acted on it – and straight away too.

In between he talked a lot to me and yes, he did know about Uni, Connor and the cat biscuit icing! At first, I was really tense and then he explained that in his world information simply flooded in and that he was interested in me because I was so different from the people he normally met and dealt with. In private, he started to call me Rachel White Tail and this was done with such affection that I liked it.

He also told me about himself and I learnt that he was very unusual too. He came from a lower middle-class family in Gallerate, in Northern Italy, and if he had not been so clever at school he knew that he would have ended up teaching or in some factory office. Instead, he had worked every second, of every minute, of every day and had become a top student.

He was also ambitious, and wanted to be perfect in English, and that's why he ended up at Durham and met Ruth. When he found himself at the epicentre of power in the new state of Kushan he took every opportunity which came his way.

As MG had said, the start of his wealth came through the oil which was discovered in the country and the Americans' obsession with getting it to

India. Then he turned this good luck into a fortune through property. In a short time, he became very rich – and without the need to be dishonest.

He had everything except the one thing he and Ruth ached for: a child. They tried everything but with no success. Then they went on a holiday to Durham, to remember their student days, and prayed for a child in the little Catholic Chuch of St. Margarets, where Piero used to occasionally take Mass. Six weeks later, Ruth told Piero that she thought that she was pregnant – and she was. The child was Margaret – or Maggie when she was with her Mum and Dad because they were both Rod Stewart fans!

So, when no-one else was present, we swapped little bits of gossip and gradually I came to like Piero – not for The Appian Way, his jet or the Lyndas but because he was a really lovely person.

*****

It was still a scary experience living with a billionaire. Margaret wanted me to go swimming with her – in the ship's enormous pool obviously! I sort of faffed about and said I didn't have anything to swim in but no-one got even a tiny bit stressed. Ruth asked if I would really like to swim with Maggie and when I said that I would, she whispered to a Lynda. A few minutes later, she said that the swimwear they always kept on the ship for guests was in my bedroom and perhaps I would like to look at it.

To be honest, I wasn't keen on wearing a second-hand cossie. Once, at school, I had been made to wear a hockey shirt from the store when I forgotten my own and it smelled rotten so the thought of wearing someone else's swimming stuff didn't appeal – at all. I still had a lot to learn about being involved with a billionaire!

Laid out on my bed were five bikinis and a full length swimming costume. There were titchy little things, like Suzie and Jenny had worn before the skinny dipping, and some which covered a lot more. I chose a lovely yellow and white striped one with a Missoni label – and it hadn't been used by anyone else either!

I swam in the pool with Maggie and then she asked if we could we go in the sea. It was another learning experience. Piero and Ruth weren't there but Avril was. She was all smiles but you could see that her mind was in full computing mode.

Avril was never without a phone – literally never – and she was on it now.

There was a smiling non-smile and then she said: "Yes, that will be fine. Just give us a few minutes."

A few minutes? A few minutes for what? I dried myself off and gossiped to Maggie and then Avril non-smiled at me again and said: "Whenever you're ready..."

Maggie insisted that we take the lift down to swimming deck. I saw the drips she left on the floor of the lift and thought of some poor Lynda, or maybe an Alissa or Rache, cleaning them up!

At the stern of The Appian Way, there was a huge swimming deck which slid out until it sat just on the surface of the water. A slide had been erected on one end and there was a ladder up to the top. It was fabulous. Maggie shrieked with delight and asked could we use the slide and of course, I was dying for a go myself.

At the top of the ladder I looked out towards Kalamos and there were two of the four guard ribs patrolling slowly off our stern. This was a very different world where a little girl couldn't go swimming without a load of guards armed with machine guns.

*****

I slept an awful lot. It wasn't just the bang to the head and the kicking which made me tired but suddenly my body said: "You know, you haven't had a day off in seven months and you're really exhausted now."

So, I slept for hours and hours and I gradually felt better.

Every morning, Dr. Sweeney examined me – and thoroughly too. It was all very jokey but I could tell that he knew exactly what he was doing. The wound on my head itched like mad but I could feel it getting better and my stomach and ribs were just sore now instead of really hurting.

On the third morning, Dr. Sweeney said: "You should have joined the Paras the way you're healing. Despite the best efforts of our security staff, you'll probably live. I'll tell Piero that from my point of view, you can go back to Tychos now."

I couldn't think of anything really clever to say so I just said: "Thank you. I'd really like that..."

At breakfast there was just Piero, Ruth and Maggie plus another ton of food that really only MG could have eaten. I was still stuffed from the previous night so I just had some fruit and yoghurt and a big glass of freshly pressed orange juice. I was tender in lots of places but feeling better by the minute – even if I couldn't stop messing with the lump on my head and touching the staples.

Ruth gently eased Maggie away as a Lynda cleared the table. I sensed that something was going to happen.

Piero spoke in the calm, re-assuring voice that I had heard so often in the last three days.

"Rachel, forgive me for being rather business-like but there is no easy way to say this so please excuse me for being so direct.

"I want you to work for me. I have said that you are unique and if you are not absolutely unique in the literal sense of the word then you are a very, very rare person.

"I can buy anything, or anyone, from anywhere but I cannot buy what you have inside you.

"I want you to work for me, not as Avril does, but by being there to represent me when I need absolute, incorruptible, honesty and integrity."

I started to object but Piero raised his hand ever so slightly from the table.

"No, I know all the objections you are about to make but you will have to trust me in this respect. I need and want what you can give me, Rachel. Please, at least think about my offer."

I woffled about again and Piero smiled. "Okay, let's have a little bet. If I can tell you what you are going to say next, exactly – and no cheating from you or the bet doesn't count – will you consider working for me?"

I giggled and agreed.

"Okay, you are about to say that you couldn't work for me for anything at all because Dave and Mike and Delfini Holidays need you and not even with the opportunity to work for billionaire Piero Bianchi would you let them down.

"How's that?"

I was shocked – absolutely amazed. "Well, yes, that's just what I was going to say...

"How could you know?"

"It wasn't difficult. White tailed wolves think differently to the rest of us.

"My offer is there now, and will be in the future, but please remember that your way of looking at the world is very different so take care not to let yourself be hurt by what is normal."

He wrote a phone number on a piece of paper taken from the notepad he always had next to him.

"Rachel, this is my personal number. Only I will ever answer it. Very few people in the world have that number so you can be sure of reaching me at any time. If you ever decide that you would like to work for me, please phone me and we can talk. I will not mention the matter again nor will any of my staff. The decision will have to be yours."

And then, incredibly, he got up and hugged me.

*****

I gathered my things together. A Lynda had put everything into a small, brown, Gucci case like the ones you take on planes. It was a brilliant case and I thought that it would be really petty to object to having it.

Then Avril smiled, a real smile full of humour, "I hope that you don't mind but we've put your pyjamas in the case too. We tend not to have a need for second hand sleeping clothes."

And we both giggled – really, Avril actually had a little laugh at the thought. So, there I was with four pairs of pyjamas and a case which probably cost more than Dave had paid me all season – not that he had paid me much so far!

There were lots of hugs from Ruth and Margaret and a handshake from Piero and Dr. Sweeney. Avril even managed something which looked a bit like another real smile.

Margaret promised that she would write to me and I promised that I would see her again. It was the sort of promise I made to clients all the time – honest and well intended at the time but with the knowledge that things change.

The security guys helped me into their rib and I had to suppress a chuckle when I saw that they had tucked their machine guns away under some anoraks. I wouldn't have noticed except that there was the black metal handle of one just sticking out a bit. I hoped that it wasn't choppy on the way back in case the gun went off and shot us all. Woohoo! The mad bit of my brain was in full working order again!

As the rib climbed up on to the plane, and we started to accelerate away from The Appian Way, I had a real mixture of feelings. Living on a Superyacht with a billionaire had been wonderful and those magical, soft, silk, purple pyjamas were a lot better than an old t-shirt to sleep in. But swimming with a boat full of guards wasn't as good as skinny dipping with clients or a beach barbecue.

You swapped one thing for another in life because you couldn't have both and it wasn't clear which was best, it wasn't clear at all.

Now, it was time to get back to being a Hostie, sort out the mess that the guys had definitely got themselves in - and to see Luke.

13

All Change At This Port

SAILING changed my life in so many ways – and all of them good. More than anything else, it taught me to look and listen – to the wind, the waves and what was happening around me. That's why when I saw Mike waiting by the ferry ramp, I knew straight away that something wasn't right.

He caught the mooring line thrown by one of the security guys and tied it to a ring. Then the guard passed him a second line from the stern and Mike pulled the rib tight against the harbour wall. I thanked them for the lift and Mike helped me up because the wall was a good height above the rib's hull.

He cast off the lines and we waved to the two Russians on the rib as it accelerated away.

I did get a hug but it was so short and distant that it wasn't worth having.

So far, Mike hadn't said a word. When he did, it was in a voice I hadn't heard him use before.

"Rache, I'm so glad to see you back – I really am – but a lot has happened in four days and I need to talk to you before you see Dave."

My first thought was for Luke – had there been an accident or problem with the boat?

"Is Luke okay? Mike tell me."

"Yes, he's fine. He got in earlier today and since then he's been going crazy waiting for you to come back. For both of your sakes, I need to see you on your own and then let you talk to Dave before you and Luke get together.

"I know that this sounds as if I am being a total bastard but believe me Rache, it's for the best – honestly it is.

"Let's go and talk on Brizo and then we'll see Dave."

Brizo was moored further down the harbour and I should have been desperate to go aboard her but, as Mike and I walked in silence, I wasn't.

Mike led the way into the cabin and the first thing I noticed was that it was tidy, and there was no sign of MG's normal mess.

Mike said, "Sit down, Rache, and let me get you an orange or something because this isn't going to be easy."

He opened the fridge, poured two glasses of orange juice for us, and sat down.

I spoke first – hesitantly, "Mike, where's MG's stuff?"

He took a sip at his orange juice and said, "Well, I might as well start with MG and get that bit over.

"Okay, MG isn't here. He left and got a job on that Austrian bloke's ocean racer. Carl Heinz has been on to him for months so MG went two days ago.

"You know Rache, he thought the world of you, he really did. He would have laid his life down for you - and he nearly did.

"When he saw that the guys from The Appian Way had you in their rib, he did no more than charge across in our inflatable like the SAS. But before he could get there, the second rib cut across him and bang, they had him on the floor with a pistol in his face.

"I thought that was it - MG was going to kick off like he always does and they're going to kill him. Thank God common sense took over and he lay still.

"When the security blokes saw that you were on The Appian Way, they said something like 'Fuck off and count yourself lucky' in Russian and chucked him back in the inflatable and took off. I couldn't believe how we'd got away with it because I was certain that we were both going to get killed.

"The next thing we know, a legal deputation came across from Bianchi and they were all smiles and apologies. Look, it had all been a terrible mis-understanding, Miss Lamb is 100% fine, and everyone is so, so sorry. How about if we give you £50k a piece and you sign this confidentiality contract saying that nothing happened?

"I looked at MG and we both thought the same thing. Look, we could either be totally pissed off with everything, and try to sell the story to some newspaper or other, or we could take the £50,000 just for doing nothing - and with no chance of meeting some Russian late one night wanting a quiet word with us.

"You were okay, no-one had been hurt and £50k, tax free, is a lot of money so we signed. Like I said, £50,000 is an awful lot of money.

"When we were sorted out, Bianchi's lot went to see Dave. They said they realised that all the fuss had caused Dave a lot of inconvenience so how about £50k for him too? Sign here, here and here now - or the offer's withdrawn immediately and watch out for our lawyers if you step a millimetre out of line.

"You know how long Dave took to decide that.

"Then the woman, Avril I think her name was, says, 'We know how important Miss Lamb is to your company but Mr. Bianchi has invited her to stay with him for a few days so how about £50,000 a day to find a replacement?'

"Dave couldn't wait to sign up for that one either."

I was shocked. I had been sold like some slave girl with no thought for how I felt. No wonder they had wanted me to stay on The Appian Way!

I sat in total silence for a long time. And then, in a quiet voice, I asked: "What happened next?"

"What happened next is shit - absolute shit - but don't take it personally Rache. It was nothing to do with you - it's just the hand of cards we've been dealt.

"Me and Dave had a meeting, like we used to do in the old days when we had a big company. I had £50,000 and he did too. Bianchi wanted you with him for another two days so that was going to be £200K for the four days – and we needed that money. With the money you brought in, and our two £50ks, we had £300,000."

I choked back the tears. Mike and Dave didn't care about me – I was just a £50,000 a day cheque. For all they cared, I could have been dead or alive just as long as the money was coming in. Mike didn't even see how hurt I was.

"The same day as he signed the agreement with Bianchi's lot, Dave was on the phone to the banks and yacht manufacturers. The bottom line is that a Qatari bank is going to loan us another £650,000 and now Dave's talking to the boat manufacturers who want to get rid of their old stock. The boats are a couple of years old but brand-new and perfect for charter. All the Servals will go and so, next year, we'll have fifteen new boats and we'll be back in the Flotilla business in a serious way.

"This bit is going to hurt Rache but, like I said, don't take it personally. Dave has hired that South African girl who's been looking for a job – the one who's been a manager for a couple of the big sailing companies…"

His voice trailed off because we both knew what that meant for me.

"Look Rache, you're never going to be Hostie long term, you're not. You're too good for that. You've been great for us this year but Delfini will have a new fleet and three, or maybe even more, flots at sea all the time. It isn't going to be like the four of us making things up on the back of envelope and living from hour to hour.

"And you've done okay out of it too. I'll bet old man Bianchi was well pleased that you'd saved his daughter."

I wasn't tearful or anything - just shocked. So, I took a few seconds to answer.

"I didn't take anything off Mr. Bianchi, not a penny. I'm sure I could have, but I didn't. I couldn't take money for saving a little girl's life."

Mike stood up and looked at me with the same hard face I had seen so often when things were messy.

"Then you're stupid. Everyone else has got a drink out of what you did but if you're too full of yourself to make the most of the opportunity, then more fool you.

"Come on, let's go and see Dave."

And with that, he stood up and climbed the cabin steps.

*****

We walked along the harbour in silence. Dave was sat outside Andreas' taverna with a tall, thin girl in her late twenties.

"Well, looking at your face, I guess Mike has told you?"

"Yes, he has. He's also said that there's no place for me next year."

"Look Rache, that sounds bloody awful, as if we don't know what you've done for us this season. But sometimes shit happens and this time it's fallen on you.

"Next year, we'll have a proper fleet again and this means a Base Manager and five Hosties who are right for the job.

"That's why I've hired Khwezi. She knows the tourism business inside out and, with a fleet of new boats for next year, we're going all out to build the business up again."

Khwezi gave me a smile which would have drilled holes in Brizo's hull…

I wanted to say nothing but I couldn't stop myself, "But haven't I, haven't I done a good job this year?" and my voice trailed off.

Dave spoke, "Look Rache, let's cut the crap. There's no-one in the world could have done better than you with what we've had. Mike and me both think that.

"Together, the four of us and Luke, we kept the job afloat when it was impossible. So no-one's saying you've not been bloody brilliant – an absolute star.

"But next year will be completely different. It won't be the four of us patching stuff up and scrounging a bit of credit for diesel or getting welding done on the cheap.

"With a bit of luck, there'll be five skippers, five engineers and five Hosties, and Khwezi will be managing them all. If you were here next year, you'd be working for Khwezi not me. You would be just another one of the Hostess team and you wouldn't stand for that Rachel. You know you wouldn't, and we know you wouldn't. So rather than bugger about and waste everyone's time with a load of bullshit, we'd better just all tell the truth."

And it was the truth. I actually smiled, "Yes, you're right Dave, like you always are. So - what do we do now?"

"Good girl Rache. You always were a good girl - right from the Boat Show. Mike said that you would throw a fit and start wailing and all that crap but I knew you wouldn't. You're too good for that."

"Okay, what now?" I asked again.

"Well, first – and you're going to be amazed at this – I've put £6,000 in your bank account in England. I'm sure that Bianchi has looked after you but we owe you the money so we've paid it. And there's a bonus."

I looked at Mike and my eyes said that I didn't want to hear about what I had taken, or not, from Mr. Bianchi – ever again.

"I'll also get you a ticket back to Manchester as soon as you want to go."

I thanked him for the gesture.

"But Rache, I don't want to part on bad terms. Like I've said, me and Mike think you're great and if things were different we'd have you forever. But they're not and that's it.

"But let's part friends. We're selling all the Servals. They're all in nice condition but the electronics are buggered on Brizo and MG's not going to be fixing them for us. So we've asked to Luke if he'll take her to that American bloke in Lefkas and get her sorted out. If you fancy a last trip in her, you'd be welcome."

I forced another smile. "Yes, I'd like that. Thanks Dave. I'll go and find Luke."

*****

I didn't find Luke. He found me. We didn't say anything, not a single word, for a long time. He just held me tight in his arms and kissed my cheek over and over again.

Then he told me how much he loved me and it was only then that I cried – not soft, girlie sobbing but just big, fat tears of relief and happiness that I was safe in the arms of the man I loved.

We didn't go to Andreas' but walked along the harbour wall and then up the rocky path to the headland which overlooked The Pool - where we had swum together and Luke had showed me how to dive, and I had first felt feelings for him.

The Autumn sun was warm, but not hot, so we sat on two bits of flat rock and just let the soft glow wash over us. I told him everything, and even explained why I didn't ask Mr. Bianchi to bring him to me. Luke balled his fists with frustration and told me, over and over, how much he loved me and how we must never be apart again.

I didn't cry this time – but I nearly did.

*****

That evening, we all ate at Andreas' but it was very strained. In fact, it was so bad that it was funny. Luke and I were the outsiders now and it was very much Dave, Mike and Khwezi who were the team.

I didn't like Khwezi at all. I didn't like her nasal South African accent. I didn't like her forced smile and I didn't like the way she treated us like a couple of Sixth Formers who were on work experience.

She couldn't sail, she couldn't cook - and she had a chest like an ironing board so I'll bet she'd never go skinny dipping. Luke and I had a good laugh at that and felt a lot better.

But there was no arguing that she did know the tourism business inside out so maybe me and Luke were the amateurs at the grown ups' party now.

Things did thaw a bit after some wine and Mike said: "Rache, I've got something for you. MG left you a present. He really did think the world of you and when he found out that you wouldn't be here next year he was gone – like a flash! No Rache at Delfini – no MG."

Mike slid an envelope across to me sealed, as you would expect, with a strip of the silver duct tape MG carried with him everywhere.

There was a scruffy piece of paper with a heart drawn in the centre. In the middle of the heart was an R clip stuck on with another piece of duct tape and underneath was a message.

"In case you ever go swimming in Sivota harbour at night and need a spare R Clip

Lots of love
MG
XXXXX"

I choked back a little tear and said thanks to Mike.

*****

Although Luke was sitting next to me at dinner, and his hand was always touching my thigh, he clearly wasn't all there – and I knew it.

As we started our coffees, he made some silly excuse and disappeared. He was really, really bad at anything which wasn't the absolute truth so I don't know why he didn't just have a big, red flashing light on his head whenever he was telling fibs: then everyone would know straightaway and we could be extra kind to him!

When there was something on his mind, I had learnt just to leave him alone because he was like a baby with wind and he wouldn't settle until he had done a big burp. I just hoped that he wouldn't be sick on me!

He came back in a real state of fussiness, which wasn't like him at all.

"Sorry Rachel, just been helping Andreas' Auntie out with her freezer and arranging things for tomorrow. Are we up for taking Brizo to Lefkas?"

Well, I certainly was. A day sailing with the man I loved wasn't exactly going to be much of a problem.

"Look, I've got to sort some more stuff out so I'll see you first thing in the morning. You're sleeping on Brizo aren't you?"

I confirmed I was.

"Okay, you sleep on Brizo tonight and I'll see you first thing."

My heart sank. To be blunt, I was getting desperate to wake up next to Luke. It wasn't just the sex, although I was aching for this, but more to feel him next to me, to touch his skin and smell his scent and just be near him.

But this was Luke – and it was driving me crazy! If he didn't do something soon, I was going to bash him on the head with a fender and drag him unconscious into Brizo's forepeak!

But there was even worse to come.

"Rachel, when we get to Lefkas, can you sleep on Brizo again? I've got to go Risto's and it'll be late when I've finished so I'll doss down there and see you in the morning."

Oh, bloody, bloody, bloody great! What the bloody, bloody, bloody hell was wrong with this man? Did he fancy me or not?

"Okay, if that's what you want…"

"No, it's not what I want exactly but it'll be the best because there are things I've got to do and, and sort out and things. Come on Rachel, you understand…"

But I didn't understand. Not even a little bit. I knew what I wanted and I knew that I wasn't going to get it until Luke was good and ready – no matter if I got undressed and chased him down the harbour wall naked.

I let out an enormous sigh - and then had an idea. If I wasn't going to get what I actually wanted then I could at least get a consolation prize.

I got my phone out and had a quick look on Poseidon. The forecast was good for tomorrow – a top end, easterly 3 in the morning running into a strong 4 later. It couldn't be better weather for a sail.

"Luke, this will be my last trip in Brizo so why don't we sail her round the outside of Lefkada? Let's leave just before dawn and then sail past Cape Ducato and come down into Lefkas through the Canal.

"Let's do it Luke. I'd really like that."

"You're mad! I'll have to be up in the middle of the night but if that's what you want, and you'll helm her while I have a sleep, then yes, let's do it.

"How about 6.30 on the dock? There'll be just enough light and then we can have a good sail to Lefkas and get Brizo on the pontoon in plenty of time for Byron, that American guy, to sort out the electronics."

✶✶✶✶✶

It was strange sleeping on Brizo all on my own and, although I never would have thought it at the start of the year, a bit lonely. There was no rumbling and snoring from MG and none of those noises from the dog kennel in the back. I could get undressed in the cabin and slide into my space as slowly as I wished with no-one in the way. One life had come to an end and I didn't know what was in the future.

I was so glad to hear the familiar slap of the waves on the hull and without these I don't think that I would have got off to sleep at all.

Because I had insisted on an early start, I actually used the alarm on my phone. That would have been all. Hey Luke, let's go for a dawn sail. Oh, I forgot and I'm still in bed.

I started the engine to get some hot water for later but just sloshed my face with some cold water in the sink. After all, I wasn't exactly going to be close to Luke today!

It was a good job I was up because he was early – all smiles and a big kiss! Grrrrr. I should have had that already, when he woke up next to me!

"Okay Captain, ready when you are…"

Getting ready to sail, I felt totally at home. It had been a wonderful seven months and now I was sailing my favourite boat in the whole wide world with the man I loved to bits. It might have been a lonely night but life was good.

"Cast off please Luke."

He slipped the starboard mooring line and then the port one, and Brizo eased forward on her anchor chain.

"Okay, anchor please…"

In the grey, pre-dawn light I could hardly see Brizo's bow as she slowly edged through the water. I listened to the noise of the anchor chain, checking that it was running smoothly – it was. The anchor finally made a satisfying clonk as it located on the bow.

Then I put the gearbox into forward and gave the motor just a fraction of throttle. Brizo crept steadily forward and we eased away from Tychos for the last time.

Was I sad or even weepy? No, not really. Helming the boat helped because I wasn't a good enough sailor not to have to concentrate totally on what I was doing. I watched Luke stowing the fenders and coiling the mooring lines and knew that I had all that I wanted – well, nearly everything - and if Dave was achieving his dreams then he could get on with them without me. For sure, he was right – I would never have worked for Khwezi – not ever, not even if a herd of polar bears had set up camp outside Andreas' taverna!

I eased Brizo down the passage and past The Pool. That bit did make me take a second breath!

Then, ahead of us, was the open sea - like Homer said 2,700 years ago, a wine dark purple at this time in the morning.

I looked across at Luke. "Ready?"

"Yes, good to go."

There was no need for discussion or explanation. We were one and it was wonderful.

"Headsail first?"

"Yes please," I answered and brought Brizo head to wind.

Luke waited until she had come to a complete halt and then hauled out the Genoa.

I held Brizo into the wind with just the slightest touch of throttle.

Luke glanced at me and I nodded. That was all: words were unnecessary.

He pulled at the mainsail outhaul and then made his way to the foot of the mast and engaged the ratchet.

The sails flapped impatiently, waiting to be released. I knew what was coming next. Since that very first time when Mike had let me take the helm, I had been in love with the wind breathing life into the boat.

I put the engine into neutral and centred the throttle on tickover. Then, gently and respectfully, I turned the wheel to port and the sails filled with the easterly breeze. Even in the half light, I could see their graceful arc and feel their eagerness to drive us along. This was the magic of sailing and the alchemy was all the more powerful in the lilac grey of the nascent sunrise.

Half an hour later the sun was a fiery red ball, more like a sunset than a sunrise, as it forced its way up and over the mountains of Kalamos. The rays lit each wave crest so that instead of being white they were a slash of red against the purple and blue black of the waves.

In this enchanted world, if a unicorn had come galloping across the sea

I wouldn't have been a bit surprised. Dave and Mike I could do without - but the Ionian would be calling me back for the rest of my life.

We turned north-west round Cape Ducato and I set Brizo on a long tack out to sea. With the electronics dead, there was no auto pilot and really, I didn't want one. I braced my left leg against the cockpit seat and let Brizo heel over in the wind, balancing her with the rudder. It was another spiritual experience.

Luke came up from the galley with a couple of coffees and a plate of cream filled Bougatsas which Andreas' Auntie had made. Wow, they made cat biscuits look a bit ordinary – even when they had my special noses!

Luke sat on the windward side of the cockpit and balanced the plate of Bougatsas. We said hardly anything at all – and didn't need to. Words can't improve on perfection and I was perfectly happy.

The light had picked up by the time we were passing Porto Katsiki. Once one of the most visited beaches in Europe, it was all but destroyed in the earthquake of 2015 but the Greeks soon got it back in business.

I held Brizo on the same tack, past Sesoula Rock and out to sea. This bit of the Ionian can get sparky but I just felt so good about Brizo, Luke and me that I wanted to sail forever and never come back to land. On the right day, sailing can get you like that.

Luke lay down on the cockpit seat with a couple of cushions from MG's cabin as a pillow. Brave boy – I hoped that he didn't catch anything! I looked at him as he slept and felt even more in love.

Without electronics, there was no way for an amateur sailor like me to accurately judge distances but I guess that we were doing five or six knots and so we must have been a good ten or twelve miles out to sea when I kicked Luke – fairly gently though because I was in bare feet.

"Come on crew, get yourself up! We're ready to go about."

He rubbed his eyes and stretched. "I can't. I need the loo. If I don't I'll wet myself."

I loved the intimacy of our relationship where, not only were we in love, we were also really good friends and didn't have to hide anything from each other.

I giggled again, "Well Baby Luke, if you wet yourself then I'll have to put you on my knee and change your little boy knickers…"

"Ooohhh. Promises, promises...

"Come to think of it, I'd rather stay dry."

I did my best skipper's glare and said: "Come on, concentrate – otherwise we'll never get to Lefkas."

Luke freed the Genoa sheets from the cleats and held them, one in each hand. He was laughing because he knew what was coming next. I never used the correct language for going about but instead had a hybrid one I'd made up. Luke found it hilarious.

First, I had good look round as I had been taught. Mike had been strict but he was one heck of teacher. There was no other boat, or marker buoy, in sight.

"Ready about in three, two, one?"

Luke nodded.

"Ready about…"

I spun the wheel hard to starboard and Luke eased the Genoa over, helping it shift sides with the leeward sheet. The mainsail followed without Luke's help and, in a few seconds, we were on a north-easterly tack heading for the long, sandy beaches which run round the edge of Lefkas Town. It was a lovely thing to do with Luke. Two people working in complete harmony – neither one more nor less important than the other: simple, beautiful and just so satisfying.

About three miles off the entry to the Lefkas Canal, I brought Brizo head to wind and Luke stowed the sails. I was glad he was so much stronger than me because the wind had picked up now and getting the mainsail in took more strength than I had without constantly using the winch.

As we motored in it was getting bumpy, with the 4 more of a 5, and I was glad that we had set off early and enjoyed the best of the weather. We'd been sailing six hours now and I hoped to catch the 14.00 opening of the bridge.

I'd sailed through the Canal lots of times with clients but this trip was special. I was with Luke but also I didn't know when, or if, I would ever do it again. I remembered the first time I had rattled over the ridges on the bridge with Mike - in the van, with my eyes as wide as saucers and my mind bursting at the thought of what was waiting for me.

If I had known the future, would I have stayed? Yes, for 100% certain. I thought of all the things I had done and I was still here – and my Dad's €1000 was still tucked away in my kitbag. I could have given up loads of times, but I hadn't, and now I was taking Brizo through the Canal with my lovely Luke.

The bridge actually floats like a ship so that Lefkada is, strictly speaking, still an island and gets loads of grants for being isolated from the mainland. On the hour, during daylight, it swings back and allows boat traffic to enter and leave the Canal.

Getting into the Canal from the seaward side always needed a bit of thought because the dredged channel is quite narrow and in summer it gets packed with yachts, like kids queuing to see Santa!

Today, there was only us so I held Brizo just off the beach, at the northern end of the harbour wall, until five minutes before the opening and then motored straight up just before the hooter sounded.

The bridge swung open as we arrived - as if the Queen was coming through - and we were in the Canal.

Luke phoned Byron, and got directions to the pier we were to moor at, so that I could take us straight to our berth. The marina at Lefkas is always packed with boats and now, at the end of the season, it was really jammed.

Waiting on the pier was Byron, an ex-American Navy techie who had been stationed at Souda Bay, in Crete, and then fallen in love with the Greek way of life - and couldn't face going back home to the cold of Oregon.

We moored at one of the lazy lines, Byron caught our stern lines first time and that was that. We were here.

Luke briefed Byron on the problems. This was easy. Nothing was working. Byron stroked his beard and made some techie noises, which no-one ever understands except another techie, and said we should come back tomorrow.

I was about to say that I was staying on board overnight but then Luke spoke - and he had that lovely cheeky grin I loved so much.

"Do you want to sleep on Brizo? You can if you want, but there might be another place you can doss down for the night…"

I looked puzzled after he had been so keen to fix all the plans when we were still at Tychos.

"Grab your bag then."

The last bit was easy. I had my wash bag, obviously with my precious minty gel and toothbrush, a pair of knickers, a towel and a spare top, in case I'd got wet. They were in a really sexy €5 bag from the cheap shop near the bank in Nydri. Oh yes, move over Mr. Bianchi!

We walked along the pier and out through the hotel lobby. By the main door, there is a little bay for taxis. One was waiting there.

Luke opened the car door and bowed low, "Your carriage awaits Racherella…"

I got in, wondering what was going on.

The driver opened the boot and Luke put the big kit bag carefully in the back.

"Luke, we can't afford this. Don't be silly. Ring Risto and ask him to send one of the guys with the van."

"Ah, Princess Racherella…Who said we were going to Risto's?"

"Luke, what's happening? What are you doing? Stop winding me up."

Luke put his finger to his lips.

"I have sworn a vow of secrecy. If I reveal what is going to happen next,

186

you will turn into a pumpkin or something like that any way – maybe a box of baklava or something else sticky and soggy.

"Anyway, something not very nice will happen to you. Probably - definitely it will, so you'll just have to be silent for a little while – and I know how hard that will be!"

We left the marina and followed the ring road round Lefkas, past the really nice supermarket on the right where I had shopped so often, and then took a left at the cross roads and out towards Nydri.

Risto's yard was as busy as ever and then we climbed the coast road after Ligia and suddenly, in the best Greek fashion, the driver swung right into the mountains, without any warning.

"Luke, what are we doing? Luke, tell me please. Please…"

"No. Can't. My bosses in MI6 would shoot me and then you'd never see me again. I'm on a top secret mission and I can't reveal a thing."

"Oooohhh Luke. You're a meanie. Tell me. Please…"

"No. And if you keep pestering I'm sending you back to Brizo."

We drove on for another couple of miles and then, on a tight right-hand hairpin, the taxi swung off to the left and on to the drive of the Hesperides - the most exclusive hotel on Lefkada. It was a place so posh that I barely even dared look at it when we were sailing towards Lefkas from Nydri, for fear of being arrested!

Luke said: "We're here."

And for once I didn't say a word.

Luke paid the taxi driver and we walked to the reception, past the marble fountains and the immaculate gardens - and me in worn out shorts, flip flops falling apart and a faded shirt - looking just like a Hostie who had been sailing all day!

The receptionist leapt up when he saw Luke. "Mr. Bickerton, a pleasure to see you. Everything is ready so please let me show you directly to your room."

We walked along the polished marble corridors and, at the very end, the receptionist opened the door and then stood back.

"If there is anything I can do to help Mr. Bickerton, please let me know."

The room was massive, with an immense balcony looking out over the Ionian and away to Kalamos in the far distance.

On the bed was a huge bunch of flowers with a hand written welcome card.

Luke took my bags and laid them on the table.

"Would you mind sharing with me tonight, Rachel?"

*****

If I live to be a hundred years old, what happened next will still be the worst thing ever – the absolute, total, complete baddest five minutes which could ever possibly happen to me: ever!

Luke took my head gently in his two hands and lifted my lips towards his. Then he kissed me, with long, firm kisses which told me how much he loved me and what he wanted to happen next. He kissed me for a long time and it's a wonder my legs just didn't give way and leave me in a heap on the floor looking up and wondering just how lucky I could be.

Then, he reached down and began to lift my shirt, with one hand on each side – and I screamed!

And that wasn't the worst bit. What followed next was even better.

First, I pushed his hands off my shirt and then I pulled it down tight around my waist. At the same time as I screamed, again, "No, you can't Luke, you can't!"

Luke stared at me completely freaked out – upset, confused and more than a bit frightened.

"But Rachel, I thought, after all this time, and how we feel about each other, I thought..."

But I interrupted him with an even bigger bash on his head, this time with the anchor off The Appian Way.

"No Luke, it's not you – it's not you at all. It's MG!"

Now Luke was horrified – just as if he had picked up a bomb and it had gone off in hands – or probably inside his head.

"What? You and MG? You've been doing it all this time and I didn't know?"

The knife was in his heart and I was twisting it round and round at the same time as pushing it deeper.

I grabbed his hands and held them tight in case he ran off.

"No Luke, it's not like that at all."

And I began properly crying, with great big sobs soaking my cheeks.

"It's not like that – not at all. I have waited so long to be with you like this and I wanted it to be so special.

"I've dreamed about looking lovely for you and you being glad that we were together and I wanted everything to be perfect and, and - and MG boiled my knickers and bras with his shorts and they're blue now and all horrible and I'm wearing them and they're terrible and I'm rubbish and..."

But I couldn't say another word for crying.

Luke took my head again and he kissed me on my wet, salty lips.

Then he laughed gently.

"Are they really blue? Come on, let me see."

The tears wouldn't stop but a funny sort of giggle came to me too. How could anyone be loved as much as Luke loved me?

I held my arms up as he lifted my shirt and then he paused, looking at me. I hung my head desperate for Luke to want me – and then he kissed me once more but now with more passion than I had ever felt.

He didn't speak but reached around my back and slowly and gently undressed me.

Then he began kissing me. Tiny, affectionate kisses along the nape of my neck, my lips and down. Luke kissed me slowly and patiently – each kiss was subtly different and he made every single one matter to me as if it were the first, and last, kiss for both of us.

He slipped off the rest of my clothes and then picked me up in his arms and carried me to the bed, our bed.

As I lay there, he continued kissing me until I was wrapped in the warmest, most intimate blanket of love.

Then he undressed and we made love. It was perfect and all that I had ever dreamed of – the two of us as one, loving each other and being loved.

Afterwards I cuddled up close to him and, with my head on his chest and his arm wrapped round my neck, I went to sleep.

*****

When I woke up, Luke was still there. I had wriggled on to my side somehow and so now he was close up against my back. I could feel him there and it was wonderful.

I went to get a shower and wash off the salt stickiness of the day's sailing. The bathroom was fantastic and, if I hadn't experienced The Appian Way, I would have believed that it had the best shower in the world. Well, it was still the second best shower anywhere!

There was no Chanel soap but there was a really nice cream coloured one which was soft and smelt lovely. If I hadn't used Chanel I would have given full marks to the Hesperides' soap.

I had a really long shower, washed my hair and then dried it with one of the great big, fluffy white towels.

Before I opened the bathroom door, I paused for a couple of seconds because I wanted Luke to see me naked - and I was desperate for him to be pleased with what he saw.

I wasn't disappointed.

"My God, Rachel – you look absolutely incredible. Truly, you are the most wonderful, beautiful woman in the world – and I love you."

Wow! Had I got the lucky lottery ticket or what?

Luke had arranged my clothes on the long seat next to the dressing table. There were all my non-MG'd undies and my Asos dress. Even the knickers were immaculately pressed so I knew that Alissa had been on this job!

I bent over to choose what to wear for the rest of the day and I sensed Luke behind me before he even touched my bottom. Then he did - and I thought that two showers in one afternoon would be great!

This time, there was a change of mood. If I had been desperate to be with Luke, well now I was sure he had been feeling exactly the same way about me! He wasn't rough but he was passionate in a way that no-one who didn't know him really well would ever believe he could be.

This time, Luke went to the shower and I lay back, wet with sweat and knowing what making love really meant.

*****

Surprisingly, incredibly is probably more truthful, we both managed to get showered – and dressed – although it was a close run thing! Luke couldn't stop looking at me and for the first time in my life I wanted a man to be undressing me with his eyes – but only this man.

I got dressed carefully and put my leather barette in just the right place. I think that I have nice brown hair and its colour matched the leather of the barette, just as if they had been made for each other.

Luke was in his smart shorts, and an Alissa shirt, but I sensed a change in his mood - and I was right.

"Rachel, I've got a table booked for dinner and I hope that you will like it. But, before we eat, there's something I want to show you. Is that okay?"

I didn't quite shrug my shoulders because if Luke had just asked me to stick a banana in my ear I wouldn't have been concerned: I just wanted to be with him every second, of every minute, of every day – for the rest of my life.

Luke had a quick conversation on the hotel phone and then said: "Come on. It'll only take five minutes and you might be interested."

We walked down the marble corridors hand in hand and I was so happy. When we reached the reception desk, the guy on duty said: "The key's in the car Luke, just park it in the same place when you've finished and drop the keys back with me."

Luke thanked him and we walked past the fountain and to the car park. There was a little red Nissan at the end of one of the rows.

My lovely man swung the passenger door open for me. That was a nice thing to do and very Luke.

"It's only a couple of miles, but there is something I want to show you."

190

I put my hand on his thigh and couldn't have cared less whether we drove for a minute or a year.

We worked our way up the mountain for a few miles and then Luke turned off onto a stony path. He eased the Nissan down it very slowly because there were big rocks sticking up everywhere.

After about half a mile, the road flattened out and we came to an old house – not quite derelict but very nearly.

Luke said: "Come on Rachel, let me show you."

We got out and Luke took my hand as we walked to the front of the house. There was a palm covered area outside, and below was a small, grassed field next to a badly neglected olive grove. I'm no good at sizes but it was smaller than our school playing fields – maybe as big as four football pitches.

"What do you think?"

My first thought was not the small, run down house or the weeds but the view: it was spectacular looking south east, right across the Ionian to Kalamos and Mitikas, if you could see that far.

"Wow Luke, what a place! This could be incredible if it was done up properly."

Luke took my hand. "It could be Rachel. It belongs to Petros who owns the Hesperides. He said that if I will manage all the hotel maintenance for him then we can have it for €30,000 – and that's nothing. Together, we've nearly got that now.

"You can forget Delfini and we can live here. You can get a qualification for teaching English and it'll be great forever."

I gave Luke a huge hug and put my arms around him.

"Oh, I love you Luke, and wherever you want to be I'll be there with you. I don't care if you live at the North Pole - I'll be your Eskimo. But, if you want the truth, this is not what I want.

"You've seen Dave and Mike and that guy Matt, who parks the boats on the Three Palms' dock. They're stuck in Lefkada for life. They can't do anything but sail and live in Greece and I want something more. I don't want to be re-living the same thing over and over again, every year for the rest of my life.

"But if this is what you want, then I'm going to be with you. Not even a hurricane is ever going to separate me from you, I love you so much."

He put his arms around my waist and hugged me tight against him. Through my dress, I could feel what he was thinking - and without any doubt!

"Rachel, you are the most wonderful, beautiful, loving person in the world and I would give my life for you every day.

"If you won't be happy here, then I won't be, and where you go I will so we're going to work something out together."

And we got back into the car.

*****

We were a little bit late for dinner - but the third shower of the day was great...

14

Worth a Phone Call?

IT'S no wonder that the Hesperides had the reputation for being the best hotel in Lefkada. They were really used to having celebs stay there and how they treated Luke was incredible, as if he was Royalty or a rock star.

The receptionist guy had a girl assistant, a bit polished and gleaming teeth for me - but with a nice enough smile. She took us through the dining area and there, right at the end, were some white cloth screens with pictures of yachts sailing across them. She pulled back one of the screens and showed us our table. Wow! It was amazing. They had opened the French windows right back so, although we were nice and warm inside the restaurant, we had a perfect, unobstructed view out over the Ionian.

"Your table, Mr. Bickerton..."

"Oh Luke, this is wonderful – absolutely incredible. But you shouldn't have spent all this money. I would have been just as happy in that little Italian Taverna on the dock front at Lefkas and we would have been fine on Brizo.

"You're a bad man Luke Bickerton, you really are."

Luke smiled. "I'm sorry, I can't pretend with you: I love you too much. I've not paid for anything, really I've not. Not the room, or the flowers or the meal or anything. It's all free."

"How? How did you get all this for nothing?"

"Well, you remember that time in August, when it was ten million degrees, and I didn't see you for three days?"

I nodded.

"Petros had a major problem with the chlorination system in the swimming pool. The pumps were giving trouble too. It was seriously bad and the clients would have gone crazy having paid top money and then not being able to swim in the pool.

"His Greek guy was up to his ears with other jobs so I worked all through the night on changeover day, and then for most of the next day down in the pump room next to the pool. It was like a furnace, and the chlorine was making me throw up, but I sorted it all out.

"Petros paid me very well but he was more than a bit grateful for me getting him out what was a real mess so he said if I never needed a room, to let him know and he'd do something special for me and everything would be on the house

"When I found out that we were going to take Brizo to Lefkas Marina that's when I disappeared and started fixing things up. I rang Petros and said could I please have the room because I was going to be in Lefkas with the woman I was going to marry and I was desperate for her to have a wonderful time."

I cut in, "What did you just say – about going to marry someone?"

"Oh yes, I thought I'd better mention that to you too. We're going to get married and live together happily ever after. It'll be great. You'll really enjoy it."

"But you're supposed to ask me on one knee and everything. I might not want to marry you. I might fancy someone else more than you – someone who can sail and dive and mend swimming pools and things like that."

"Okay. Rachel Lamb, will you marry me? Or would you rather me take you back to Brizo now and you can sleep in the forepeak, where you belong?"

I giggled, "Oh go on then, I'll marry you just this once – but only because I want to stay here."

And Luke held my hands in his. "There will only ever be once, Rachel Lamb, because we will be together forever and ever…" and he leaned across the table and kissed me.

I would have had another sniffle - but it had taken me ages to put on my Estée Lauder mascara and I didn't want to smudge it.

*****

Petros came to the table and said, "Well, have you asked her?"

Luke grinned and said: "Yes, and she said she would - but only because she wants to stay here for the night and she can't find anyone better."

Petros clapped, "Yes! Congratulations to you both – you are a lovely couple and deserve each other."

Then he glanced towards the screen and an immaculate waiter appeared from nowhere with a bottle of champagne in a polished ice bucket.

One of those mad thoughts which invade my brain galloped into view. I just can't stop them, no matter how hard I try. What would have happened if I had said no? The champagne was already open so would Luke have had to pay for it or perhaps the staff would have all had a drink?

If Luke knew what went on in my head he would never, ever want to marry me!

The waiter poured two glasses of the French champagne, better even than the stuff we had won in the Sivota bet, then Petros left and we were on our own.

Luke said, "I haven't got an engagement ring for you yet but I do have a bit of a pressie. It was given to me, but it's not quite my style so perhaps you might like it?"

I smiled and got a real tickle in my tummy at the thought of what might be coming next.

"Okay, shut your eyes tight and no peeking. Now, hold out your hands and make sure that the cheap plastic bag it's in doesn't stick to them..."

I shut my eyes, tightly too, and then put my hands, one over the other, on the table.

It's difficult to describe what I felt next. It was quite heavy and hard, like a stainless steel nut, but at the same time soft and warm. There was more weight in the centre of my hands and less towards the edges.

"Okay, open your eyes..."

I did – and there, on my hands, sat the necklace Mr. Bianchi had offered to me - and I had refused. It gleamed gently in the warm, evening sunset and as the diamonds caught the light from the ceiling they reflected it back in tiny, fiery showers. Truly, it was the most beautiful thing I had ever seen.

All that I could say was, "Luke..."

"I know what you're going to say and Mr. Bianchi warned me what was going to happen but it's not a present from him – it's from me. He gave me the necklace and I tried it on but it didn't suit me at all. So I thought, maybe Rachel will wear it for knocking about in just until she gets something decent."

This time I did have a little cry - and got mascara all over the starched, white napkins.

"Would you wear it for me? Please?"

And I did my best Cabbage Patch doll nod.

Luke got up and came to my side of the table. First, he put the necklace on to the front of my neck, lifted up my hair, and kissed me very softly and gently. Then he closed the clasp at the back and kissed me again.

The necklace sat beautifully filling the space above my dress perfectly. It was heavier than anything else I had ever worn but felt so utterly and completely natural, as if it been there all my life.

Throughout the meal, I kept on touching it in case it evaporated and I never saw it again.

*****

The meal was wonderful and Petros popped in at the end for a chat. Having the owner of such a posh place coming to see us was nice and made me feel very special. Wow! Luke was worshipped here!

We walked slowly back to our room, with Luke's hand around my waist. I took the necklace off and laid it on the dressing table. For a long time I just looked at it, and occasionally touched the golden flowers, wondering at its perfect beauty.

But then we got undressed…

*****

The following morning we had breakfast, unbelievably in the private area again. I really was beginning to feel like a princess.

During the night, I had been thinking. I told Luke and he said: "Yes, I spent a lot of the night thinking too – but you were fast asleep!"

"Oh, you cheeky boy! Not thinking just about that – although I have, a lot! No, I've been thinking about something different. Mr. Bianchi seemed to like me a bit…"

Luke interrupted me, "You're mad Rachel, completely bonkers. He thinks you're wonderful."

"Well, he said some nice things about me and said if I ever wanted to talk to him about a job then to ring him. I said I couldn't because I didn't want to let Dave down but he still gave me his personal number and I put it in my phone.

"But… after what's happened with Delfini…"

"Luke, what do you think? Should I phone him?"

I liked Luke taking my hands in his and this is what he did now. "Rachel, you just don't realise who, or what, you are. Mr. Bianchi couldn't stop praising you – he thinks you're unique.

"I do too.

"Of course you should phone him. You don't want a quiet time in Lefkada so you've got to get life heeled over and see if you can handle it."

"But I don't want anything without you…"

"Let's worry about that when it happens. Yes, give Mr. Bianchi a ring and at least you can hear what he has to say."

*****

I counted the rings. One. Two. Three. Four and then Piero's voice. "Good morning Rachel White Tail. How are you today?" I could hear him smiling down the phone.

I didn't know what to say so I just said what was on my mind. "Good morning Mr. Bianchi, I mean, Piero. How's Maggie?"

196

"She's fine – but she keeps talking about you. You really made an impression on her."

"Please tell her that I look at her picture every day and it makes me very happy," that sounded a bit stiff and formal but it was true and what I meant.

Piero replied: "I will Rachel. I will, and thank you for being so thoughtful. But is there something else I can help with?"

"Yes, thank you so much for the necklace and thank you for giving it to Luke for me. I wore it at dinner last night and it was very beautiful – the most beautiful thing I have ever seen in my life."

There was a slight pause. "I am so pleased that you decided to wear it. Ruth and I were nearly offended that you wouldn't have it directly from us but then I explained to her that you were a special person and she understood.

"And is there anything else?"

I was stuck for words – embarrassed I suppose because no-one had ever actually offered me a job before without me applying for it.

"Well, you mentioned that, perhaps, you might have something I could do for you? Like a job?"

"No Rachel, not like a job – but, actually a job. I want you to work for me – directly for me and for no-one else in my organisation – do you remember?"

I answered quietly that I did.

"Rachel, please stay on the line for a moment. I'll be a couple of minutes but please don't go away."

I raised my eyebrows to Luke and we played a game of chase around the flowers on the table with the sugar bowl and milk jug. In the background, I could hear Piero speaking quickly – shifting to and fro between English and Italian.

"Okay Rachel, everything is sorted out. A car will pick you up at two o'clock and take you to Preveza. The Gulfstream will be there and then we can meet this evening for dinner.

"Could you please ask Luke if he would come with you?"

My mouth went dry. "Well yes, but what about Brizo and my things on Tychos and our passports?"

Piero's tone changed instantly. Now it was the flat, calm but unequivocal voice I had heard him use in meetings on The Appian Way.

"Look Rachel, I am prepared to try to see the world through your eyes because I want your special way of looking at things so much. But I'm not prepared to discuss trivial things.

"Do you want to be on the Gulfstream or not? Decide now and we can then go forward - or not. It's your choice." The tone of his voice made it clear exactly what his words meant.

I gulped. "I'm sorry Piero – really sorry. Yes, I – we – will be ready at two o'clock."

"Thank you Rachel. You are learning at the speed I knew you could and would. We will work well together.

"Everything, including your passports, and your Madonna from Brizo, will be at Preveza when you arrive.

"I'll see you and Luke for dinner this evening."

I gulped again - and the phone went dead.

Wow!

*****

We were waiting in the hotel lobby nice and early – really excited but more than a bit apprehensive. Luke was holding my hand and I was so glad he was beside me.

"This is going to be great, Rachel – what an adventure. I can't wait."

I smiled – but in my head, I was getting ready to climb some more big mountains!

I was thrilled at what was ahead too but filled with so many powerful memories of this season. Would I ever see the Ionian again – the places I knew so well, the winds I had come to love and the waves which were so much a part of me? Could I let go of everything which had changed me and still be who I was now? Maybe it would be all too much.

Luke sensed my tension and gave me a big cuddle – and I felt better.

Then my phone rang. It was a number I didn't know. My first thought was that it was Mr. Bianchi, saying that he had changed his mind and I had better start looking for a job as a cat nose icer. That cleared my head and got rid of any doubts I had about working with Piero. I really did want this job – whatever it was!

It was Avril. Oh God, I was right. I had been sacked before I had even started!

"Hello Rachel. It's Avril. How are you?" There was almost a hint of a smile in her voice. Wow again! She must have had a bowl of niceness muesli this morning – either that or she'd just finished beating someone up and was enjoying wiping their blood off her knuckles.

I waffled a bit and made some non-conversation and then Avril said: "Rachel, we need your advice. We've just bought a little yacht – it's a Serval 34 called Brizo. I believe you might know it?"

I was stunned – just as if some big Russian security guy had given me a good kick and I knew exactly how that felt!

"Yes, I know her very well – she's a lovely boat."

"Well, Mr. Bianchi thought that someone on our team might like to sail in it next year but he wants the boat sorting out properly so that it is ready to use. Who would you recommend?"

I knew that she was playing with me but I sensed not in a nasty way. Brizo was worth £60,000 - an impossibly large sum for me but for Mr. Bianchi it was the equivalent of a cup of coffee – probably not a full one either. It was a nice gesture, almost playful and very subtle. Piero had read my mind as if he was inside it and what he had done was very clever and very reassuring. I wasn't going to lose everything which had come to mean so much to me – not sailing, the Ionian or even Brizo – and this made me feel so much better about the future.

*****

The Mercedes taxi arrived and we sat in the back together – not cuddling but close. We followed the tight hairpin bends, like coming back from Karya after the party or leaving Porto Katsiki that time when Julie and Stephen had a giant, mega row on the beach and I'd had to take her back to Lefkas in a taxi. What a day that had been!

We reached the Lefkas road – dusty, with potholes here and there but so full of memories of running back and to from Nydri, begging favours and scrounging bits to keep us in business during those first few months.

I was very quiet. Luke read my mind and didn't try to speak to me.

Risto's boatyard was jammed now and I thought of all the work that was going to be done before the next season – the welding, the painting, the cleaning and evicting the rats!

Then past the marina where I had been in awe that there could ever be so many yachts in one place.

We turned right at the end of the harbour wall and ran alongside the first bit of the Canal. Once, we'd been early for one of the bridge openings, and there was a strong cross wind, so I'd taken control of Zephyrus from the clients and held her at an angle against the wind with just a touch of throttle. Mike had said that I had done okay – and I nearly burst with pride.

Now there were the rattles of the bridge and then past the Venetian fort where I had walked with one group of guests who were pretty fed up with boats and sailing, and wanted some heavy duty culture. A good Hostie can do everything – and I was proud of this too.

The open Ionian was on the left. When I had first seen it, the sea had looked impossibly huge and I couldn't imagine anyone sailing on it without drowning. Today there was just one yacht, making slow progress under sail, heading for Paxos. I looked at the sails and had bitchy thoughts that the boat would have sailed better reefed. I was a bit ashamed of myself for thinking this – but not a lot!

There was one of my favourite supermarkets in Agios Nikolaos opposite the left turn to Preveza. The guys there always had a smile when I stopped for some Pringles – the Hostie's compulsory comfort food – or a bottle of water.

We dropped downhill with the taxi driver just banging through the potholes as if they didn't exist and there was Preveza airport ahead. I gulped. I had collected clients from here all season but now this was me - leaving, and it felt really scary.

The old fighter jet was still there, on its pole at the start of the perimeter fence. It was all getting very emotional and I squeezed Luke's thigh for re-assurance - and he held my hand tighter.

The Mercedes swung in front of the main door, alongside the tour coaches and taxis waiting for trade, and we were here.

My God! What do we do next? We'd no tickets, no passports and I didn't have a clue where check in was for a private jet.

I was sitting on the pavement side of the car so I got out first. Luke, as kind as ever, gave the driver a tip and they went round to the back of the car together. For a moment, I just stood there and stared around, like a lost infant looking for her Mum.

It was only seconds, but it felt like months, before a girl slightly older than me appeared out of nowhere and said: "Miss Lamb? I'm Eve and I'll be assisting you today."

Actually, she was a bit like the girl I'd first met at the Boat Show in January but, instead of having an icy smile which would have frozen the Ionian in August, she seemed genuinely pleased to see us.

All that I could say was a really weak, "Thank you…" and then carried on with my lost infant impersonation.

Eve was quite chatty and, as I have said, really keen to please.

"Here is your passport, and Mr. Bickerton's…"

And she passed them over.

"Mr. Bianchi has also asked me to give you this."

There, carefully wrapped in some tissue paper, was the Madonna which Alissa had given to me all those months ago and who had done such a good job, all through the season, watching over me in the forepeak. There were grooves around her neck and waist, where MG's zip ties had kept her secured to the bow but, other than this and a bit of a battered nose, she was fine.

I giggled and said thanks – but I was also starting to understand just how careful and thorough these people were. Nothing was too difficult, no detail escaped them. This thought both scared and excited me at the same time.

Eve spoke again. "We've already loaded your luggage on to the aircraft…"

Neaaggghhh! Not my boiled blue knickers and bras! Please tell me that you've either not seen them or you've chucked them all in the bin. Please don't say that you've been looking at my MG'd undies…

"But perhaps you might need this?"

I took the small, fabric wallet which my lovely Dad had given to me in April. Immediately, I could feel the ten, new €100 notes - still untouched. When things were bad I had often felt for those notes, checking that they were still there for me – but I had never opened the wallet.

The parachute hadn't disappeared and me and Luke could do a lot of escaping with €1000 if we didn't like what Mr Bianchi had to say. I said a silent thanks to my dad and felt my eyes watering.

A guy appeared with a luggage trolley and loaded the bags we'd brought with us on to it. I said another silent prayer when I saw my €5 bag on top. Please Madonna, don't let Eve have noticed my cheapo bag!

Eve didn't because she set off at a cracking pace. The luggage guy followed her and we speed marched behind.

We didn't go to the check in on the right-hand side, where everyone else was queuing, but through a little door, by Passport Control. The security guard waved us in and there was a small desk with a smiling police officer.

Eve asked if she could have our passports. The policeman took the briefest glance at them, thanked her and we headed through the Arrivals' Hall where I had come in April, out of the door at the end and on to the tarmac.

It was only a short walk to the most beautiful plane I had ever seen. It had a very sharp, pointed nose and wings which swept up at the end, like a bird's, and it was big too – almost like a small commercial aircraft.

At the foot of the steps was a tall, blond haired and drop dead gorgeous guy in a white shirt with epaulettes on the shoulders. He had a lovely smile – no, grin is more accurate – and held his hand out to me.

"I'm Mike Harrop – your Captain today and I'm looking forward to flying you. If there's anything you need, or we can do for you, just ask. We're all here to help."

It had to be a Mike didn't it? It just had to. I mean, what other name in the world could a stunning guy who was a super star pilot be called? I bet he sailed too and was a brilliant skipper. Aren't all Mikes?

Inside the Gulfstream was just incredible – I mean absolutely mind-blowing. The nearest thing I can think of to describe it was The Appian Way. The plane had the same soft, relaxing colours with very light brown leather armchairs, wooden tables and a speckled, nutmeg coloured carpet. Everywhere, there was loads of space – an unimaginable amount of room, compared with a normal plane.

But it wasn't the space or the monster sized chairs which impressed me the most - but the light. I'd never been in a plane which had so much natural light pouring through great big windows on either side.

We sat down and fastened our seat belts without being told. Even the clunk on the catch was smoother and quieter than the cheap planes I had always flown in.

Luke was next to me, holding my hand as usual, and I was feeling better by the moment – more confident and starting to believe that I could handle this new life - and even like it. That's why I decided to take a chance.

Eve was hovering and I caught her attention.

"Could I please have a word with Mike?"

The outside door was closed now and the engines were running so maybe I had left things late but Mike came back to us immediately, all smiles.

"How can I help?"

"Mike, I've spent a wonderful season on Tychos and, if it's not too much trouble, I wonder, if we're going in that direction and it's not too much trouble or anything, I wonder if we could fly over the island, if that's possible?"

"I'm sure we can. Preveza is very quiet at this time of day but I'll still have to check with Air Traffic and get clearance.

"We're eventually going north-west but there's no rush, so how about if I fly along past Palairos and then down the Ionian because I guess that's a route you will have sailed many times?"

There were no secrets here.

I smiled and thanked him.

*****

Taking off in a Gulfstream is like a ride at Alton Towers because you just zoom up into the sky like a rocket. We thought it was great as Mike turned the plane right and over the mountains.

The door to the cockpit was open and Mike turned to me: "OK, Miss Lamb. Here we go. I'll drop down a bit and Palairos will be on your left – but you're probably a better navigator than me so you'll pick it up straightaway."

I grinned and thanked him. Flying in your own jet was great.

I couldn't see Cathy's place but the little harbour and the Club Vounaki building were easy to spot.

We banked over towards Meganisi. I nearly cried because there was the road to Nydri - and I was sure that I could see Risto's.

Then we turned again and now Kalamos was in sight and another flood of memories of swimming, and barbecues, and glasses of wine with lovely clients.

Mike levelled the plane out and we passed the tip of Meganisi. I was certain I could see the very, very special little bay right at the end – as if I could ever forget what happened there!

Kalamos was there, green in the Autumn light, but, probably fortunately, I couldn't see where "The Appian Way" had been moored. That would have been just too much!

We flew on, over Arkoudi, and then Mike said: "Tychos is just to your left. Would you like me to fly right round the island so that you can get a good view all the way?"

I quickly said I would - and thanked him.

It was great being able to get out of your seat and swap from one side of the plane to other for the best views without treading on anyone!

We were quite low as Mike banked the Gulfstream gently over, and there was the entry to Porto Tyche, and The Pool and the little dock and everything which had been my life for the last seven months.

Mike turned the plane around the eastern side and I could see the twisting, narrow channel which we had rushed down to rescue Dan and Sophie. Cape Ducato was in the distance where we had been sailing just one day before, me in a faded shirt and threadbare shorts and Luke asleep in Brizo. All that so near – and yet such a long way from where I was now.

Mike looked back to me again: "Okay?"

Luke grinned. It was the same lovely, mad smile he'd had when he teased me into getting Notus cranked over, and then pretended to drown in the cockpit. Maybe that was when I first saw something special in him – the very first hint of what a wonderful man he was.

He squeezed my hand: "Yaaaay, Rachel. A trip round Tychos in a plane and a free tea somewhere tonight. How good's that? We're going to have a brillo time!"

And he leaned across and gave me a great big, silly kiss which made me laugh too.

The plane climbed rapidly, through grey streaked wisps of white clouds and then towards the indigo blue sky as Tychos disappeared behind us and into the distance - and our new life began.

Frank Melling – In His Own Words

You hear about kids who could sing and dance before they could walk - well, I was a bit like this with telling stories. The snag was that working class kids like me were supposed to get their hands dirty and do real work – not mess about with typewriters.

This is why I became a motorcycling journalist – a profession where my background didn't hold me back.

So far, I have written something in the region of 1500 full length feature stories and 17 books. I'm still writing about bikes today and I enjoy every single article.

As well as bike magazines I wrote for posh publications such as "The Daily Telegraph" and "The Guardian".

I also found that I could write more than stories about bikes. So in between getting paid, and very well too, for motorcycling features I produced everything with words from film scripts to advertisements – science fiction to satire.

Instead of the Infant being told to shut up and be quiet, I found that people actually liked me telling them stories.

This brings us to my latest book: "Hostie". Writing in the voice of a 22 year old woman has been a very different experience. Yet Rachel, the book's heroine, remains one of us – an ordinary person who, through her own efforts and with a little help from fate, achieves remarkable things. In this way she is you, and I guess me too in some small way: I do hope that you enjoy her story.

Thanks for reading.

A PENGUIN IN A SPARROW'S NEST

The Story of a Freelance Motorcycling Journalist

FRANK MELLING

Wyrd bið ful aræd

A Penguin in a Sparrow's Nest is the first part of Frank Melling's hilarious, and very moving, autobiography. It's been a best seller since its publication in May 2015 with over 100 five star reviews and has been critically acclaimed.

Available now from www.frankmelling.com for £12.99 including free post and packing.

What the Reviewers Say About
A Penguin in a Sparrow's Nest...

"Autobiographies are usually clouded by false humility, massive egos, and the natural inability to see ourselves as others do. What results is rarely more trustworthy than a ghost-writer's fantasy.

"A Penguin in a Sparrow's Nest is different. Frank suffers from none of these conditions and this inspirational meander through the life of an ordinary man proves that he is anything but ordinary.

"Adversity, sackings, hard work, determination, love, success, and the ability to cheat death all play their part – under the umbrella of Fate – and leave you convinced of two things above all else: Penguins are categorically superior to sparrows and life is very much what you choose to make it."

Richard Newland – Deputy Editor Motorcycle News

"A Penguin in a Sparrow's Nest" is the fascinating story of Frank's early life. It is warm, funny and informative - and told by a master story teller. I could not put it down."

Jim Redman MBE – Six Times World Champion

 "A funny and observant personal account of what a man can learn, and do, in his life - in such an easy and enjoyable read. Every page is packed with fascinating stories."

Frank writes beautifully. I cried with laughter and I cried.
If you are into motorcycles and life in general, you **MUST** read this book.

Mr Melling should be running the country!
Robert Bentham

THE FLYING PENGUIN

More Stories of a Freelance Motorcycling Journalist

FRANK MELLING

Wyrd bið ful aræd

The Flying Penguin is the second part of Frank's autobiography. There are plenty of near death stories, from almost drowning under a Honda enduro bike to looking down the business end of a Colt .45 in the backwoods of Missouri.

There's the vital information you need to become an imitation World Champion – but only when there are free hotel rooms on offer!

But more than anything else, you'll be amazed at how far self-belief and determination can take you in life.

Available now from www.frankmelling.com for £12.99 including free post and packing.

What the Reviewers Say About
"The Flying Penguin"

Frank Melling tells a mean tall story. Broken bones, broken bikes, broken relationships – all precariously balanced on the knife-edge of a freelance journalist's permanent state of financial insecurity.
Out of the occasionally all too real fires of experience emerges if not a phoenix then certainly a Flying Penguin…
Rowena Hoseason – Editor "Real Classic Magazine".

I got my copy of "The Flying Penguin" as soon as it came out – and three days later it's finished!
"A Penguin in a Sparrow's Nest was truly brilliant but, dare I say it, this book is even better.
The stories about working with Giacomo Agostini, Jim Redman and the modern stars were fascinating and now I know the real reason the Thundersprint came to an end.
Obviously, there's a lot about bikes in the book, that's to be expected, but it's not just a book about motorcycling. It's more like a thirty year travel journal of a journey through one man's life.
Highly recommended – and definitely worth five stars
Screen Genie

This book is a must read, not only for all who enjoyed "Penguin in a Sparrow's Nest", but also for those who have yet to be turned on to Melling's addictive writing. I only hope that there is more still to come.
Frog777

Both of Frank's Penguin books rank right up there at the top and take a place of honour on the bookshelf. "The Flying Penguin" is a terrific book!
Ian Easton